CW00470430

THE CHESHIRE RING

THE CHESHIRE RING

Annemarie

with love

John Oliver

John K. Oliver

Book Guild Publishing

Sussex, England

First published in Great Britain in 2010 by
The Book Guild Ltd
Pavilion View
19 New Road
Brighton, BN1 1UF

Copyright © John Oliver 2010

The right of John Oliver to be identified as the author of
this work has been asserted by him in accordance with the
Copyright, Designs and Patents Act 1988.

All rights reserved. No part of this publication may be
reproduced, transmitted, or stored in a retrieval system,
in any form or by any means, without permission in writing
from the publisher, nor be otherwise circulated in any form
of binding or cover other than that in which it is published
and without a similar condition being imposed on the
subsequent purchaser.

All characters in this publication are fictitious and any resemblance
to real people, alive or dead, is purely coincidental.

Typesetting in Baskerville by
Norman Tilley Graphics Ltd, Northampton

Printed in Great Britain by
CPI Antony Rowe

A catalogue record for this book is available from
The British Library

ISBN 978 1 84624 498 8

In appreciation for their hard work

Margery

Richard

Jo

The Crew

Jane Langan
for her expertise

John Hill
for his hard work

1

'You're goin' the wrong way!' shouted a spotty-faced youth as he reluctantly raised his perch pole to let us pass. 'Some people just don't know what the hell they are doin'.'

He sat on his fishing box surrounded by a confused pile of tackle, tins, macs, flasks and nets. An open plastic container of maggots lay near to a packet of sandwiches, which were in such close proximity to his left hand that he could grab either with consummate ease. Some cans of lager were just discernible, cooling in his keep net.

He wore scruffy tattered jeans and a T-shirt proclaiming to the world, 'I Luv Sex'. Though quite where he was likely to find it was a complete mystery to me.

In actual fact we were not going the wrong way at all, but we were going backwards; and although that is the story of my life, in this case it did have a purpose.

We, Margery and I that is, hadn't been on holiday with either of our children for many years. They wouldn't be seen dead with us. In an expansive moment which he no doubt instantly regretted, Richard, one day last winter, suggested we should go on a canal holiday with him and his wife Jo. We had taken canal holidays a number of times when the children were younger. At the age of 14 Richard had always wanted a narrowboat. Over the ensuing years he had probably changed his mind. But, as all parents do, thinking of him still having the desires of a 14-year-old, I booked a 62-footer for the four of us. This was partly, I have to admit, because I like my creature comforts, and the boat

1

had two cabins with double beds, and en suite facilities. There was a spacious lounge, with huge picture windows in the front – sorry, bows – and an ultra-smart galley.

So on my birthday we set out for a week's leisurely cruising around the Cheshire Ring. I proudly announced the chosen route, advising that it was 97 miles and, to sighs of anguish, that there were 93 locks. In actual fact I could only count 92 during the trip, so have a feeling I was let down by the publicity blurb, and really want another one.

We were intending to travel north, through Manchester. I arranged with the boatman to pick up the boat early so that we could steal a march on the tunnel at Preston Brook, and reach it before four o'clock, when the traffic flow changes from north to south. I intended to give us a good start.

A Ford Sierra was parked across the entrance to the boatyard. Stan, in a loud shell suit and dark glasses, was clutching his mobile phone as if his life depended upon it. And speaking animatedly.

'They've gone into the boatyard at Acton Bridge.'

'What the hell are they doing there?'

'I don't know yet, they are getting out and talking to the boatman.'

'What bridge number is it?'

'I dunno! What do you mean, bridge number?'

'Canal bridges are all numbered. Usually fixed to the arch of the bridge on one side or the other. Didn't you know that?'

'No.'

'Well, what is it?'

'I dunno. I can't see from here. I daren't go into the yard now, or I'm blown.'

'No, suppose not.'

'They're being taken towards a boat, *Colette*. It's a big one painted grey, and facing down … er … south. Towards … er … Northwich. It's right up to the bridge as far as I can see. Some of them are taking on cases and boxes. Looks like they're going for a trip. Perhaps they're going fishing.'

'The cunning sods. They are going to take it by canal. They know we wouldn't think of looking for them there. Can't be seen, can you?'

'No chance.'

When we had approached the boatyard, the road had been blocked by a Ford Sierra, with a driver in very loud attire. Margery sounded her horn, and Richard pulled up behind. The driver ducked hastily from sight, and with a grinding of gears reversed into the hedge and out of our way, keeping well down behind the dashboard.

We drove majestically into the yard, parked our cars and went in search of the boatman. To my dismay the boat was facing the south, not north as we needed, so that my crafty manoeuvre of being early fell flat on its face.

Then, horror of horrors, there were four muscular blokes carrying luggage and boxes aboard our boat. Drawing near, up to the canalside, I was able to see that they were not boarding our boat, merely going across it to another, smaller boat, which was tied up to our boat and completely obscured by it. This boat was also facing south.

'Sorry about that, some cocky old trout sounded her horn at me. So I had to move quick.'

'I told you not to make yourself conspicuous.'

'I'm not. It's all right. Struth! That couple and another two are also going towards the same boat. What do you make of that?'

'Can't be.'

'They are, I tell you. A grey-haired elderly couple in an estate car, and a young couple in a flashy BMW. It's them all right. Tall, smart-arsed athletic type, and her … my God, she's all right. If I moved the car out again I could get a better gander at her.'

'Never mind her. Keep your mind on your work. It must be the whole lot. Altogether in one fell swoop. We must play this very carefully. Don't want to lose any of 'em.'

'Is that grey-haired old codger the boss then?'

'Must be!'

'No chance. He looks such a prat. Yes, they're taking luggage on board now. Can see why they've got such a big boat.'

'Keep your eyes open. They are going south, you say?'

'Yes, definitely south.'

'OK. I'll get a boat at Anderton, and we can follow them until they make their move. In the meantime, keep quiet. Tell me when they are off, and then follow them as best you can by car.'

Stan put down his phone. As best as I can by car? Silly bugger.

The smaller boat untied from us and slipped quietly away under the bridge, going south towards Northwich.

Whilst Richard learnt all about the boat, Margery and Jo stored the food away, putting too much in the fridge, but not before I managed to store the essentials, two bottles of Chardonnay, a wine box and four cans of lager for emergency use. I then sat back and checked that everyone had done what they had been delegated.

Luggage stowed, cars parked, and we were off under the instruction of the boatman, steering us backwards for half a mile, swinging the rudder backwards and forwards, like one of the Nile dhows, to the winding point where he turned us around. Easy when you know how.

'George! George! Where the hell are you?'

'What's all the excitement?'

'The flaming boat's going off backwards.'

'Nonsense. Can't be.'

'It is, I tell you. Going up to the covered area over the towpath.'

'Going to fill up with diesel, I expect. Tell me when they come back down.'

The spotty youth lowered his perch pole when we had passed. He threw some maggots on the water to encourage the fish, and took a bite of a sandwich.

'With the same hand,' said Margery. 'Ugh!'

Richard was passed out by the boatman as efficient, and duly appointed Captain. But then admirals don't actually man the boat they sail in. If, that is, admirals ever go to sea at all. The boat turned, the boatman jumped agilely onto a boat moored against the towpath, from there onto dry land, and waved us 'bon voyage'. And off we sailed under our own steam, with a week of blissful relaxation ahead.

The sun was shining as we glided through meadows where cattle leisurely grazed. The reeds bowed their heads to us as we passed. Quite regal.

'No sign of the boat, George.'

'Patience. We've got a small boat, enough for the two of us waiting at Anderton. We can pick 'em up, and follow 'em from there.'

'Hang on, here's the boatman on foot. Where's the flaming boat?'

With that Stan flung down his phone, rushed past the boatman, almost knocking him over, through the yard and along the towpath. In his hurry he tripped over the end of the perch pole, which the spotty youth had withdrawn across the towpath, and fell headlong, face downwards in the plastic container of maggots.

'You clumsy sod,' shouted the spotty youth.

'I'd screw you if I wasn't in such a hurry,' spluttered Stan as he spat out a mouthful of maggots.

He reached the next bridge, breathing heavily and just about knackered, just in time to see *Colette* disappear northwards around a bend.

This was the life. Carefree easy boating. Not a care, not a worry in the world. We met our first oncoming boat, which was well out in the channel. Sticking to the rule of the canal, we pulled hard right towards the bank, and away from the towpath. We all looked at each other as we heard the steel hull grinding along the bottom.

'George! George! They've turned the boat and are going north. I had to run after 'em to see.'

'Why the hell couldn't you tell me that sooner? You were supposed to be keeping a look-out, and you let 'em go. Our boat at Anderton is no flaming use at all now. Get after them as best you can, and whatever happens don't lose 'em, or I'll string you up by your bollocks.'

'But I can't follow a boat by car.'

'Look at your flaming map. You can see where the roads cross the canal. You check 'em out at every bridge. Don't lose 'em again, or I'll kill you. Keep in touch. I'll try and get another boat, seeing as how you messed up this one.'

'Yes, George.'

Stan put down his phone and straightened himself up. You clever dick. Follow 'em by car? Don't lose 'em? Bugger 'em.

We didn't run aground, much to our relief. But half a mile further on we did.

I did the obvious thing, and panicked. We couldn't go forwards, and we couldn't go backwards. There wasn't anything else to do but panic.

6

There were four fisherman on the towpath opposite who were in two minds over whether to be delighted to see one of the boats stranded, or to be annoyed because we must certainly have been disturbing the fish over a quarter of a mile of canal.

Three of us went to the bows, leaving Richard with less weight in the stern to steer us off backwards. I tried to help by pushing into the mud on the bottom with a mop. Then we all rushed to the stern to try and float the bows off, whilst I valiantly tried to push into the mud at the stern with my mop.

What on earth brought us on this silly trip? Whose idea was it? We must be idiots, and we hadn't even seen a lock yet. All thoughts of sublime cruising vanished, and remembrance of hard slogging work came back to numb the senses. We could have been sitting on a Mediterranean beach, sipping pink gin and doing nothing.

Stalemate. We had tried everything. The shame of it, beached, and we had only been on the damn thing 20 minutes. What could we do? I saw us stuck there until high tide, or even the whole week. Rescued by helicopter. Stop! Think logically. But only panic came.

Richard was beginning to get fed up with our antics, which were, minute by minute, making matters worse as he was busy with the throttle and tiller, trying to ease us off the bottom. He told Margery to take the tiller and the throttle, and to take instructions only from him. With that he jumped onto the roof of the cabin, grabbed the boat pole and stuck it firmly into the mud halfway down the boat.

'Full throttle reverse, and throw the tiller right over,' he ordered. 'Not that way. The other.'

Margery, with full throttle reverse, swung the tiller right over the other way, whilst Richard, pole on his shoulder, started to walk steadily down the boat. With all the weight in the stern, with more crunching and grinding, we slipped quietly into the water again. Cheers all round were premature. The boat pole was stuck firmly in the mud.

So keeping a firm hand on the pole, and easing the boat gently backwards and forwards, taking great care not to run aground again, it gradually loosened and we were free again. We were relieved and chastened. It had lost us 15 vital minutes, and we still wanted to take the tunnel on time.

We ran aground a number of times after that, and somehow extracted ourselves with ease. Strange, isn't it? Why was that one such a marathon? Or was it?

The four of us relaxed in the stern, relishing our newfound freedom, as we chugged quietly towards the tunnel. Margery, practical as ever, put us at our ease, producing, right on time, mugs of coffee and ham sandwiches.

A traveller should always have a map, or better still, half a dozen. They show you where you are going, or intend to go. Remind you of where you have been. Indicate places you might wish to visit, or avoid, as the case may be. Afterwards they will show you what you have missed.

I had a full half-dozen. A 1971 map book of what was then the whole of the canal system. A 1992 book of the Cheshire Ring, our proposed circular route taking in six different canal systems, and ending up where we started. There was an AA map of Manchester and district with, on the reverse, a detailed map of central Manchester. Our route was to take us right through the heart of the city. To top it off, there were three Ordnance Survey, Landranger series maps. 'Chester' covered only $3\frac{1}{2}$ miles of our route across the top right-hand corner. In fact the very bit we were travelling on now. 'Manchester and surroundings' covered the north part of the Cheshire Ring, and 'Stoke on Trent and Macclesfield', the southern portion. We had the lot. Difficulties could not occur. Everything in detail at our fingertips.

Before setting out I had made a summary of our route, with copious notes, and sub-notes. Working out our approximate daily run, with possible overnight stops. I could, however, only count 92 locks on the maps, and was determined to find out for myself the correct number.

We glided under the last bridge before our first lock, now less than half a mile ahead.

'George, I'm on bridge two hundred and thirteen. They've just gone underneath.'

'OK. Check them into the tunnel. We don't want them to have any problems there. Then come on to Preston Brook. I'm trying to organise another boat, seeing as how you messed up.'

'It wasn't my fault. I didn't know that they were going out backwards.'

'You should've checked. They haven't got much here. All damned well out. Flamin' holidaymakers cluttering up the whole place, and getting in our way.'

'Yes, George. Funny, you know, but there are only the old codgers on show, with the two flashy young ones. No sign of the chaps I followed into the boatyard. Perhaps they are lying low, but there is certainly no sign of them.'

'If you've lost 'em …'

'I haven't lost 'em. There hasn't been anywhere for 'em to go, now has there?'

'You'd better be right.'

'This lot just looks like holidaymakers.'

'They'd better not be.'

'OK. I'm off to the tunnel, or they'll be there before me.'

'Leave your car at Preston Brook, then I want you under the M56.'

'Under the M56? What the hell for? Can't I ride on the boat? I fancy that.'

'We're not here for a nice time. Check your map, and

9

you'll see the canal splits into two, to Runcorn or Manchester. Can't you read your flamin' map? I want you to
point them out to me, and indicate which way they go. I
may pick you up if there is time.'

'What do you mean, "if there is time"?'

'What I said. And don't be cheeky with me. If I don't have
time to pick you up, you follow me up along the towpath,
until I do have a chance to get you on board.'

'But I can't take the car along the towpath.'

'You can jog along, can't you? But whatever you do, keep
me in sight, because I'll be following them.'

Stan flung his phone down, ground his gears, and
skidded off in pursuit.

'Stand under the M56 ... jog along the towpath after him.
Cheeky sod. Every time I ask for a holiday he cancels it.
God, I wish I was an insurance salesman, anything would be
better than this. I hope he bloody well sinks!'

Colette glided gracefully round a bend into a wide grassy
sloping cutting, ringed with trees. Ahead was a small hill,
and the little black dot just above the water level was the
entrance to the tunnel. To the left of it stood a small
cottage, beside a track leading down to the towpath.

A large sign indicated traffic movements: open northwards until 4 p.m. Twenty minutes to go: we had made our
first port of call on time. On the right was an old dry dock,
once used for the repair of barges belonging to the North
Staffordshire Railway, the one-time owners of the Trent &
Mersey Canal upon which we were travelling. Its valanced
canopy was reminiscent of railway architecture.

It appears that for some strange reason, a few yards just
inside the northern end of the tunnel, the Trent & Mersey
Canal system ends and turns itself into the Bridgewater
Canal. Why should anyone in his right mind, I thought,
decide to link the two systems inside a tunnel?

Apparently the owners of the canal systems did other strange things as well. The two canals meet at the lowest point in both these systems. Such, however, was the trust each had for the other, that to prevent the Bridgewater Company stealing the Trent & Mersey's water, the latter put in a stop lock just before the tunnel so that there should be no free flow of water from their system. Nothing, seemingly, changes in business. So we had to go through the whole process of negotiating a lock of only 6 inches in depth because years ago two idiots didn't trust each other.

So: wind up the paddles on the two lower doors with windlasses, to allow the water through the gates and lower the water level in the lock by 6 inches. Open the gates, shove the boat in. Close the gates again, lower the paddles, this time to keep the water in. Rush to the other end. Wind up the paddle in the single gate to raise the water in the lock by 6 inches again, where it was in the first place. Open the gate when full. Push the boat out to the other side. Close the gate again and lower the paddle to keep the water in. One down and 92 – or 91 – to go.

We looked up as we approached the tunnel. There was a red car parked on the bank beside the warehouse.

'George, where are you? Answer me, George.'
His phone just crackled.
'They're entering the tunnel, and I'm off. George! Answer!'
The only reply was more crackling.
'But I've still only seen the four of them. George! George!'
The crackling continued.

Lights on and extinguish gas appliances. It looked such a small arch cut into the hillside as we approached. The water shimmered gently at its mouth, its brick roof reflected in the water. There was total darkness inside, cold and uninviting, damp blackness, eerie and sinister. We edged nearer; surely it's not large enough to take us. We can't possibly get in there. But somehow, we did.

Quiet stillness and a sudden chill, as we moved from the bright, hot, sunny June afternoon, into this dark, dank, subterranean world. A world which never sees daylight. Odd, that. It never has seen daylight, it never will. Yet we were travelling through this world, which was so unreal. I wondered if fish ever penetrated very far into the tunnel, or have ever navigated right through all of its almost three-quarters of a mile, 1,239 yards to be precise. But I didn't count them.

There was no towpath. The barge horses of old had a gentle walk over the hill, without their load, while the poor bargees, on their backs on the roof, walked their craft through the tunnel by means of their own leg power. Foot by weary foot. A daunting prospect.

We chugged gently on. I could put my hand out and touch the damp walls, or stretch up to the sometimes leaky roof. No speck, or spot, of light ahead, just damp, cold blackness. The four of us entombed alone on our boat. Strange, there should be some pinpoint, one would have thought. Unless ... it's not straight, and if it isn't, poor Brindley didn't get it right.

Every so often there were distance marks pointing in either direction. Gradually we found ourselves approaching the midpoint. A pinpoint of light suddenly appeared, and got larger. It is much more reassuring when there is light at the end of the tunnel. More drips landed on my head, but the pinpoint of light made it more reassuring. That was my world out there, the real world.

The hundreds of yards turned to tens, and my world grew nearer. As it did so, a magnificent picture emerged, as the bricks of the roof were clearly reflected in the still water, merging with the actual bricks of the roof as the water mirrored light onto them. We were approaching an almost complete circle of brickwork.

'Quick, take a photograph.'

But the camera cannot capture the beauty, the magic. We travelled through it, and a moment of sheer magic was gone. We were out into the world again. My world, where magic only exists in storybooks.

2

We were blinded momentarily by the bright sun, whose rays soon breathed life into us again as we chugged out into the real world. Warmth melted the chill, and extinguished the eerie, sinister feelings which had so recently enveloped us. A few cirrus clouds moved very slowly high across the sky. Nothing now stopped the warmth reaching us on our little boat. I could swear *Colette* was smiling.

There were grassy banks again, and green trees. How beautiful it seemed after our recent dreadful incarceration. A mother duck quacked, and quacked again to try and frighten us away, whilst at the same time trying to gather her fluffy little brood together as they darted all over the place, bobbing up and down like fluffy little brown corks. She managed to round up eight on one side of us, whilst two dived for the far bank.

'Oh, they are lovely,' sighed gentle Margery, and she was right, they were lovely.

After we had passed, the two separated ones joined the rest of the brood, and they darted all over the place again, looking for food, as if nothing had happened. We had been an alarm, which was soon forgotten.

Suddenly there were more boats about, moored and moving. They grew considerably in number as we approached the junction, where the Bridgewater Canal forked left for Runcorn. We were, however, Manchester bound, straight ahead. The crew were duly appraised of the situation.

We slipped under a bridge and were soon approaching the huge M56 viaduct. No single-span bridge this, as it stalked across the countryside, striding on a number of legs.

Our attention was drawn to a little man in a bright shell suit, wearing dark glasses. He was waving furiously, and held a telephone in his hand which he occasionally put to his ear and spoke into.

'I don't recognise him, but he seems to be waving at us,' I said, and started to wave back.

The others joined in, and we all waved furiously back. The man, seeing us, suddenly stopped waving, and looked quickly away, as though he had never seen us before in his life.

'Perhaps we've embarrassed him, and he wasn't waving at us at all,' said Margery, feeling sorry for his embarrassment. 'He may have been waving at someone else. I think you'd better stop.'

'Rubbish,' I replied, and continued to wave at the poor man, who was covered in confusion. He occasionally took a sly look in our direction.

'There are some funny people about, aren't there?'

'There are some funny people on this boat,' whispered Richard to Jo, at the same time raising his eyebrows. They both burst into laughter.

The man just stood there glumly looking anywhere but directly at us. We soon overtook him, and were into pastures new. A thing of the moment, almost instantly forgotten, as new vistas opened up before us. I took one last look back, and thought I saw him pointing in our direction. Funny, why would he be pointing at us? But then, perhaps he wasn't.

'We are approaching Daresbury on our right,' I announced.

'Oh, are we?' was the uninterested reply.

'Charles Dodgson was born here.'

'Oh.'

'Lewis Carroll's father was the curate here. There are *Alice in Wonderland*, and *Through the Looking Glass* windows in the church.'

'Oh.'

'Shall we go and see them? We can stop at a bridge up here.'

'No.'

Strange to hear, 'no' from children who had in former years so eagerly run all over Beatrix Potter's house at Sawrey. Perhaps they are growing up, I thought. Sad, that. I had long ago decided that I was never going to grow up. It had always seemed – and still does – so boring, growing up.

'Stan. What the hell are you doing? You start to wave all over the shop, and then stand like a zombie stuck in the mud. Finally, you start pointing vaguely into the distance. Where is our bloody boat?'

'Where are you? I've been pointing and waving for ages.'

'Well which way did they go?'

'Straight on. You can just see them going straight ahead. There.' He pointed again. 'Anyway, where are you?'

'I've got a little boat, *Blue Belle* of all stupid names. It's really small and wobbles all over the shop. They didn't want me to have even this damned thing, until I'd passed my driving test. Christ, I'm heading for the bank again.'

'Is that you across the other side? Just going to hit the bank? Look what you're doing, or you will hit the bank.'

Crackle … crackle …

'Is that you?'

Crackle … crackle …

'Is that you, George?'

Crackle … crackle …

'George is that you just managing not to hit the bank?'

'It's all your bloody fault anyway, messing me about. Of course it's me. Who the hell do you think it is?'

'Are you coming to pick me up? I'm getting fed up just standing here like a wet lettuce.'

'You're the nearest thing I've seen to a wet lettuce. I'm coming over now to pick you up. Stay where you are – got that?'

Blue Belle had seen better days. She was a small, very old, wooden cabin cruiser. The varnish was peeling badly, and she was barely seaworthy. With the air of one who had been doing this for years, George made straight for Stan on the opposite bank.

'George!'

Crackle … crackle …

'George.'

Crackle … crackle …

'George! George! Look what you are doing.'

'What's up? Don't worry me now, I'll be there in a jiffy.'

He switched off the phone. He heard a horn but did not think anything of it as he waved to Stan. He hadn't, unfortunately, seen a steel-hulled narrowboat approaching, full ahead.

'George! Turn back! Turn back!' Stan waved furiously.

George waved back. The horn sounded much louder, and nearer. God forbid! There was a huge craft bearing down on him. The helmsman was pulling further to his right, waving angrily, and furiously shouting abuse at George.

Seized by disbelief at the position in which he found himself, George just stared wide-eyed. Then, with a bold gesture stemming from sheer panic, he swung his rudder hard round to the left. Thinking he was going in reverse, which he couldn't, he thrust the accelerator forward with such force that his small craft rocked furiously, completed a 90 degree turn, just missing the narrowboat, which was almost grazing the towpath.

'You useless sod!' shouted the narrowboat helmsman. 'Your mother shouldn't let you out on a tricycle.'

It is doubtful if George heard the lurid description of him that flowed from the lips of the helmsman. True though it was. He was by now heading straight for the offside bank again, which he had so recently missed. This time he made it.

The boat crunched as its wooden hull ground into mud and gravel. Stan looked on in horror, to see George high and dry on the mud bank.

A middle-aged man with receding hair, wearing overalls and considerably out of breath, stared on in disbelief.

'Who is that bloody maniac? I knew I shouldn't have let him have my boat. The smart-arsed clever dick said he knew all about boats. I'll call the police to him. Get him dragged off before he does any more damage.'

'I should,' said Stan, trying to look disinterested.

By now a crowd had gathered to see what new feat George was going to perform next for their delectation. George struggled to free himself with his boat pole.

Stan made himself scarce, lest anyone should associate him with the maniac. He crossed the bridge over the Runcorn arm of the canal and started to walk along the towpath towards Manchester.

'George, can you hear me, George?'

Crackle ... crackle ...

We were now gliding through Moore and on to Higher Walton. The traffic after Preston Brook thinned considerably, but as we approached Higher Walton it built up again. There were a number of boats moored on the towpath side, and even more on the private moorings to our right. We had to slow and jostle with oncoming traffic, as the boats on both sides made navigation difficult at times.

The reason soon became obvious. The private moorings

19

were having a barbecue. A midsummer party. There were crowds thronging the bank, sitting, standing and leaning.

At this point the canal does a left turn just before a bridge, which is slightly at an angle. I feared we might graze the towpath under the bridge.

My attention was drawn to a very attractive lady on one of the moored boats along the towpath, with long blonde hair down to her shoulders. She was standing nonchalantly at the stern with a flute of white wine in her hand. I couldn't help noticing her long, slender bare legs. She was wearing open sandals, through which her scarlet toenails peeped, red shorts, and her ample – nay, very ample – bosom was most inadequately covered with a silk scarf tied across the valley. It barely covered the essentials, but that didn't matter. The sight was well worth seeing. But how on earth did she keep it up, I wondered. Will power? If so, whose will power would win?

Unfortunately we were quickly through the bridge with inches to spare, and she was gone. Pity.

Onward now, to my celebration birthday dinner. We were going to dine out, and I was beginning to feel in need of a little something. Gliding through Stockton Heath, it soon became clear that we were not going to get as far as we had intended. I had in mind reaching Little Bollington, and trying Ye Olde No. 3 Inn for a meal, but we wouldn't even make Outrington, where, according to the map, there was at least a fish and chip shop.

Stan jogged along the towpath towards Manchester, occasionally stopping.

'George … George.'

Crackle … crackle …

Jogging gradually gave way to a brisk walk.

'George … George.'

Crackle … crackle.

And then a dawdle.

'George … George.'

'Where the hell have you been? You've got a lot to answer for.'

'What have I done?'

'Done!'

'Yes?'

'Got me into one bloody mess after another, that's what! Where are you?'

'I'm walking along the towpath towards Manchester.'

'Can you see 'em all right?'

'I lost them ages ago. They must be miles ahead by now.'

'What! I told you to jog after them, and not let them out of your sight. And now you tell me you've lost 'em.'

'I've jogged for miles, and now I'm walking. In fact, I'm waiting here until you come, because I'm bloody knackered. I have no idea where I am.'

'I've just passed Daresbury. You can't be far ahead. I'll pick you up in a minute, and don't mess me about. You know I'm beginning to like this boat now I'm getting the hang of it. Life on the ocean wave …'

Stan sat down on the towpath and lit a cigarette. He considered how nice and peaceful it was, and contemplated his sore feet and smelly socks.

The canal took a large right-hand corner and then a left, in open farming country. Grappenhall church stood out across a field to our right. I remembered the name, for I had read in the newspapers recently of the tragic death of a poor young boy from there. Out of respect, I felt we should not stop, attractive though it appeared.

After reference to my book, I suggested we went on as far as Thelwall aqueduct and, if we liked it, stop for the night. It was described as a peaceful 'lost' village, with two good

21

pubs that supplied food. The crew approved my choice; they were, by now, also feeling the need for some sustenance.

We glided on through peaceful meadows. A heron flew up from the water ahead of us, and perched for some time on a hillock away from the canal bank, but before we reached it, it was off again into the distance.

'Stan ... Stan ... Why don't you answer?'

Crackle ... crackle ...

'Stan.'

Stan awoke from his reverie, feeling a little refreshed and very hungry. He picked up the phone.

'George.'

'Where the hell have you been? I've been calling you for ages.'

'Haven't moved since we last spoke.'

'I can see you. Stand up, I'm coming for you.'

George steered *Blue Belle* towards the towpath, this time keeping an eye out for other traffic. He was, however, very fearful of running aground again, and the boat was about 3 feet from the towpath as it drew close to Stan.

'Jump on,' shouted George.

'How can I? Slow down and come into the bank,' called Stan, as he now had to trot to keep up with the boat.

'I can't, or we'll lose 'em.'

'We've lost them anyway. So pull in.'

George slowed the boat a little, but not enough. He pulled slightly closer in, but not enough.

'Jump on now!' he yelled.

'I can't,' snarled Stan, becoming puffed again. 'You're going too fast, and you're too far out.'

'Why are you so bloody awkward?' snapped George, easing the boat a little nearer, and slowing it slightly.

Stan jumped, caught the handrail around the cabin roof,

but failed to get a foothold on the gunwale. His feet splashed into the water.

'Help me up,' he shouted.

George leaned across to the side and caught Stan's wrist, but by putting all their weight over the side of their small boat, they caused it to lean heavily over to that side. Now not only Stan's feet were in the water – it was up to his knees. With a heave from George, he was aboard, but the effort had put the boat off course again. It was heading, once again, for the offside bank.

'You silly bugger,' said Stan. 'Why couldn't you have slowed down and pulled in like a normal person.'

He pulled off his soaking trainers, which he put on the cabin roof to dry, along with his socks. He also took off his shell suit bottoms, attaching them to a cleat on the stern bulwark. They floated behind them like a pennant.

'You're not going to stand there in just your jock strap, are you?'

'What else can I do? The rest of my clothes are soaked, thanks to you.'

An air of disagreement was apparent.

The approach to the Thelwall Viaduct was through a lovely quiet wooded glade. We nearly missed the aqueduct, which turned out to be a small bridge carrying the canal over a quiet country road. Just beyond, some boys were fishing. This was it! We all agreed on a beautiful, quiet, tranquil wooded glade for our first overnight stop. What could be better?

Some 50 yards ahead there was a moored boat facing in the same direction as ourselves. It appeared to be unoccupied. *Colette* glided to a halt beside the towpath. Jo and I jumped ashore, and took hold of the mooring ropes fore and aft. The Captain turned off the engine, and all was quiet. Richard collected the mooring stakes and lump hammer from the locker beneath the seat at the side of the cockpit nearest the towpath. After that, they were to remain under the seat at the stern, as we found it easier to land and board from there, rather than the bows. The bow locker was now otherwise empty, apart from an old plastic sliced bread bag and two empty beer cans.

Securely tied, we cleaned ourselves up, changed our clothes, and were ready to go out on the town. Well, the peaceful 'lost' village.

Whilst waiting for the others, I watched a boat come towards us round the bend ahead, and pull in to moor beyond the other boat. The family aboard seemed to have a great deal of trouble mooring. First the bows swung out into the centre of the canal, then the stern. Eventually they appeared to have moored the boat successfully, but they had made such a meal of it, I wondered how long it would stay tied up.

'There isn't much room in this tub. Couldn't swing a cat.'

'All I could get at the last minute,' said George. 'So you'll have to lump it. Your trousers dry yet?'

'No.'

'Well, we're meeting a lot of people ahead. I think you'd better put them on.'

Against his better judgement, Stan put the still wet shell suit bottoms on again. From the knees downwards they were cold, wet and clinging. He did agree that it would look better if he had them on, rather than just his underpants, as there was a large party just ahead.

George found it extremely difficult negotiating the moored and oncoming craft. Bump. *Blue Belle* shuddered.

'Get away from my boat,' shouted an irate member of the barbecue party. But by that time he had collided with another.

'My God, get a look at that.' Stan's eyes were glued on the

tall leggy blonde in red shorts, who was still sipping white wine from a fluted glass. Her flimsy silk scarf seemed to cover less of her essentials than it had done a short time earlier.

Crash, again. She turned quickly, her attention being drawn, as were the barbecue party, to George's antics with *Blue Belle*, as she crashed into one moored boat after another. So strong was the centrifugal force of the blonde's movement that the flimsy silk scarf could no longer take the strain of the surge of the two magnificent orbs. With a final tear it gave up the ghost, split asunder, and fell into the water.

Stan's jaw dropped. 'They're bloody marvellous.'

George couldn't help but be drawn towards the statuesque figure.

'Struth, what tits.' His eyes bulged, his breathing quickened and his Adam's apple gulped in his throat.

The eyes of the barbecue party all swivelled towards the blonde in stunned silence, as they took in all of her 42 inches.

'Sod it,' said Rose, and she proceeded to increase the blood pressure of all those around by stretching out over the side of the boat to try and retrieve her silk scarf. But the more she tried, the more the scarf moved away in the wake of George's boat. The scene was breathtaking. They were truly magnificent.

George knew he was moving towards the bridge. Easy, he thought, having already negotiated some eleven without difficulty. A piece of cake. He glanced away from the girl for a moment, just in time to see the front of the cabin roof collide with the arch of the bridge. There was a tearing, grinding sound as the roof timbers of the cabin tore and splintered. George ducked just in time, as the boat grazed its side all along the inside arch of the bridge, just missing his head.

They were through the bridge, but the offside of the cabin roof was badly shattered at the front, and severely grazed over its length. The canal behind them was strewn with floating matchwood that had once been part of *Blue Belle*.

'Now look what you made me do.'

There were cheers, and applause, from the barbecue party, but whether this was for George's robust feat of destruction, or some further unbelievable antics of the blonde, was not clear.

'My God, it was worth it,' replied Stan, whose eyes were still wide with wonder and disbelief. 'Bloody marvellous!'

The crew looked smart and passed muster in their casual summer clothes. We closed the curtains, as we didn't want anyone prying in, locked the cockpit doors, and went out through the back hatch, which we firmly padlocked.

The boats ahead were quietly moored. There were children about on the one I had seen mooring earlier. The boys had given up their fishing and gone home for supper. We now had very healthy appetites, and were looking forward to a good dinner.

Blue Belle limped slowly into the wooded glade and pulled into the side.

'Better have a look ahead, we don't want to come right up on them unawares.'

Stan jumped off, and ran, squelching along the towpath. He saw *Colette* ahead, stopped and ran back.

'They are moored up ahead, and the old fogies and the young 'uns are walking along the towpath. The others must still be aboard,' Stan reported.

'Better stay here, as we are out of sight of them. We can then make a recce later, when it's dusk.'

They moored their craft, and began to survey the damage.

'What a mess,' sighed Stan.

'There are two sleeping bags, but I only hope it doesn't rain,' said George.

'Anyway you're sleeping on the damaged side.'

'Thanks! What's for tea?'

'Pork pie past its sell-by date, and some cheese and pickle sandwiches. All I was able to get.'

'Thanks,' said Stan, as he took off his sodden trousers again.

3

From the towpath a flight of steps took us under the railway, down to the road. There was a rather smart, fussy new house, built above the road level, with a curved drive through immaculate lawns to two separate entrances, each flanked by opulent brick pillars, surmounted by sitting lions. The home of a TV star, or minor royalty, at least. I looked up the drive expecting to see a row of Porsches, but there was only one of those four-wheel drive vehicles, so much in favour nowadays with green wellington-wearing country persons. I might never have given more than a cursory glance, but out of the corner of my eye, I saw the inner lion on the lower gate pillar wobble.

My God, it's loose, I thought. That's dangerous. To my horror there were three men beneath the lion, very close to the pillar. I looked back at the lion. It was quite still. Perhaps it hadn't moved at all. A figment of my imagination.

My attention being drawn to the men, I had another look. They were, I must say, an odd group, for they kept their backs to us. All were in jeans, T-shirts and trainers. Their hair was close cropped except for the one in the centre, who was short, fat, bald and somewhere in his forties. Of the other pair, one was about the same age, and the other a good ten years younger.

Nearing the group, I noticed that the lion was standing at an angle, not facing directly outwards. It was certainly loose. So it had moved. I looked back at the men again. They seemed very keen that we should only see their backs.

Margery, reading from the guide book, advised us that Thelwall Station used to win prizes for its floral displays, but it was closed in 1956. Another political blunder, I thought.

These men weren't politicians, I was quite sure of that: they were not oily enough. But I still didn't trust them. Two of them appeared to be holding up baldy. One of them was also holding a heavy leather bag. The other had a lighter one. They gave baldy a heave up again, as he seemed to be wilting. Drunk, I thought. A bit early in the evening for that, but perhaps they start early in these parts. Yes, drunk. No doubt about it.

We walked on and the lion on the other gate pillar winked at me. Did it really wink? I looked back up at it again, but it just stared out straight ahead, with a poker face.

We crossed the A56, and spread out before us was a large open village green, surrounded by trees. It was remarkably beautiful and inviting on a warm summer evening. A sign indicated that the son of King Alfred, of the cakes fame, founded this 'city' in AD923. I surveyed the scene. Better than most cities I had visited, I thought.

'Thank God they've gone. I didn't expect to find anyone along here.'

'They didn't notice us I'm sure. You all right Fred?'

Fred said nothing, but his knees sagged again.

'Give him a heft up, Sam, and we'll get going.'

Ern helped pull baldy upright again, and they started to make a few faltering steps.

'It's all right for you, but I've got the flaming heavy bag as well. It's damned heavy I can tell you. What with him as well.'

Fred only gave a gurgle. It became clear that between them, they were going to have to carry Fred, if they were even going to get him up the steps. Inch by inch, foot by foot, they reached the steps, and started to negotiate each one with difficulty. The bag was heavy, and Fred was a dead weight.

'I can't carry him and this bag. You must carry it for a bit,' sighed Ern, 'or I'm done for, like him.'

'OK.' Sam took the bag, and they tried a few more steps, and had to stop again.

Fred just gurgled. There was foam around the edges of his mouth. There was a red stain on the T-shirt over his stomach, and it ran down his jeans. He was in a bad way.

The raid on the bank had gone quite well. They brandished their guns, which weren't loaded, or shouldn't have been. All went like clockwork until Fred got excited, and started to shout at the manager, who wasn't being quick enough for him.

The truth was that it was very hot in mid-June for a balaclava helmet. He was sweating profusely; perspiration was soaking down from his forehead, and running into his eyes. He couldn't see, and his eyes smarted, He wiped them again with the back of his left hand, but it didn't do any good. Fear took hold of him and he started to panic. He shouted again to speed things up, and hit the manager with his left hand as he waved the gun at him. Stinging sweat filled his eyes again, and it seemed to drive him mad. Shouting furiously at the manager again, he fired his gun, which shouldn't have been loaded. He didn't want to hurt anyone, just liven them up a bit.

Sam and Ern went cold with disbelief. This now put them in a different category. They wanted to look like gangsters, without actually going quite that far. Now they were for real.

'You stupid sod.'

Unfortunately, blinded by the smarting sweat in his eyes, Fred's bullet struck, at almost point blank range, the backside of a bronze leaping horse which decorated the counter,

31

and ricocheted right back, striking him in the stomach. He gave a cry and started to crumple.

Wasting no more time, Ern grabbed the only moneybag that was ready. He didn't dare wait for a second.

Sam dragged Fred out through the doorway, picking up a second lighter bag as he did so. Pulling off his and Fred's balaclava helmets, he bundled him into the back of the getaway car, which had been sitting outside the bank, unremarked, for 15 minutes, on double yellow lines. Adjacent to it some men were making a great noise digging a hole in the road with a pneumatic drill. Ern jumped into the front seat with the bag, and they were off.

No one seemed to give chase. No alarm appeared to have been given. The use of a firearm must surely have alerted someone, but perhaps the pneumatic drill had drowned out Fred's futile gesture. They raced around the outskirts of Manchester, eventually being stuck in a traffic jam around some major roadworks for nearly an hour.

'For Christ's sake get on,' shouted Ern to the driver.

'What the hell can I do? The traffic is stuck.'

'Well you should have checked out the route better.'

'Well, it was all right last month. I tried it.'

'Last month! It looks like we picked a right load of amateurs, Sam.'

'All right,' said the driver, 'do you want to get out now? Go on, get out.'

'Shut up you two, or you'll attract attention,' snorted Sam, 'Fred doesn't look too good. So just make it as quick as you can.'

'Right, as long as he shuts up,' replied the driver. 'And don't let him bleed on my car. I don't want to have to clean that up. Horrible. Ugh.'

'Your car?' shrieked Ern.

'Yes.'

'You stupid bugger.'

'Right. Get out.' He jammed on his brakes sharply, but the car was already stationary and nothing happened.

'We're not getting out,' said Sam from the back seat. 'You should have knocked off the getaway car, not used your own.'

'Why?'

'Because they can trace the car, you stupid git,' shrieked Ern.

'That's it. I'm not going any further.'

'We haven't moved an inch for five minutes,' said Sam. 'Just you two shut up, or I'll brain you. Now get us as quickly as you can to the dropping-off point.'

'Right. As long as he shuts up,' said the driver.

Ern snarled, but as he did so the traffic moved off again.

Apart from the strange men, we hadn't seen a soul in the 'lost' village, and it certainly was peaceful. Then we approached a large public house, surrounded by a high, thick hedge. We heard a great deal of shouting, yelling of children and some breaking of glass. We turned in at the gates and walked up the drive. The noise came from the beer garden, which was jam-packed. People everywhere. The car park was full, but there was a smart restaurant. I felt instinctively that this was the place for my birthday dinner.

On enquiring, however, a pleasant but overly made-up young lady advised that the restaurant was full. I was starving. We went out again along the drive, among the shouting, yelling and breaking of glass, in search of some-where else.

Sam and Ern managed to drag their companion up the steps to the towpath. But it took some considerable time, and they constantly had to transfer the heavy bag from one to the other.

Fred by now looked very sick indeed. His mouth was

frothing, but the froth was tinged pink. They were virtually having to carry him, as he had no strength to move on his own account.

'Its up there, about a hundred yards. Won't be long now, Fred.' But Fred didn't hear.

They reached *Colette* and stopped for another rest. Sam, who was now carrying the heavy bag, rested it on the lid seat which covered the locker at the side of the cockpit. It seemed that the seat had not been replaced properly, with the result that it slipped and the bag fell into the locker.

'No one about,' said Ern. 'Leave it there for now, while we get Fred seen to. We can easily collect it later. This boat isn't going anywhere tonight now, and they aren't using this locker.'

He replaced the lid carefully. They then lifted Fred and continued along the towpath. But Fred's limbs were now limp, and they were simply dragging him along, his shoes scraping along the gravel.

'God, he's some weight.'

We sauntered quietly down the lane. The next pub would be all right, but there were still no pedestrians. Where were they? But perhaps one doesn't find pedestrians in 'lost' villages.

In the heart of the village we soon found the Post Office, and a proper, old-fashioned pub. It was a quaint, olde worlde pub. Just the thing. There were some seats outside, but there wasn't a soul using them. This is going to be the place. There wouldn't be many people inside if there wasn't a single one outside. So in we went.

We soon found where all the pedestrians were. They were inside. It was packed to the doors. There was standing room only, but precious little of that. There was food, according to the notice board and some people were eating. But there wasn't a seat anywhere. We looked and pried into every nook and cranny, and went out again.

Outside there still wasn't a soul to be seen. So in sheer disbelief I went in again. We must have been wrong, it couldn't possibly have been that full, but it was. My birthday meal was receding fast. There were only these two pubs, and there wasn't a chip shop.

On coming out a second time, we actually saw two pedestrians. They dashed our hopes. We wouldn't get anything here tonight. There had been a fete, and the whole village was celebrating. They were too. Why didn't we try Grappenhall? said one, but we'd come through there, and couldn't go back. Despondence fell about us. How were we going to eat? What were we going to eat? Where were we going to eat?

I could sense mutterings among the crew. He's mucked up again: I could read their thoughts.

'Well, that's easy,' said Margery.

Easy! I thought. This is a major crisis and it's my birthday.

'I've got a whole roast chicken with all the trimmings in the fridge. It won't take long to do a few veg.'

Saved! Thank heavens I had had the foresight to place those two bottles of Chardonnay in the fridge!

'George.'

Crackle ... Crackle ... Stan was loitering near the aqueduct, keeping an eye on *Colette*.

'Yes.'

'It's all very quiet. Curtains drawn, no lights on. Dead quiet, it is.'

'I only hope you haven't let them get away with the goods. If you have I'll bloody crucify you.'

'When the old ones went out with the young couple, they looked as if they were going to the pub. It is Saturday night.'

'They'd better be.'

'They didn't take anything with them. So the goods must be aboard.'

'Have you seen anything of the gang you followed to the yard?'

'Nothing, I suppose they must be lying low.'

'Yes …'

'They wouldn't want to advertise.'

'Yes … Clever that, arranging for the others to work the boat, looking like they were tourists. Bloody clever.'

'Can't I come back now? I'm still very damp, and I'm damned hungry.'

'Always bloody moaning, you are.'

'Well they aren't going anywhere now, are they?'

'OK, come back. I'll put the kettle on.'

We had a few more drinks while the vegetables cooked, and then a few more. Richard and Jo sat down to watch the Olympics on TV, and Margery joined them.

I realised that I must do something slightly more elevating, and opened my wine bluffer's guide, so thoughtfully sent to me by my favourite cousin for my birthday. I chortled and read aloud to them interesting anecdotes. Strangely, no one seemed to want to hear.

'We can't do anything more for him,' said Sam.

'Do you think he will pull through?'

'No … Not much chance. Look at him, poor sod.'

'He brought it on himself, silly bugger. What the hell are we going to do with him?'

'We can't go anywhere tonight. We'll drop him in town tomorrow. He'll be looked after all right then.'

'He won't make it.'

'We'll have to hope he does.'

'We shouldn't have used him. You know what a useless

git he is.'

'Not now, please, he's very sick. Just shush a minute.'

'Remember what a mess he made of things in the Strangeways riot? Almost let the screws in, and he was supposed to be helping us.'

'Oh, do shut up! Go and collect the bag, before they come back.'

Ern looked down disdainfully at Fred and, with a grunt, left.

Sam sighed and shook his head. Fred's face was ashen, and his breathing was irregular. Suddenly he opened his eyes for the first time in over an hour, and gurgled unintelligibly as he struggled to speak. He knew Sam, realised where he was for a moment.

Sam wiped his face and tidied him up, after dressing his wound. The pink froth was back again, only now it was scarlet. Fred tried to lift himself up, struggling hard and trying to speak. But still only a gurgling throaty rattle emerged.

'What is it, Fred?' asked Sam, as he put an arm underneath Fred's shoulders to take his weight.

There were simply more gurgles. He was alive, awake, enquiring. Trying to say something. Sam tried to soothe and coax him.

Then, just as suddenly as he had come to, Fred slumped back, shuddering with a loud exhalation of breath and gurgles. He lay still and silent, his eyes open. His arm fell limply from the bunk and hung down towards the cabin floor.

'Fred.'

Sam shook him gently, but there was no response. He shook harder.

Ern came running aboard noisily. He could be heard jumping into the cockpit, through the lounge, banging the doors, and lurched into the cabin, where Sam stood quietly beside Fred.

'They're back,' he shrieked, in a very agitated state.
'They're back already. What the hell are we going to do
now?'

'He's gone,' said Sam quietly.

'What?'

'Fred's gone.'

'Where's he gone?'

'He's passed on.'

'Oh, dead,' was all he said. 'They're back and eating
supper. I can't get the bag. What are we going to do?'

'Show some respect.'

'Yeah, well … But we got business to do, or have you
forgotten?'

'Nothing we can't handle.'

'You're sure he's dead, anyway?' enquired Ern, looking
for the first time at Fred.

'Yes, quite sure.'

'What we going to do with him?'

They left Fred in peace, after Sam had lifted his arm and
laid it along the bunk beside his body. They went quietly
into the lounge area.

'I'll make a mug of coffee.'

The kettle quickly boiled, and Sam made two mugs of
coffee. They sat at the table, and helped themselves to
sugar, but Ern was still in a state of near panic.

'What *are* we going to do?' Ern enquired with considerable feeling.

'It's quite easy.'

'Seems a bloody mess to me. Fred's dead, and the money is
on the other boat. Been a flamin' shambles from the start.'

They sipped their coffee. It was strong and hot, helping
to calm their nerves a little.

'If you stop panicking, and thought a little, you'd see how
easy it all is,' said Sam, trying to calm the excitable Ern. But
with little success.

'Well this time, you've organised the biggest balls-up I've ever seen. Fred shoots off his gun, and manages to kill himself. So now we have a body on our hands. The getaway man uses his own car, so that any fool can trace him, and then gets us stuck in a traffic jam for an hour, so we're here too late to move as planned.'

'Who suggested Fred?'

'Well, I've worked with him before.'

'Who introduced me to the getaway man?'

'All right, all right. You've got the brains, what do we do?'

'When it's dark, we take poor old Fred out, and lay him down on the grass under the hedge, alongside the towpath. He'll be found in the morning, but by then we'll be long gone.'

'What about the bag?'

'Easy too. When they've settled down for the night, we quietly collect the bag, we needn't disturb them. Then we take off before first light. We can then have the cash back in Manchester, under their noses, by a route no one will ever think of.'

What slight breeze there had been, as the evening drew on, dropped completely as darkness fell. All around, it was calm stillness, barely a sound to catch the ear. The moon was now waning fast, and had almost reached its last quarter, so that night brought a dark blanket down over the canal. There was a slight glint on the water, which fractured as a ripple caught it, and then it was still again.

After dinner, the Olympics again took over. I tried a few more gems, which were generally greeted with disinterested silence. Once Richard said, 'You've already told us that one.' Then I got no further response as muscular men and nubile girls performed amazing feats.

*

39

Sam put out what little light they had allowed themselves. He took Fred's shoulders whilst Ern pulled his feet off the bunk, and grabbed his ankles.

They started the long struggle, carrying their heavy burden, which was now a dead weight, through the darkened boat. The companionways took twists and turns and were often narrow, so that it was, at the best of times, necessary to duck and almost walk sideways.

Sam placed his arms under Fred's, and closed his hands together over Fred's chest, and Ern firmly clasped Fred's ankles, on either side of his own body. They set off but, quite simply, were too wide to fit. They turned around with considerable difficulty, and tried with Ern leading with Fred, feet first. But that didn't work either.

In the end they took him out as they had brought him in, upright, with one on each side. They walked him sideways through narrow doorways, negotiating the galley with difficulty, where he was rested head first in the sink. The lounge, with its fixed table, gave them even more difficulty.

Eventually, sweating profusely and cursing under their breaths, they reached the cockpit, puffing like Olympic athletes who had come first in the marathon.

Another short rest, and they started out for the bank. Ern decided to go ashore first, and then let Sam lower Fred's head and shoulders over the side. He stood on the seat at the side of the cockpit, and took a step over the gunwale on to dry land. It was almost pitch dark outside, but as their eyes became accustomed to the darkness he realised, too late, that instead of stepping onto dry land, he was actually stepping into water.

Sam's wife had, for convenience, moored the boat earlier in the day. The stern, by means of which they had gained access, was tight into the bank, but it was shallow, and the bow end could not be drawn right up to the bank, though it was tightly moored.

'Oh Christ,' breathed Ern, but he did have the presence of mind to spring on his one foot still onboard. He landed heavily on his hands and knees, but he had not been quick enough to prevent his one foot dragging the waters of the canal.

'Shhhh …'

'Its all right for you.'

'Shhhh …'

They weren't, as it happened, too far out from the bank. Ern leaned forward as Sam lowered Fred's head and shoulders over the side towards him. Sam then jumped ashore himself, and joined Ern at Fred's shoulders. They gradually pulled Fred ashore, but in the process he got wet feet too.

From then it on it was plain sailing. They carried him over the towpath, and laid him respectfully on his back in the longer grass under the hedge. They crossed his hands over his chest, then quietly slipped away.

'Midnight now. We'll keep a watch out until that lot are safely in bed. A quick snatch of the bag, and we can be ready for off. Don't put any light on.'

'Why not?'

'We don't want to draw attention to ourselves. Keep your eyes open. Get the goods, and be off.'

'We're going to get bored to death.'

'Hey! What's this?'

'What's what?'

'There's someone with a torch getting off that boat behind.'

'So what? I expect they're just checking their moorings, before going to bed.'

'Quiet. Don't, whatever you do, let them know there's anyone aboard this boat. Pay attention.'

*

Before turning in, I decided to take a short walk. No doubt the Olympics inspired my burst of activity. The others were still engrossed with the even greater feats portrayed. I walked along the towpath towards the moored boats. The first was still in darkness. Still unoccupied, I thought. There were still some lights on the boat I had seen moor near the bend ahead.

The air was still, balmy, and it was invigorating to be out in the fresh air again, the slothful effects of the evening's intake of alcohol lifted from my shoulders. I was alive again, enjoying the still night, as the little cradle of the moon peeped from above.

I didn't keep my torch on all the time, but used it occasionally to make sure I was on the right tracks. I could still see the canal as the wasted moon still had a few gleams left to cast upon the waters.

The towpath was dry and gravelly. It made easy walking, and I increased my stride. Suddenly, as I lowered my right foot to the ground, it slipped forward. I checked my balance, righting myself, and shone my torch.

'Oh hell, dog shit,' I swore to myself. 'Might just as well be at home.'

I gingerly raised my foot from the moist, slimy, obviously recent motion. With my torch still on, I moved off the grass walking on the outer side only of my right shoe. Once on the grass I energetically wiped my shoe on the grass. I checked thoroughly with my torch, and when it was more than fully clean, I started to walk back through the grass, still continually wiping my right foot as I went. Just in case I had missed some. When almost adjacent to the empty boat, my foot struck something, 'Not again!'

I shone my torch. A man, lying on the grass. A tramp, I thought, sleeping under the hedge. A drunk sleeping it off. Best not to wake him up. Get away before he comes to, lest he should ask me for the price of a cup of tea.

Starting to move quietly away on tip-toe, my attention was drawn to the red patch on his T-shirt, running down into his trousers. I stopped, looked closer, shone my torch all over him. His eyes were open. His hands were crossed over his chest. No sign of life.

My God. It's blood. He's dead!

4

I stood glued to the spot, staring at him, stunned. I don't think I have ever been so terrified in my life. When I came to, I shone my torch around, expecting any moment to be the next victim of some maniac killer. The towpath was quiet. Not a soul about. The boat adjacent to me was quite definitely still empty. There was no one about.

Taking my courage in both hands, I ran back to our boat. As I climbed aboard, there were ecstatic cheers from the television, and the rest of my crew, over some race. I popped my head in through the cockpit door. I told them not to go out and instructed Richard to take care of everyone. He gave a grunt, but didn't move.

I bravely jumped ashore again and ran down the steps from the aqueduct, to do my duty and phone the police. I had never dialled 999 before.

'Hell! Now we've got to move fast,' said Sam, 'come on.'

'There's no movement down there,' Ern pointed to the boat. 'Shouldn't we just scarper?'

'Thank goodness there is no movement from the rest of them. They're watching television by the look of it. The old codger's gone for the police, though, bet your life. We must be quick. Come on, we must collect Fred again.' Sam jumped ashore, this time from the stern.

'Why?' whined Ern, but following.

'If the police find Fred up here, by the canal, they'll soon put two and two together and realise we are making our getaway on the canal. We can't risk that.'

'What about the loot? We can't leave that. I'll run and grab it, shall I?'

'That can wait, this can't.' They picked up Fred and started to carry him back to the boat. 'They are going in our direction, we can watch out for them tomorrow, keep an eye on them and grab it when the opportunity arises.'

They carried Fred aboard at the stern, with comparative ease, and laid him on the open stern deck. Then they quickly went ashore again, quietly removing the mooring stakes.

Sam pushed the boat out into the canal, grabbed the boat pole, and started to push the boat forward, by punting it along. He did it with such ease that he was obviously used to it. The pole moved quietly in the water, with no splashing and no banging. There was still no movement from the boat behind them. The towpath was quiet.

'Why don't you use the motor?' enquired Ern.

'We don't want to attract attention.'

Sam manoeuvered the boat out into the centre of the canal. Using the boat pole very gingerly, the boat started to glide forward. It reached and, like a spectre in the night, passed the boat near the corner. Onward they went into the night, and darkness enveloped them.

The police were very helpful, and they told me to wait for them at the boat. I could then take them to the scene. They didn't want me to hang about there by myself.

In a state of bewilderment I walked up the steps to the canal, looking carefully over my shoulder, lest the maniac should be near. There! What's that? I swung my torch beam back again over the viaduct. I was sure I had seen something, but I couldn't see anyone now. Perhaps I was mistaken, but was I? I must be ready for anything. I hope they are all right on the boat, I thought, quickening my step. I started to run. Suppose something had happened? I urgently needed to see the family, see that they were all safe!

They were! Still lounging about watching the Olympics, just as I had left them, except there were more cans of lager about. This was becoming an obsession.

'Everything been all right?' I enquired.

''Course,' came the disinterested reply.

'I've just been to report to the police.'

'Police?'

'About the body.'

'Body? What body?'

'The one I told you about.'

'You didn't tell us anything about a body,' said Richard. 'You asked me to keep an eye on them,' indicating Margery and Jo. 'They haven't moved except to get some more lager.'

'Body?' said Margery, unbelieving.

'Body?' repeated Jo, looking concerned.

'Where is it?' asked Richard. 'Show me this body.'

'The police are coming. They don't want me to go out there again. They said to stay here.'

'Whereabouts?' enquired Richard taking the torch from me.

'Up by the next boat. I went on to the grass. His eyes were open and there was blood on his shirt.'

Before we could move there were sounds outside. The boat lurched as someone climbed aboard. The maniac was here. I rushed to the galley and grabbed the carving knife. A policeman's head appeared through the cockpit door. I tried to hide the knife.

'No need for that sir,' said the officer. 'Mr Oliver.' His eyes ranged over all of us, taking in the empty wine bottles and lager cans. 'Sergeant Tooth.'

'Yes,' I replied, trying to hide my confusion.

'I'm sorry to have to ask you, but perhaps you could show me where it is.'

'Is there really one?' asked Jo.

'Don't worry, miss. No need for you to come.' He turned to me. 'But if you could come with me, sir. Once we've found it, you can come back here. The rest is then up to us.'

'I'll come with you,' said Richard, realising my reluctance.

'What about them?' I said, indicating Margery and Jo.

'Don't worry, sir, PC Nonelly will look after them.' He turned his head as someone else clambered aboard.

A very attractive woman PC came into the cabin. Woman? Girl! I would rather have stayed, but went ashore nevertheless after the police sergeant, and Richard followed. There were two other policeman on the towpath. All had torches.

'George. George.'

Crackle. Crackle.

Stan was again by the aqueduct, keeping vigil.

'Yeah.'

'Hell of a lot of activity here.'

'Are they making a move? I'll be there.'

'I got here just in time to see the old fella trotting up from the village along to his boat. He almost caught me in the beam of his flashlight. He was shining it everywhere as though he was looking out for someone.'

'Perhaps he's scared that someone is after him. Can't say I'm surprised.'

'Well, he went to his boat, but since then four local police have arrived, and gone to their boat too.'

'We don't want them mucking in. I'll be there soon.'

'They're off again, all of 'em, up the towpath again. They didn't stay at the boat long.'

'Can you get a bit closer?'
'I'll try, but I don't want to be seen.'

'On holiday are you, sir?' enquired Sergeant Tooth.
'Yes, we started from Acton Bridge this afternoon.'
'Been here before, sir?'
'Never.'
'Any reason for mooring here, sir? Visiting, meeting anyone?'
'No. It seemed a nice spot.'
'It is, sir.'
'Thought we could just find somewhere nice to eat. My birthday.'
'Thought you ate on board, sir? Or am I wrong?'
'We did, Sergeant. Couldn't get any food in the "lost" village.'
'Lost village?'
'That's what the guide book called it.'
'I see. Never heard that before, although I've lived in the area all my life. Had a good celebration did you, sir?'
'Oh yes, thanks. Lovely.'
'They are police. Shut up,' whispered Richard to me under his breath. 'Just stick to the facts.'
We walked up the towpath. I shone my torch carefully.
'Know anyone in the area, sir?'
'No one.'
'Had any trouble down here? Seen anyone acting strange, that sort of thing?'
'No. Very quiet and peaceful.'
'We don't normally get much trouble here.'
'No, Sergeant.'
'What were you doing out here?'
'Just taking a walk after dinner. Getting a little fresh air.'
'Working it off, clearing your head, so to speak?'
'Yes. That's right.'

'Shut up,' whispered Richard again. 'He thinks you're tight.'

Me, tight? I'd had a couple of glasses of wine … Well, a few more, but I wasn't under the influence. Was I?

My torch beam caught the squashed dog turd.

'That's it, officer!'

'What?' said Sergeant Tooth, in a rather shocked tone.

'That's the dog muck I trod in.'

'I see. What did you do then?'

'I flashed my torch onto the grass beyond the towpath. I went on to the grass to wipe it off, and as I was doing that I knocked into … the …'

'Yes, sir.'

We could see the streaked marks of the dog dirt, where I had wiped my shoe.

'Yes, I see, sir. Now whereabouts was it?'

'It was further back. Under the hedge.'

'Why did you go right back there, sir? I can see you wiped all the dirt off within a yard of the towpath.'

'No, I was wiping my feet.'

'Did you need a pee, sir?'

'No, I was wiping my shoe.'

'He would go on wiping his shoe long after it was clean. Just in case,' confided Richard, trying to ease my embarrassment.

We moved further back towards the hedge. Looking carefully, sweeping our torches. But we didn't find anything untoward.

'Nothing here, sir,' said Sergeant Tooth. 'Can you identify the area specifically by anything?'

'No, I don't remember anything. I just saw this body. I thought it was a drunk at first, or a tramp.'

'Oh, I see. A tramp, or a drunk. They are not usually dead, sir. You reported a body!'

'It was. I looked carefully. His eyes were open. He wasn't

breathing, and had his hands clasped across his chest.'

'Oh, come, sir. Bodies aren't found with their arms clasped across their chest as though they had been laid out.'

'But they were. And there was a red patch of blood across his stomach, running down into his trousers.'

'Well, sir, where is he, then? Do you really think he got up and walked off, sir?'

The policemen went up and down in a sweeping movement, minutely covering the whole area. There was certainly no body there.

'You sure this is the place, sir?'

'Quite sure. Yes, this is the area, adjacent to that parked boat.'

The torches flashed towards the canal, but there was no moored boat.

'Boat, sir?'

'There was one. It was in darkness. Unoccupied, and it was parked right there.'

'Been spirited away like the body, has it, sir?'

'No, it was right there.'

'Did you see the boat, sir?' Sergeant Tooth asked Richard.

'There was only one ahead of us when we moored, and there is only one now.' He indicated the boat I had seen moor whilst the others were bathing and changing.

'No, that one came in just before we went out.'

'You haven't seen any other mysterious boat?'

'No,' said Richard.

Sergeant Tooth sent an officer to the moored boat to enquire if they had heard, or seen, anything untoward. A further sweep of the whole area was carried out again. We walked slowly, in a row, and our torches covered the whole area.

'There!' I suddenly shouted, pointing at a crumpled crisp packet. 'That was in the hedge, by his … pelvis.'

Sergeant Tooth went over to it, but there was no sign of

anything. A small gust of wind rose, and carried the crisp
packet further on up the hedge. We all watched. Silently.

'If you marked it by that it could have been anywhere.'

'Yes.'

The policeman returned and reported that the occupants
of the other boat had seen and heard nothing.

'Mr Oliver, are you sure you saw a body? A real body?'

'I think so.'

'You think so.'

'Yes. And there was a boat.'

'I think we should go back to your boat, sir.'

We walked back in silence. When we were all aboard,
Sergeant Tooth asked the ladies what they knew of the
matter, but they knew nothing.

'If you saw anything, Mr Oliver – and, in view of your
remarks about the mysterious boat, I have very serious
doubts – I think your first thoughts were probably correct, it
was a drunk or a tramp.'

'I'm sure he was dead,' I said weakly, but I was by now
beginning to wonder if, by chance, I had been mistaken.
Perhaps I was.

'You must realise this is a serious matter, sir. Wasting
police time is taken very seriously indeed, I assure you. I
have alerted the CID, and now I've got to tell them to stand
down, it was all a mistake. Won't go down well, sir.'

'No,' I said weakly.

'Celebrated a little too much, did we, sir? You get my
meaning.'

I was, by now, feeling a complete idiot in front of everyone.

'I think we'll go now, sir.'

'Yes. Thank you, Sergeant. Sorry to have troubled you.'

Sergeant Tooth's portable phone rang.

'Spriggs here, Sarge. I'm still near the aqueduct where
you left me.'

'Yes.'

'Well, there's a chap here spying on you. Trying not to be seen, but he's not very good at his job. I've had my eye on him for some minutes. And there is definitely something fishy about him. Shall I nab him?'

'Yes. Apprehend him, and I'll be there in two minutes.'

He looked at me and shook his head slightly.

'I think we've got your tramp, or drunk, sir. But no sign of the boat yet. Goodnight, sir, madam.'

With a nod of his head he left, taking his entourage with him.

Stan was watching intently for further activity when a voice close behind him almost made him jump out of his shell suit.

'Excuse me, sir.'

He spun quickly round, and PC Spriggs's torch shone full in his face, blinding him.

'What is all this then, sir?'

'I'm just out for a stroll, officer,' said Stan, trying hard not to look in any way concerned. The police were the last people he wanted to see at the moment. 'A nice night for a stroll.'

'I've been watching you for some time, and you're certainly not out for a stroll. You've been spying on my colleagues. Watching their every movement. Why? What's the game?'

'I just wondered what was up, so I stopped to see. Nothing else, I assure you.'

'Any identification?'

'Not on me, no. I'm just going back this way.' He pointed in the opposite direction from *Colette.* 'All right if I go now, officer?'

'No, it isn't. I'm not satisfied at all. You're not going anywhere at the present.'

53

'Well, what have we here then?' Sergeant Tooth's voice boomed out behind Stan. 'A tramp, or a drunk, he said. You been drinking, eh?'

Stan turned to see Sergeant Tooth towering over him, and three other officers now surrounding him.

'No, officer. I've not been drinking.'

Sergeant Tooth leaned forward, and sniffed hard. 'Hmmmm.' He looked with distaste at the scruffy figure in front of him.

'No identification, Sarge,' said PC Spriggs. 'Shall I frisk him?'

'That's not necessary. I'm only out for a stroll.' Stan backed away from Sergeant Tooth, but into PC Spriggs.

'Mind where you are going, sir.' PC Spriggs pushed him forward again, into the centre of the circle of policemen and woman.

'I'll be the judge of what's necessary,' rejoined the Sergeant. 'Frisk him. See what he's got.'

'Not much,' sighed WPC Nonelly, looking quite disinterested.

'He's got a red patch on his stomach, like that bloke said,' one of the officers pointed out. 'But it's not blood, its just part of those ghastly togs he's wearing.'

Sergeant Tooth studied the red patch intently. PC Spriggs went carefully through Stan's pockets. 'He's got a phone.'

'No identification, and a portable phone, strange combination. Who are you, and what are you doing here?' enquired Sergeant Tooth.

'He's all wet,' said PC Spriggs. 'What the hell have you been doing?'

'Haven't peed yourself have you, lad?' enquired Sergeant Tooth.

'Christ, I hope not.' PC Spriggs backed away, shaking his hands.

'He looks like a tramp, all right,' said Sergeant Tooth. 'Now then, let's have it straight from the horse's mouth. What were you doing down there by that boat?' He indicated *Colette*.

'I haven't been down there.'

'Don't start lying to me. You were seen down there, lying on the ground.'

'I haven't been any further than this. I walked up here, saw all the activity and stayed to watch.'

'You were down there. I know. I've got a witness.'

'No I haven't. I've never been down there. I was just out for a walk. This is as far as I got, when I saw the activity.'

'Who were you phoning while you were doing your spying? I saw you, so don't deny it,' said PC Spriggs.

'I was just talking to my friend.'

'Been casing the houses on the bank round here, have you? Or are you looking, with your accomplice, for some nice pickings from the boats? Big posh boat that one.'

'No, I was just out for a walk.'

'Take him down the station. I'm not wasting any more time with him here,' instructed Sergeant Tooth. 'Our rather squiffy friend on the boat may have been some use to us after all. This is undoubtedly the bloke he saw. Take his phone off him. Don't want him giving any signals. Jones and Nonelly, you stay with Spriggs, and have a good look around the canal and the properties nearby. I want his accomplice.' He looked closely at Stan. 'I don't know what we've got, but I reckon we've got something.'

I felt a lot better when I realised that the poor tramp, a drunk, had been found. He was certainly in need of protection, and now he would get it.

'Anyone want cocoa?'

'No thanks.' The Olympics had taken hold again.

Clutching my cocoa I went very contentedly to bed,

knowing that I had been able to help that unfortunate man. I settled down with my wine bluffer's guide.

Sam kept up his steady poling, and the boat, once it was in motion, kept going, although the poling was hard work. Ern had given a hand, but splashed so much that Sam kept him on the tiller, and did the poling himself.

Brooding trees overhung the banks, forming grotesque lowering shapes against the lighter sky. Their sinister fingers caressed them with eerie approval, shrouding further their clandestine mission. On they went, and on. It seemed like miles. It felt like miles to Sam, but on he kept, on and on.

'This is far enough, surely.'

'Not yet. We must get as far away from that spot as we can. In case there are any nosy parkers around.'

The lights of traffic on the M6 were reflected upon them as they glided silently beneath its huge span, towards Ditchfield Bridge. Shortly before it they steered *Hyacinth* towards the bank and moored, muffling the hammering of their mooring stakes.

'Let's get Fred in, out of the way.'

They carried him, upright again, sideways through the stern door, down into the cabin. They re-laid him in the same bunk, this time putting the coverlet over him.

With everything tidy, they put on the lights, and tried to look like boaters, out for the weekend. The television was still showing the Olympics, the cockpit door was open, and they sat back with a few cans of beer.

At the police station, Stan was permitted, under very strict supervision, to ring George. Sergeant Tooth quickly took the phone off him.

'I can't get much sense out of your friend. I want to see you!' he ordered.

'Is your Superintendent in?' enquired George.

'Yes. What about it?'

'Send a car to the aqueduct for me. I'll come in. Tell him I want to see him, alone. Urgently.'

'Oh yes?'

'I will not talk to anyone else. Is that understood?'

'Who the hell do you think you are? Giving me orders!'

'Just say to him, "Powder Puff",' said George.

'I'll have a car there,' snarled Sergeant Tooth, and slammed the phone down. 'Bloody cheek!'

He paced up and down, his face livid with rage. 'I've got officers out, along the canal, looking for his conspirators,' he said, pointing at Stan. 'And I'm to tell the Superintendent bloody "Powder Puff". He'll think I'm cracked. Anyone would imagine I'm organising a poofter outing.'

'Better had,' suggested the Police Constable with him. 'May be rubbish, but suppose it's MI6, or some of that stuff.'

'Christ, MI6, that's all we need. They're all bloody nancy boys anyway. "Powder Puff", MI bloody 6! Ye gods!'

He went off, reluctantly, to speak to his Superintendent.

Sam emptied one can of lager, and reached for another. A young police officer came walking along the towpath from Lymm, clambered aboard, and put his head around the cockpit door.

'Sorry to trouble you, sir. Seen anything suspicious or untoward on the canal?'

'Nothing, officer. Quiet as the grave.'

5

The dimpled sun danced backwards and forwards across the water as we woke to our first morning on the canal. The trees in full leaf, rustling gently, were full of the joys of morning, their flowing branches affording ample shade along the banks. Although at present unneeded, it would prove a welcome refuge as the heat of the day wore on.

Sheer tranquility, I thought. What could this idyllic spot possibly have to do with the previous evening's adventure? Perhaps it hadn't really happened. It could not have taken place here, not in this happy wooded bower. I breathed deeply and sighed with contentment, standing in the cockpit, drinking in the sheer magic of it all.

There was a good deal of activity about the boat I had seen moor with such difficulty last evening. Children's voices were raised, laughing, shouting with joy. But of the mysterious boat in front of us, there was not a sign.

A tall thin young man in his mid-thirties, from the boat ahead, walked slowly towards us down the towpath. His daughter was on her tricycle, and he had a toddler by the hand. We exchanged pleasantries. He commented on the nice quiet night they had, and said even the police had called to see if they were all right. It was most reassuring to see how they were looked after on their first night on the canal.

He had woken up, he said, to find his boat floating out into the canal, not moored tightly to the bank. Had we had any trouble? Young lads perhaps?

'No, none,' I lied. Having seen his effort to moor last night, I was not in the least surprised.

He went on his way to the village, and Richard returned with the Sunday papers. I was anxious to get going, but the crew refused to move without a cooked breakfast, which was just as well in view of what was later to befall us.

Suitably sustained, the crew, now in shorts and bright T-shirts, set our nose for Manchester. We passed the boat ahead. They stood in the stern and waved. Soon we were round the corner and on to pastures new.

Sergeant Tooth stood mute when, late into the morning, the Superintendent had, without any explanation, ordered him to release Stan and George and arrange for a car to return them to the aqueduct.

He was heard to mumble audibly, under his breath. 'Powder Puff! I'll give 'em, Powder Puff!'

Sergeant Tooth didn't go straight home for his breakfast. He was still overstrung and annoyed. Instead, he stopped at the aqueduct and went up onto the canal. *Colette* had gone, the scene was serene. What had it all been about? he pondered.

He heard a boat approaching from the Grappenhall direction, and saw, to his absolute horror, a very sad and dilapidated *Blue Belle* crawling along at snail's pace. George and Stan acknowledged him shyly as they passed.

Sergeant Tooth's jaw dropped, in disbelief, and that turned into a scowl of anger.

'Bloody Powder Puff,' he snorted.

Sam and Ern were sitting quietly in the stern, ostensibly sunning themselves.

'I don't see what this is going to do for us,' said Ern, with an air of indignation. 'They've got our money, and we should be getting it back.'

'If we tried now we'd get nicked. Either talk sense, or shut up.'

Ern shut up.

It really was rather restful, relaxing in the sun, particularly after the exertions of the night.

'They're coming,' said Ern. 'Shall we ram them?'

'They outnumber us two to one. Shut up. Look as if you're dozing. Don't look up, or say anything.'

As *Colette* glided quietly by, Sam watched intently from hooded eyes. Barely a breath, or a movement, was perceptible.

'We should have done something,' moaned Ern, in considerable annoyance.

'We have,' said Sam.

'What 'ave we done? Just sat here like Christmas puddings, and saw our lolly go sailing past.'

'You may have done, but now I'm sure I know where they are going. Which means I know precisely what to do.'

'What do you mean? They didn't say where they were going.'

'Oh yes they did. They're going through the centre of Manchester. We've got them. By this evening we'll have the cash.'

'How do you know that? Not many people go right through the middle of town. Castlefields is usually far enough.'

'No, not many people do go through the centre of the city. And it's Sunday. That's what's going to make it easy for us.'

'But how do you know they're going through there?'

'You really are thick. Didn't you see the old man chuntering, giving orders out of a guide book in his hand?'

'Yes. What of it? He had something in his hand. I didn't look.'

'If you did look, just once in your life, you might get

61

somewhere. They are tourists if ever I saw any, and it's a hired boat. He had in his hand a guide book of the Cheshire Ring, and that runs straight through the centre of the city.'

Ern still looked puzzled.

'When they are through the bridge, we can get going behind them. But we must do it quietly, stand back at some distance. I expect they'll stop for lunch, or something, then we can sneak ahead and lie in wait for them.'

'Where?'

'Oh, I know where.'

Colette disappeared beneath Ditchfield Bridge, and *Hyacinth* slipped her moorings.

We cruised quietly through the picturesque little village of Lymm, with its very opulent, select Cruising Club, as the sun moved higher into the heavens.

'There's water at Little Bollington, we can fill up there. We'll also see what we missed with Ye Olde No. 3!'

After Oughtrington, the canal steered straight out into the wide open country. The trees had, for the most part, gone. Private moorings galore crowded the right-hand bank. Seemingly, all Mancunians must have a boat. There were moorings of all types and sizes. From a few boats moored at the edge of a field, with the odd uneven plank out to the boat, to elaborate staging, to which the boats were tied, all within a high fenced compound.

Often there were numerous people on, in and around the boats, with highly polished parked cars behind. Boats, I learned, were not just for cruising. On some, people just sat in the sun drinking tea, or sometimes an alcoholic beverage. Others were a hive of activity. People were washing down, painting, polishing, cleaning brasses, sawing wood, hammering. Refurbishment was at fever pitch. Still others were busy gardening, for every self-respecting boat had tubs and trays of plants, which appeared on roofs, in the bows, across the stern. Some people were lunching, whilst others just sat. Out for the day. filling in Sunday. Just like having a caravan, I surmised. The only difference is that they float, whilst the others didn't.

One small field had five rather old and battered boats moored uneasily to the bank. Their rickety landing stages had seen much better days. In fact they looked distinctly unsafe. Here there was no one in attendance, these craft were left alone to fend for themselves. One had a scruffy sheet of cardboard in a window, with a price tag and telephone number, whilst another had sunk onto the bed of the canal, leaving just the superstructure of the cabin above the water. Through the still glazed windows one could see some of the internal fitments. Just the place, I thought, to find a body! That would make a good start for a thriller.

Blue Belle, despite her decrepit appearance, chugged valiantly on under the M6.

'Good job they gave us some grub at the station. There's nothing left here.' Stan was feeling sorry for himself again.

'We'll stop in a moment at Lymm. Just for a few essentials. We haven't any time to waste now. Thanks to your stupid antics last night, you've lost us too much time already.'

'You sent me out there. How did I know the police would be called out there?'

'Should have kept your distance, and not been seen. You are supposed to be using some gumption, but clearly you haven't got much.'

'Thanks,' replied Stan sarcastically. 'Posh place, this.'

'Very posh. So behave yourself. God, you do look a scruff. Go below and tidy yourself up before you go ashore.'

'Yes, Captain,' snapped Stan as he went below.

George just scowled. 'And I have to be landed with him,' he thought.

They made a quick stop for vital stores, and were off again, in minutes, without a hitch.

Outrington was still very sleepy. 'It's a beautiful day, so why rush,' Stan sighed to himself. But it was not to be.

George pulled towards the towpath, without reducing speed.

'I want you to drop off now, and have a brisk jog along the towpath, to see if you can catch sight of them.'

Stan face dropped. 'Oh, not again.'

'They can't be that far ahead. We must keep them in our sights, otherwise we won't be able to pounce at the right moment. We don't want to lose them.'

'Don't we?'

'Do we!'

Pulling close into the bank, but still without reducing speed, George shouted, 'OK, jump now, and don't forget to take your phone.'

Stan looked aghast. 'Well, slow down then.'

'We can't afford to lose time.'

'If I try and jump off at this speed, I'll break my neck as well as my leg.' Stan was determined to hold his ground. He had put up with too much nonsense already.

George grudgingly reduced speed a little.

'I'm still not trying, until you slow right down.' Stan really was digging his heels in. And getting results.

'You really are,' grumbled George, as he slowed right down, 'a useless bloody shambles.'

'Thanks,' said Stan as the boat, this time, slipped quietly in towards the bank at a reasonable speed.

He jumped ashore, and started to jog up the towpath.

Little Bollington proved a rather bleak, open stretch of water, very exposed, built up on an embankment. It was nothing like the beautiful spot where we had stayed overnight. But there was no body either. We looked down onto Ye Olde No. 3, a small former stagecoach inn which was now flanked by a large beer garden. It meant a longer trip today, but I was glad we had not reached here for my birthday dinner. The aqueduct had been far more inviting, until I found that tramp. But the tramp was now a thing of the past. A fleeting moment.

We pulled in at the watering point. The hosepipe was stored in the locker under the seat in the cockpit, on the opposite side from the one in which the mooring pegs had stood. We coupled up the hose line, and started to fill up.

As the morning was wearing on, traffic increased considerably in both directions. Manchester was on the move.

'There we are. They've pulled in for water.'

'Do we need to get some as well?' Ern stretched himself and came to life.

'No time. If we run out, we run out. At the moment it's full ahead at top speed,' snapped Sam, throwing the accelerator full ahead. *Hyacinth* heaved herself together, and set off full steam ahead.

Sam was determined not only to catch *Colette*, but to get way ahead. He didn't mind in the slightest if a few of the recognised rules of the canal were broken in the process. One irate occupant of a moored boat shouted abuse as his boat was battered roughly against the bank in the huge wake created by *Hyacinth*, as she ploughed steadfastly onward, like a bull in full charge. Sam just smiled and waved back, as though exchanging a greeting. Ern, who just didn't have the style, merely raised two fingers, which only brought forth further abuse.

Fishermen were again out in force along the banks, enjoying a Sunday in the open air. Some were accompanied by bored wives, who read their books while ignoring everything around them, or eager girlfriends, valiantly look-ing after the needs of their men, providing sandwiches, drinks, worms or maggots, at their masters' whim.

It is quite clear that fishermen hold no regard whatsoever for the boating fraternity. They are tolerated, but certainly regarded as a nuisance. The canal was obviously designed for fisherman, and the boating intruders were looked upon with disdain. They raise their rods, or perch poles, to let the craft pass, but always with a superior air of contempt. If a helmsman nods in thanks, or speaks, he is ignored. There can clearly be no communication encouraged between the rival armies. They sit quietly, looking straight ahead as though completely unaware of a boat's approach, and just at the point where a collision between boat and line seems inevitable, the rod is quietly lifted, without a glance in the boat's direction, and calmly lowered into the self-same spot of water, as soon as the interloper has passed.

The wash from *Hyacinth* turned indifference into annoy-ance, for she was certainly creating a great disturbance to the waters and, perforce, frightening the timid fish. So they would be even less enthusiastic than usual about jumping onto the waiting hooks of the fishermen.

Far from ignoring Sam, they shouted abuse at him, to which he replied by smiling benignly, and waving back. Only Ern was to lower the tone in the way he knew best, inciting them to greater annoyance, so that wives were even disturbed from their books, and looked up in annoyance.

'We aren't far off now,' said Sam. 'Put on your dark glasses and, whatever happens, sit with your back to them and don't move.'

As they approached *Colette*, Sam slowed slightly so that there was no great wash to disturb her whilst she was water-ing.

'Three of them are ashore, looking out over the village. Can't see the old lady. I expect she's making the tea.'

Hyacinth slipped quietly by, without anyone even looking in her direction.

'Gently does it,' smiled Sam.

Once clear of *Colette,* the throttle was thrust fully forward again, and Sam was away with as much speed as *Hyacinth* could muster. This was not without some annoyance, again, to those Sam passed, but he was still cordiality itself. He was unaware that all his benign sociability was immediately undermined by Ern, whose crudities, if anything, became more explicit.

Onward over the Bollin Aqueduct.

'George … George.'

Crackle, crackle.

'You there, George?'

'Yep. Now what have you got to report?'

'I've found 'em. They're taking on water at Little Bollington. I'm a bit down from them.'

'You sure nobody joined 'em?'

'No. The young 'uns, and the old codger, are ashore. The old woman must be inside with the rest of the gang. No sign of them, reckon they're still lying low.'

'If you didn't lose 'em last night. And I hope you didn't.'

'Nowhere for them to go. They must be there. I'll wait here for you until you come up. Or do you want me to get closer and have a gander?'

'No. Stop where you are. Keep a close eye on them, though. I'll be there soon.'

Stan lay down on the towpath, turned on his right side, feet towards the canal edge, watching the watering continue for a few minutes, then lay back fully to take advantage of the sun. After the hectic night, the brisk trot had invigorated him. He now felt on top of the world, tired but content. If it weren't for George, this wouldn't be all bad, he thought.

*

It was nearly midday and we still had 14 miles to go to meet our – my – target. The first 7 miles were plain sailing, but the last 7 miles would be relentless hard work for there were no less than 27 locks, and one swing bridge, to be negotiated. We had all determined to be through Manchester in the day, but it was going to take the full measure of us. We now had to see if we could do it.

The fishermen were out in force. None deigned to look, or acknowledge us, as we passed. With the fishermen, and the moored craft, speed had of necessity to be reduced.

From the high vantage point of the Bollin Aqueduct, the open park land of Dunham Massey unfolded, a magnificent hinterland on the Cheshire border, before the urban sprawl of Greater Manchester enveloped us with her huge smoke-darkened wings.

One boat, anxious to be first, accelerated hard to overtake us fast, just where the aqueduct narrows very sharply over the Bollin River. Heavy reinforcements were necessary after a serious breach of the canal wall in 1971, which took two years to repair. But there is no sign of that now, apart from the short narrow stretch.

Broadheath. Sale. We were now into the heartland of industrial Manchester. High fences, old weatherbeaten brick, factory walls flanked us on either side. Some were in occupation, others falling into decay and ruin. Warehouses, once a scene of high activity in the heyday of the canal in the nineteenth century, were now derelict, an eerie reminder of past glories.

As we ventured further into the heart of the city, boat traffic dropped away, until we were alone on the canal. The Sunday trippers clearly didn't get this far. Neither, it seemed, did the holidaymakers. Are we being foolhardy? I wondered. But the only way to reach the Peak Forest Canal was straight ahead, through the middle.

The Bridgewater tributary to Wigan Pier bore off to our

left as we burrowed further into the teeming city. Pamona Strand and Salford Docks, once the hub of the huge Manchester Ship Canal, now lie idle and derelict, awaiting the developer's hand.

A mixture of feelings flooded, and re-flooded, through me. The excitement of being at the industrial heart of a major city. The sadness at proud glories, now decaying into dust. Shelley's words came to mind:

> And on the pedestal these words appear:
> 'My name is Ozymandias, king of kings.
> Look on my works, Ye Mighty, and despair!'
>
> Nothing besides remains, Round the decay
> Of that colossal wreck, boundless and bare,
> The lone and level sands stretch far away.

'Stan ... Stan!'
Crackle ... Crackle ...
'Answer me! Stan!'
Crackle ... Crackle.
There was no reply. George was becoming rather worried. What was he up to now? Where was he, for heaven's sake?

Frantic now, he sailed past the moored Sunday boat sitters. He was somewhat self-conscious, as they looked askance at him and the sad little *Blue Belle* as she chugged valiantly onward.

He noticed a sleepy figure lying in the grass beside the towpath, but took no notice. He was past before he realised it was Stan. Throwing the accelerator into reverse, in an urgent attempt to stop quickly, he successfully managed, yet again, to force the stern out into the canal so that he was head on at right-angles to the towpath.

Shouting, swearing and phoning, did no good at all. Stan was out for the count, and wasn't going to be disturbed.

The only thing for it was to go ashore, and wake him. Eventually George eased *Blue Belle* into the bank and stepped ashore, remembering to hold the mooring line carefully in his hand. He wasn't going to lose the boat. There had been enough calamities on that front. He was being careful to do it right.

So wild was George that he kicked Stan's feet. 'Get up you lazy sod!' he shrieked. 'Get up!'

'What is it?' Stan rubbed his eyes. 'Oh, it's you. Must have dozed off.'

'Dozed off! I'll give you dozed off. Where are they? Eh? Where are they?'

Stan looked towards the watering point, which was now empty. 'They must've gone.'

'That's nothing to where you are going. Get on the boat.'

Stan slowly got up, and looked at the boat. 'Which way are we going?' he enquired.

George turned towards *Blue Belle*. He had been careful to keep a tight hold of the mooring line, but it was the stern line, and by pulling the line tight into the bank, the little craft had swung round, and was now facing in the direction from which they had come.

'Now look what has happened through your stupidity,' George roared.

Stan just quietly stepped aboard, and waited for George, who looked as if he was going to have a heart attack.

Sam strode out, through the short tunnel under Deansgate, along the towpath beside the Rochdale Canal, in the heart of the city. Ern trotted by his side.

'Why did we leave the boat down there, to walk all the way up here?' Ern enquired.

'We don't need the boat up here. We'll go back to it when we get the bag. Now keep quiet, and come on.'

'What about Fred?'

'Tonight, when we're back, we'll see to Fred.'
Under Albion Street.

Huge warehouses surrounded the Castlefields Junction. Reminders again of past glories, but here, all was tidy. The whole area has had a facelift, refurbished, bright as a new pin. It is now an urban heritage park. High above, the railway was carried on castellated bridges over the old potato wharves and the Hulme Lock, which seals the River Irwell from the canal.

Nostalgia flooded back again, with youthful memories of rowing on the black treacly waters of the River Irwell at Agecroft Regatta. We were knocked out in the first race, and spent the rest of the day in the beer tent. I don't think I would really fancy that now, but at the time, it was great!

There were a number of moored boats, but none, except for ourselves, was moving. We hadn't seen a moving boat now for some time, nor a fisherman for that matter. We were the only moving object on, or beside, the water. Why no one else? It was as though we were entering a little-frequented area. What was lying in wait ahead for us, in the centre of the city? It had, at one time, a rather uninviting reputation, but the guide books now gave it the all clear, and a recent article in the *Telegraph* had been positively effusive. But why were we the only moving boat, nothing in either direction? Just us ... Alone ... Strange.

Castlefields was built by the Duke of Bridgewater as the basin into which his coal was delivered by canal. To the centre of his major market. Manchester. My mother was born here, nearly a century ago, in a now long-gone, public house, The Rainbow, in Hulme. Somehow I feel that I have a link, an affinity, with this city, although I don't really know it at all.

The basin widened out into a huge bright clear area, under the hot June sun. This must truly have been a centre

71

of intense activity. Certainly the largest basin we had seen so far. Ahead of us now we could see a lock, the lock that would take us from the gentle Bridgewater Canal into the 2 mile stretch of the Rochdale Canal that cuts right through the very heart of the city. Two miles that once formed a vital artery, throbbing with life, across the business and commercial centre of this great city. Nowadays most visitors, and even many residents, don't really know it exists, except when they come upon it face to face. Two miles also that contain nine locks, and for which we will need a licence to traverse.

But the strangest sight of all met our bewildered eyes. The whole area surrounding the lock was crowded with people of all shapes and sizes, brightly dressed, in the gayest of moods. The strains of an operatic tenor filled the air with an aria from *Tosca*. Where were we? Was this another planet?

Sam strode down into the darkness, under London Road.

'Give 'em another hour, and we've got 'em.'

6

Stan was only too eager to get away from George, and his incessant carping. Jogging happily along the towpath beside the railway, through Hulme. Barely a mile now into Castlefields.

'Keep a good look out, and let me know as soon as you see 'em.'

'Yeeees, George.'

If he had been told once what to do when he got there he'd been told 20 times.

He took Pamona Strand in his stride. Under the railway. Then at Woden Street footbridge he started to hum to himself. A tune from *The Sound of Music* filled his head. He had picked it up from the regular showings on television over Christmas. He now knew it by heart. His mother loved the film, and was looking forward to seeing it again this Christmas. He hoped they would be showing something else. Anything else.

'The hills are alive,' he hummed, throwing out his arms, just like Julie Andrews, and spinning around, as she had done to make that good opening camera shot. A nearby fisherman looked up and shook his head.

As he spun he lost his balance, stumbled and fell headlong along the towpath, his head hanging over the edge of the canal into the keep net containing two perch and a roach.

'Silly sod,' muttered the fisherman, and went on with his work.

*

73

The waters were quiet, but the whole of Castlefields, and around the lock, were crowds of people in holiday mood. What was it? Were they awaiting our arrival? Anyone would think we were royalty, at least. The atmosphere of Carnival was everywhere. There were agile jugglers, colourful clowns, all surrounded by admiring groups. Children held balloons, adults beer glasses. The tenor's enthusiasm for *Tosca* filled the air. He was really quite good, I thought.

From the bridge over the lock entrance they looked down upon us with wonderment. Strange people arriving, and by boat of all things! A group of onlookers on the landing stage stood like a welcoming committee to greet us. 'That's Pavarotti, that is,' a smart, brown-suited elderly man informed us, with genuine pride.

That's Pavarotti. No wonder he was quite good!

The poor man must have been sweltering in the afternoon heat, for in addition to his smart brown suit, he was also wearing a raincoat. That was really taking pessimism to the extreme; there hadn't been even the slightest sign of rain for many days now, not even in Manchester.

He had in his hand a three-quarter full glass of beer, and did I detect, by chance, the very slightest slur in his speech? 'Tha's Pavarotti' indicated that this was not his first glass.

Richard jumped ashore to hold the boat, as Jo and I went ashore to open the lock.

The brown-suited man was very insistent that I should realise whom I was hearing. 'Tha's Pavarotti, tha' is.' He clearly felt that I should show due appreciation for what Manchester had laid on especially for our arrival. I assured him that I did appreciate Manchester's gesture to us. But somehow I don't think he was convinced. Instead of standing reverently and listening, I followed Jo ashore to open the lock gates. The poor man convinced himself of my complete philistinism where music was concerned.

He was soon lost in the crowd, who watched, mostly glass

or balloon in hand, these two strange beings as they moved among them towards the two large gates that open the first lock on the ascent of the Rochdale Canal.

Jo stayed on Pavarotti's side. I slipped over the bridge, up some steps onto a large open wharf, thronging with people behind which an old warehouse had been turned into a pub. Now it was clear where all the drink was coming from. I caught the eye of the juggler, surrounded by an admiring group, and ran down the same number of steps I had just gone up, to reach my side of the lock.

In an effort to reduce vandalism in Manchester, boatmen not only need windlasses to open the sluices, but a special 'Manchester Key' to allow the sluice mechanism to be operated. It seems that naughty lads had been opening the sluices and letting the water drain away, and this is an effort to stop them.

The key proved easy to operate, but added to the operating time. Something, in our case, we could have done without. We soon had the water level in the lock down, but from then the fun started. The two arms on the lower gates are normally pushed to open, or pulled, but these gates were different. The arms are chained to a revolving drum and the windlass is necessary to wind the gates open. Another anti-vandalism device. The chains creaked and groaned on the drum, once we had discovered which way to turn it.

I looked at my watch: 3.30 p.m. We were all right for time as no boats were allowed through the Rochdale after 5 p.m., or before 9 a.m. Two and a half hours through Manchester, and four hours beyond. Ten o'clock. We had to get a move on, if we were to do it.

Colette edged her way into the lock. The crowd surged around to watch. This was a canal, a pretty stretch of water. But a boat on it, that was something different, something new.

*

'George … George.'

Crackle, crackle …

'George. Come on, George.'

'What have you to report,' snapped George.

'Oh! It's like that, is it?'

'Well, do you have anything to report, or don't you? If not, I've got work to do.'

'They are just entering the lock to go through the city. What the hell are we going to do now?'

'Are they, by God. I see!'

'But you said they'd stop here, as it was an ideal pick-up spot for them. You said.'

'Well they haven't, have they. We'll have to go on, that's all.'

'But how do we do these lock things?'

'You'll have to find out. Won't you.'

'Do you know?' enquired Stan.

'It can't be too difficult, can it.'

'I don't fancy it at all. Where are you? Thought you'd be here by now.'

'Hulme.'

'Hulme! Only Hulme. You should be here by now.'

'I, er … had a … er … slight mishap.'

'You did what?'

'I ran aground.'

'Not again.'

'Never mind what I'm doing. Where are you and what have you to report?' George was getting on his high horse again.

'I'm standing right beside the lock watching them go in.'

'You are not exposing yourself, are you?'

'What the hell do you mean? Oh, I see. No. There are crowds here, they won't notice me.'

'Keep your eye on them, and see how they do it. I'll be along soon.'

'Yeah.' He put his phone down and looked around. 'I could do with a drink.'

The boat, all 62 feet, glided in beautifully. Margery waved to me, and much to her surprise, everyone around me waved back at her.

Richard took the precaution of running round closing the cockpit doors, the side hatch, and pulling all the window blinds down. Luckily we had two blinds for each window: one for night use, and one for day use, which allowed light in and us to see out, but no one could see in.

I wound my gate closed on its chain, and hoped I wouldn't see another like it. Poor Jo wasn't so lucky. Being a pretty, and obviously 'helpless' girl, with such hard work to perform, she was soon surrounded by many eager middle-aged men, all willing to help. Each had his essential equipment with him, a glass in one hand, and therein lay the problem.

One offered to hold the huge arm, which was quite capable of holding itself, another held the slack chain, which needed no help either. The simple job of winding the drum was left to Jo. She started to turn the drum, the gates creaked and groaned, started to close and then with a judder stopped with a jarring, grinding sound. It wouldn't move.

The man, quite uselessly holding the loose chain, simply dropped it. Quite accidentally I'm sure. But he didn't drop it on the drum, or directly down off the drum. Of all places, he dropped it between the drum and the metal frame in which it was running, successfully jamming the whole mechanism. The gate refused to move, try as Jo might. In fact the more she tried the tighter the chain became jammed.

I went round to help. It wouldn't take long once I was there. But try as I might, I couldn't budge it either. Sweat poured down into my eyes, stinging them, but I still couldn't move it. What a start to our trip. Twenty-seven locks, and we were stuck on our first.

Advice was profuse, as one hand after another tried to help. There was only one hand per person. The other was required to hold his beer glass. The suggestions became more and more fatuous, and I was getting more and more annoyed.

Suddenly Richard was there. He had jumped onto *Colette*'s roof, and climbed the metal lock ladder. He looked at our major problem, took the windlass out of my hands, and simply rammed its metal handle between the revolving drum and its cradle, prised them apart, and pulled the chain out. The gate closed easily. I wondered if the mysterious helper had done it on purpose.

'George ... George.'

'Yeah.'

'They're in the lock, but they had a hell of a lot of trouble with all the gear. You sure you can do it? Looks very complicated to me.'

'We'll be all right. Piece of cake.'

'Well, the girl couldn't do it, or the old chap. Only the young bloke, and he had half a dozen helpers.'

'Ah, you've seen 'em. They came out to help.'

'No, not them. Haven't seen sight of them. No, the folks round here helped.'

'Don't worry, we can do it,' George said confidently.

'Have you got one of those winding things?'

'Yes. And there's a bit in a book here shows you what to do.'

'They're filling the lock with water now. Boat's coming up very fast. They've got all the doors shut, blinds down and curtains drawn. Looks very odd for mid-afternoon. They must be inside there all right. I tried to look in, but I can't see anything.'

'They must be in there. But if they've skipped, you're for it.'

'I reckon they're making sure no one sees them. The old 'uns, and the young 'uns, do all the work. They're keeping well out of sight. Fancy having all the blinds and curtains drawn.'

'Damned clever, you know. You've got to hand it to them. Fantastic cover.'

'Don't be long.'

'Be there in twenty minutes.'

Stan put his phone down. 'Unless you run aground again.'

Seeing every other person with a beer glass in his hand was giving Stan ideas. To hell with it, he thought, and went to the pub, returning shortly with a pint and a bag of crisps.

'Can we get on now?' a lady with two small children asked Margery.

'No, I'm afraid not,' she replied.

'It's a trip isn't it?'

'No, it's not a trip, sorry.'

'We want a ride. How much is it?'

'It's a private boat. We don't give rides.'

''Course you do. It's a trip, and we want to get on.'

'I'm sorry, it's a private boat and we don't give trips.'

'Seems funny to me. You're going up here for a trip, and you won't give us a ride.'

'Sorry, no rides. This is a private boat. We're on holiday.'

'That? A holiday?' said the lady in disgust, but she was still eager to step on given a chance.

The lock was still surrounded by crowds of people who obviously had never seen a lock operated before, nor a boat on this canal. It was soon filled, and ready to open on the upper single gate, which was on my side. Richard and Jo jumped aboard and left the job to me.

My attention was drawn to a middle-aged, balding man, busy taking photographs of us. I wondered why anyone would want photographs of us. We were very photogenic, I knew, but that didn't seem an adequate reason. In my paranoia I thought of MI5, but dismissed it. Next year's 'Come to Sunny Manchester' brochure, more like. He moved on round, and out of sight.

Some ten or more people were resting while they drank their beer, sitting all along the arm of the upper gate. I asked if they would mind moving so that I could open the gate. They looked doubtfully at me, but moved quietly, without demur. They very kindly left behind for me a whole row of beer glasses, all empty of course, in a straight line all along the arm from the lock gate itself to its outer extremity.

'Open the gate,' shouted Richard, but before opening it I first had to move all the glasses, and stack them on the side of the steps leading to the upper wharf. Backwards and forwards I scuttled, like a bee after pollen.

'Hurry up,' reminded Richard.

My task completed I was now confronted by a new obstacle. The arm was clear, but the area between the arm and the lock side, within the arc through which the arm had to move to open the gate, was crowded with all the people I had disturbed from the arm, and more. I didn't particularly want to push them into the lock, so again very politely asked them to move. They moved and the gate swung open.

Colette moved serenely out into the Rochdale Canal. I closed the gate, jumped aboard, and we moved slowly. High soot-blackened walls now hemmed us in on either side. Certainly not very inviting, rather sombre after the burst of colour at Castlefields. The crowds did not venture along the towpath. As we moved off they watched us go, then turned to get another glass.

I became aware of the photographer now walking along the towpath ahead of us, still taking photographs of us as he went. I felt a little uneasy. Why all these photographs? What was he up to? He wasn't doing all this for fun, had he got some sinister motive? He kept ahead and never let us catch up. He just went on clicking shot after shot. All of us?

A bus conductor walked along beside us for some distance, asking questions about the boat, the canal, the city, but he knew more about the city than we did. He was a likable, cheerful chap, who was obviously interested. He knew the canal was there, but boats were new to him.

There were also two pretty girls. I was very anxious to talk to them. Students, I thought; one was French, the other Asian. They were good company, and chatted amicably as they walked beside us.

But, by the second lock, just before Deansgate, we were quite alone. There wasn't a soul. A few moments ago we were surrounded by hundreds of people. Now there were none at all. In the heart of Manchester, and there wasn't a living soul, apart from the four of us. Up above, the world went on like a merry-go-round, but down here on the canal, flanked by the high, dank walls, there was no sign of life. We were quite alone.

After the fourth lock, approaching the bridge, which took Oxford Street over us, we could see to our right, high up on a wall in white lettering, 'Palace Theatre'. Margery spotted it first, and shouted to me, pointing upwards and smiling. I looked up, and was immediately taken back some years.

We had fond memories of the Palace Theatre. One Christmas, on two consecutive days, the two parts of 'The Royal Shakespeare Company's' production of *The Life and Adventures of Nicholas Nickelby* had been shown on television. Some two years later we learned of its revival at the Palace. It was so long an epic that it was staged in two halves on alternate evenings, but on Wednesdays and Saturdays they did both parts. In a fit of mental aberration we booked for a Wednesday 'blockbuster'. Act 1 started at 1.30, until 5.30. An hour and a half of refreshment, and then 7 o'clock until 11 o'clock for Act 2.

I didn't think I would make it. I remember loosening my shoelaces and expecting to find my legs twitching, which does happen to me in theatres when I get bored, or shows go on too long. But this wasn't too long. As soon as the music started we were gripped. Transported on a magic carpet, they carried us hither and beyond, with such consummate ease. No curtain, no lavish sets, and the cast played numerous parts. You knew you had seen them as six other people already, but it just didn't matter. The Kenwig's poor, cramped little house, was a single dais crammed with chairs, and people, who trod on each other's toes in the centre of a huge empty stage. But the congestion was so intense I can still feel it.

At the end, the audience rose as a whole to their feet, and gave the only really spontaneous standing ovation I have ever known. The memory is for me as sharp today as it was then. I know it is still with Margery. I grinned at her, and she smiled back. Happy memories, a moment of sheer joy that can never be taken away.

'Which one is this?'

'Er …' I tried to gather my thoughts.

'Which one is this?' Richard and Jo had now taken over the lock-keeping activity, and were walking hand in hand along the towpath to the next lock.

'Number five. Half way.'

George still hadn't arrived. So Stan went for another glass. After all, everyone else was drinking. He felt quite justified in doing so. He had been told to wait, so wait he must. Anyway it was a hot day and he was in need of refreshment.

*

Under Charlton Street, and into a fresh lock. This lock was, however, different. It had two upper gates, instead of the usual one. As we rose with the water in the lock, we noticed that they were chained together, and fastened with a padlock.

Now what have we got? I pondered. The guide book said to pay the car park attendant at the top lock, and there were two locks after this.

A man was sitting on the stone-flagged towpath, his knees up, and his back against a wall. He was just silently sitting there, saying nothing, and taking no apparent notice of us.

'This is the Rochdale Canal,' he suddenly said. 'You going through it?'

A strange question. Why else would we be here?

'Yes,' I politely replied.

'You'll need a licence,' he said.

'Yes. I believe so.'

The man still sat there without moving or, apparently, taking any more notice of us. When the lock was almost full, and I was about to enquire where we could find the lock-keeper, he stood up. He was a tall, bearded man with a cap, and I could now see he had a leather money bag on his shoulder. He was the lock-keeper. He took a pad out of his bag, looked at the boat, taking in its name and number, and started writing on his pad.

'How much is the licence?'

'Twenty-six pounds.'

I proffered £30 in notes. He gave me four £1 coins and the licence, which he tore from his pad, carefully moving the carbon down the pad for the next boat. Next boat! How many did he see in a day? I wondered, or more likely, how many days went by without seeing any?

He then proved very helpful, and gave us some useful advice. He enquired how far we intended going tonight. All the way to Fairfield, we hoped. He thought that wise.

'You can stop at Paradise Wharf just up here. It's quite safe, but I'd go on further if I were you.'

He clearly thought we still had time to go the whole way, and obviously didn't think it would be too much for us.

'The kids are terrible up there, though. So watch out for 'em. Lock your doors, close your curtains, and don't let them on board.'

We had managed all those so far. It was nice to be re-assured that we had been doing the right thing.

'If by chance you do have to stop overnight, don't moor to the towpath. The kids are terrors. They won't do you any harm, but they'll strip the boat of anything moveable. If you do have to stop overnight, tie up under a factory wall on the opposite side to the towpath.'

With that, he unpadlocked the upper gates, and we went on our way, feeling all the better for having a licence to travel these waters. He had reassured us in one way, but left us wondering what ogres we were going to meet.

7

Stan was on his fourth pint, and sitting among a carnival group on the arm of the upper lock gate. Certainly better company than George. What more could anybody want?

Blue Belle came into view of the spectators at Castlefields. Two boats. Incredible.

George looked around in bewilderment. He slackened speed, and looked in vain for Stan.

'Stan … Stan.'

Crackle … Crackle.

'Stan … Where the hell are you? … Stan.'

Crackle, crackle.

He edged in closer to the landing stage, and tried phoning again. But in vain. He tried again.

Stan was on his fifth pint when a jovial, pot-bellied man with a small beard said, 'Have you got a phone that needs answering?'

'Christ,' muttered Stan, 'more bloody trouble.'

He pulled the phone out of his pocket. 'I didn't notice. I was enjoying myself so much.'

He put the phone to his ear, and switched on, carefully holding his half-full pint glass with his other hand.

'Yes, George. Where are you now?'

'I'm bloody here. Where the hell are you?'

'Waiting for you. Where's here?'

'At the landing stage. Get down here at once.'

'OK.' He put the phone in his pocket, being especially careful not to spill any of the contents of his glass.

'Cheerio, I've work to do now. Nice to meet you.'

On cloud nine, clutching his half-full glass, Stan moved towards the landing stage. He was a little unsteady on his feet, and certainly incapable of moving too swiftly. He waved to George, with his free hand, as he descended to the landing stage.

George threw him a rope, which Stan tried to catch with one hand, but he missed it, and it fell into the water. *Blue Belle* started to float away from the landing stage. George was becoming furious. He recoiled the rope and threw it again. This time a small boy caught it for Stan, and he helped him pull the boat in and tied it to a ring. After all, Stan did have only one free hand.

'You're drunk,' screamed George. 'You're bloody drunk on duty. Put down that beer at once.'

At this command, in deference to his superior, Stan lifted his glass and downed the remaining half pint in one long gulp. A crowd was now surrounding Stan, in admiration. It was clear to George that the crowd were on Stan's side, and didn't think much of his outburst.

Stan put his glass among others on a nearby wall. 'Oh do shut up, George,' he sighed.

George's jaw dropped and he didn't say another word.

'That was useful,' said Sam as he and Ern, for the second time, followed the towpath into the murky gloom under Piccadilly, 'We've got 'em now by the short and curlies.'

'Yeah. This is going to be a cinch. They won't know what hit 'em.'

'They won't know anything hit them,' corrected Sam.

'No. Quite right. I've got to hand it to you. Foolproof.'

They walked on up to the pound between the two locks. Water dripped from the ceiling on to the towpath, and, with an eerie plop, onto the water of the canal. Sam had very carefully chosen the site of his attack. The penultimate lock, and the pound beyond, were underground. Or, more properly, high-rise city blocks had been built over them. The top lock just emerged into the open again. But the whole prospect was uneasy and far from inviting.

'What about Fred?' enquired Ern anxiously.

'Never mind Fred. We'll deal with him tonight.'

'We could tip him in here. Be ages before they found him.'

'I thought he was a friend of yours, and now you just want to chuck him in the water. Anyway, he's two miles away. Are you suggesting giving him a piggy back all the way along the towpath? Use your head. We aren't going to need to come up here again, when we've got the loot.'

'See what you mean.'

'Now,' said Sam firmly, 'let's run through it all again. We've just seen that the young couple are working the locks, and walking along the towpath. Just leaving the old folks, as I thought, on the boat.'

'Suppose they change over?'

'Hardly likely. Anyway, I don't think the old man is capable of opening a lock gate.'

'Useful the muscle won't be on the boat.'

'Precisely. Now then. We go above the top lock, and keep an eye out for them back down the canal. Then when they are in the first lock we saunter down, very casual like, and say we've got a boat coming down the other way. So if the young couple go to empty the top lock and open it, it will speed things up for them, and the old couple will be alone on the boat.'

'Yeah. Brilliant.'

'We tell them we'll open the bottom lock for their boat, and we'll leave it open for our boat, if they'll leave the top lock open for ours.'

'Suppose they see we haven't got any tools to open the locks?'

87

'You really are thick. That's the beauty of it. Ours are still on the boat. We're merely recycling, see. So we can't open the top lock for them as we'd liked, but we can open the lower one, when full, and help the old folk whilst they are opening the top one, and are out of our way.'

'Clever.'

'Then I'll go over the gate, so that we can help them from both sides. That is the side, you remember, where the cash bag is hidden. When the lock is full, you start to open the gate slowly. I, being very helpful, step on to the cockpit to help guide the boat out of the lock without it banging the side. I lift the lid, take out the bag, jump ashore your side, with the bag. Wave them goodbye, and hope they have a nice trip.'

'Sounds a piece of cake. But supposing they see you're up to something? What do we do then?'

'Easy. We push 'em in the water out of the way. The young ones will be ahead at the top of the lock, and won't be able to see what's going on down in the dark where we are.'

By now they were out in the open above the top lock. They sat on the towpath, and awaited their quarry.

We approached Piccadilly Bridge, and slowed gradually to a stop. Richard went up the steps to the lock.

'My God, this is weird,' he said, pulling a face.

'Spooky,' sighed Jo.

'Hope there aren't any winos.' Richard looked carefully around. 'I'll be glad when we're out of here.'

Margery looked at me. We could only wait in doubtful anticipation of what was in store for us.

Ern pulled a wallet from his pocket. 'I forgot this,' he said opening it.

'What is it?'

'I picked the pocket of that customer in the bank yester-day.'

'You stupid bugger. I told you, just take the cash, nothing that we could be traced by. And here you are running around with evidence that could put both of us back in Strangeways again, in your bloody pocket.'

'Two credit cards. I could use them.'

'You bloody won't. I'm having that destroyed as soon as we're back.'

'Only twenty quid, driving licence, summons for unpaid Poll Tax. Cheeky sod, I paid mine.'

'More fool you. I don't exist, except on police records. And this is going to be the perfect crime. Or was, until I got mixed up with you and Fred. God help me.'

'Hey. What's this,' he said, taking out a Polaroid picture of a very well-endowed blonde, who was wearing a broad smile, and a very small leather G-string.

'Bloody hell. Look at those tits. He looked such a mild old sod. Wonder who she is?'

He turned it over. On the back was written in a bold hand. 'Come and float on your dream boat again, Love Rose. XXX.'

'His girlfriend, I expect. The randy old sod. By God, I wouldn't mind floating on that dream boat.'

'Some tart, I expect.' Sam turned quickly. 'They're here! Put that away, I'll get rid of it later.'

Ern quickly pushed the wallet into the back pocket of his jeans, as he also turned to see what was happening under-ground. He did it so quickly that he left almost half of it sticking out of the top.

They were very quiet and attentive to what was going on below them.

The gates opened, and we moved slowly, further into the darkness. Behind us the gates closed, and the cloak of night enveloped us. All we could see dimly was the gloomy concrete ceiling above us.

'It doesn't look very pleasant,' I ventured.

'It's worse up here,' replied Richard, looking around again. 'Doesn't appear to be a soul, as far as I can see.'

'Spooky,' said Jo, with a shudder, and a thin smile.

Water flooded in, and we started to rise. Soon we would be able to see for ourselves.

Brian and Steve were already bored with Sunday. There was nothing interesting to do, and they had the rest of Sunday to kill. Nothing until school tomorrow. But that wasn't very interesting either. Except Miss Spinks, the French teacher. She was gorgeous. Brian had a pash on her, but she didn't seem to be reciprocating, although he offered her sweets, and showed her his poems. They sauntered idly by the canal.

'We'll have a fag when we get underground.'

Approaching the top lock, they saw Sam and Ern intently looking underground. Their backs were to the boys. They eyed the wallet sticking out of Ern's back pocket. They eyed each other.

Moving forward, Brian stretched out his hand, about to remove the wallet carefully. He knew he could do it without the owner knowing. After all he had done it before.

'Let's go,' said Sam, standing upright.

Ern moved also. But in moving he felt something move in his back pocket.

Brian quickly snatched, and both boys turned tail and ran for dear life.

'Hey! Come here you young buggers. I'll bloody kill you,' Ern shouted, giving chase, away from the lock

'Come here, you fool,' shouted Sam, going after him. 'Let it go. It's no damned good to you anyway.'

But Ern continued after the boys. At first he made up ground very fast.

'Come back, you bloody idiot. We've got a job to do.'

Ern was by now only keeping up with the boys, he was no longer gaining ground.

'I want my wallet. I'm not being robbed by a couple of kids.'

He ploughed on regardless, with Sam cursing him a couple of yards behind.

When almost at the top of our lift, we could see the gloomy, eerie pound ahead of us. A large pool with round concrete pillars, rising from the water supporting the roof above us. No light penetrated from behind, which was now below us. Some 150 yards ahead was a letterbox of light, where the top lock stood. There were lights in the roof, but they were not lit. To our left was an open shaft between the high buildings, from which the majority of the light which illuminated this concrete and water tomb filtered down to us.

All in all it had an uneasy atmosphere. Richard was right, just the place to find winos sleeping it off. But perhaps they didn't have any in Manchester.

Richard and Jo stood together on the towpath side, pushed open the door, and *Colette* glided out into the pound. The gate closed behind us.

'Be glad when we are out of here,' Richard said, as he and Jo trotted off towards the letterbox of light, and to open the top lock.

We stood, close to the pillar, gently rocking. Rising and falling slightly, as the water flooded down from the top lock. The pillar had some fairly large pieces knocked out of it. Some boaters had certainly given it a rough time. But how, I wondered, could anyone in this restricted area have managed to do so much damage? How could such speed have been attained in so short a distance, to gain such force to cause damage of that magnitude? It wasn't in danger of falling down, but it was intriguing.

Off the canal route, the pound extended to our left, beyond the pillars. It washed the foundations of the buildings around the open shaft. Beneath one building there was a small opening onto the canal. A boat house perhaps. What appeared to be a bicycle cum paddleboat was stored inside. Was it used by some strange troglodyte to run up and down the canal, to clear rubbish perhaps, or was it just a toy?

There was no time for conjecture. The lock gates opened, and we rose up to daylight again.

The boys left the canal, and ran up into the town, with Ern in hot pursuit, but by now he was losing ground. However, his pride insisted that he should follow them, and give them the hiding of their lives.

They turned, suddenly right into a side street, and Brian, still with the wallet in his hand, ran straight into the arms of PC Spriggs, who had been up too late last night, and wasn't in the mood for any nonsense.

'What's all the rush, then?' he said, taking Brian's wrist firmly. 'Stay just where you are,' he ordered Steve.

Sam and Ern stopped abruptly at the corner, took in the scene, and very quickly turned back the way they had come, without being noticed.

'A wallet, eh? Now where did that come from?'

Brian hung his head. Steve didn't move a muscle.

PC Spriggs called for a car, and the boys rode in state to the police station. Brian and Steve's Sunday was certainly beginning to liven up. It wasn't boring now.

'Now the police have got it. You know, you really are a stupid sod.'

'They took my wallet.'

'Not your wallet at all. One you pinched. They'll wonder now who the kids got it from. We can only hope he didn't report his loss yesterday.'

'He wouldn't have done, not with that picture in it. I'd have kept that.'

'We don't know that, do we. And because you were daft enough to chase them, they've run straight into the arms of the police, the very last people we wanted to see that wallet.'

'Sorry.'

'Too late to be sorry. You've made more problems for us. But what is worse, you've loused up our opportunity getting the money.'

'We can still catch 'em, if we rush.'

'They'll be through that section by now. We'd have four of them on the boat now if we tried to intercept, and we don't want four against us. Lastly, the police may soon be down there looking for the bloke who was robbed.'

'OK then, what do we do?'

'Go back, overground, to Castlefields. Now we have got to take the boat up that flight after them, and you can operate all the locks. You know what you are, don't you? A bloody loony.'

8

From the top lock we cruised leisurely into Paradise Wharf. A large car park was beside the canal, with large modern office blocks beyond. I thought I was back in London at Canary Wharf: another similar approach to a derelict dockland site, with the same uninspiring results. Anyway, it was soon over. A sharp right under Dulcie Street, then almost immediately left onto the Ashton Canal.

Nicely laid-out gardens flanked the waterway, making an attractive setting for a group of pleasant, modern maisonettes. A number of old people waved from windows as we passed. We waved back. A happy little spot.

Around a bend, and there ahead of us was the first of 18 locks, to ascend over the next 4 miles. Not to mention two swing bridges.

Three boys were fishing close up against the gate. Here we are, I thought. They gave up fishing, and followed us up the three Ancoat locks. Despite the warnings we had been given, they were well behaved, and merely watched us with apparent interest.

Half a mile further on, and Richard and Jo were ashore again, for the four Beswick locks. Here we met a group of six girls, aged 12 to 14 years. No problems here, I thought, no lads in evidence.

How wrong I was. Very wrong. They were absolute she-devils. It really was a good job everything was nailed down tight. They hung onto the boat. Tried to jump onto it. Rocked it.

95

'Can we get on?'

'No.'

'Why not?'

'Do let go. Don't hang on. It could be dangerous.'

One let go, as another grasped hold. The rigmarole of the exchanges was repeated all over again, and again.

With the boat in the lock, Richard and Jo closed the gates behind us. They opened the paddle on the gate in front to let the water into the lock, only to find that the girls had, for fun, opened the gates again behind. And the water was just flowing out down the canal.

Always so close, but always out of reach. They had done this before, many times. If they had got nearer I'm sure they would have been murdered.

One smiling little girl, with buck teeth, was standing on the iron bridge over the lock gates. She smiled, and asked Jo, as the boat went underneath her, 'Can I spit on it now?'

'Certainly not, you little horror,' Jo replied.

It did no good. We found gobs of spittle in different places on the boat, when eventually we had time to stop.

After three locks, where the same procedure was repeated each time, they eventually got bored with us and looked for someone else to torment. What a relief. I didn't wish them on anyone else, but I was glad they went. I now appreciate fully what the guide book, and lock-keeper, had told us. But it wasn't the boys, it was the girls who were the trouble. Perhaps that should tell us something.

'The worst kids I've ever seen,' said Jo, with obvious relief. 'What a nightmare.'

The discovery that in addition to the windlass, a special Manchester security key was required, caused George even more consternation than usual. Eventually, having found one, at something after 6.15 p.m. they started their ascent of the Rochdale Canal. Stan had delicately pointed out the instructions, clearly indicating that no one was to enter the canal after 5 p.m., but George put his mind at rest assuring him that this did not apply to them.

It was proving a particularly tortuous and agonising journey up through the locks, Stan doing all the work of opening and closing, never quite quickly enough for George, who scraped and crashed poor little *Blue Belle* in and out of each. Every bump, of course, resulting from Stan being casual, inattentive, or just plain sloppy in accomplishing every part of his easy job.

Perspiring hard, and badly in need of another pint, Stan opened the seventh lock, and *Blue Belle* again lost some more paint. The problem then became apparent. For instead of one upper gate, there were two, and they were chained and padlocked together.

'It said we weren't to come up here after five.'

'Shut up.'

'I did point it out to you,' said Stan, with a self-righteous smirk.

There was no one about. No one to ask. No one to open up. No one to see what was going to happen.

'Well, we've got to go on. We can't be held up by this.'

'You can't break it. It's chained up.'

'To think that some stupid moron would be so irresponsible as to chain up the gate. Break it open!'

'I can't do that, it would be vandalism.'

'It's vandalism, pure and simple, to chain it up in the first place. The route might be needed in an emergency. We can't have people held up.'

'There isn't anybody to hold up,' interjected Stan.

'We're being held up. It is our duty to keep the waterway clear. To undo this act of wanton vandalism. In any case, it is essential that we get on. Our work is vital. Open it,' ordered George.

'I think you'd better do it. You're in charge, after all.'

George said no more, but with the aid of the windlass he started to prise the lock and chain apart. It wasn't easy.

Up above on Chorlton Street, the city property was not all unoccupied, as George had supposed. The lock-keeper's house is carefully perched above the lock. The lock-keeper had gone to the off-licence for some cans of lager, whilst his wife cooked his tea. Her attention was drawn to some noises emanating from the canal, unusual for this time of the evening.

'Vandals again,' she sighed, and shook her head. She wasn't going to confront them, and simply rang the police.

WPC Nonelly and PC Jones, in a patrol car, pulled up adjacent to the canal.

'Not another mysterious body, I hope,' said WPC Nonelly.

They took the steps down the towpath and found Stan standing beside *Blue Belle*, with his hands on his hips, watching open-mouthed at George's furious antics. With each attempt his language got steadily worse.

'You again,' said WPC Nonelly to Stan.

'Nothing to do with me. He's in charge.'

'You know you're not supposed to be here after five.'

'I told him. He would just insist upon coming.'

'And you, aided, and abetted him, in trespass. And that,' pointing at George, 'is vandalism.'

The chain suddenly gave way, but in the process the gate sustained some superficial damage.

'What's all this then?' PC Jones asked George.

'Some damned vandal had chained the gate, stopping free access along the canal,' replied George. 'He ought to be locked up.'

'This is private property, and you are trespassing. I agree that there is vandalism, and you've done it.'

A slight altercation ensued, but PC Jones wasn't having any nonsense.

'I'm taking you both in for trespass, and vandalism. The magistrates here don't like vandalism. Into the car. Both of you.'

For the second time in 24 hours George and Stan were on their way to the police station. As they drove through the city, WPC Nonelly phoned Sergeant Tooth.

'Just bringing in two friends of yours. I'm sure you will be delighted to see them.' With that she hung up, leaving Sergeant Tooth in eager anticipation.

On the way back to Castlefields, Sam phoned his wife.

'May. Bring the car to Castlefields, and pick me up. I'm up to my ears in problems. I've got a recce to do. I'll tell you more when I see you.'

'You told me this was going to be a cinch. I expected you home for tea, and now you've got problems. I told you your friends were liabilities. OK, give me an hour.'

Sergeant Tooth had seen Brian and Steve, and it had come to light that the owner of the wallet had, strangely, not yet reported it as stolen, or even lost.

'Aha! We know him, don't we. He was a witness at the bank raid yesterday,' Sergeant Tooth said, with a knowing look.

'I've found out something else interesting, Sarge. The credit cards are not his. The kids insist that they hadn't opened the wallet before I nicked them,' replied PC Spriggs.

A smile broke out on Sergeant Tooth's face. 'Well, I don't know what exactly we've got, but we've certainly got something.' He leaned back in his chair with his hands behind his head. 'I wonder if he was implicated in the raid. I think we must see Mr Paul Boakes, mustn't we.'

He mused for a few moments, and then said, 'I wonder what Nonelly has got for me?'

He soon found out. George and Stan were pushed before him.

'Trespass and vandalism,' said WPC Nonelly.

'And we witnessed both,' added PC Jones, with a broad smile.

'Gotcha! You miserable squirts,' beamed Sergeant Tooth. 'Your "Powder Puff" has really got up my nose this time. Book 'em.'

He got up to leave, but was suddenly pulled up sharp.

'I want to see your Superintendent,' said George.

Sergeant Tooth's jaw dropped. He was livid with rage.

'You were caught in the act. And now you have the affront to ask to see the Superintendent. Bloody cheek. Book 'em,' he ordered.

WPC Nonelly whispered to him. 'Remember last time, Sarge. Better had tell the Super. Suppose they are MI6. They'll be bugging your home phone, and lord knows what, if you're not careful.'

'They probably are anyway.' Sergeant Tooth eyed George and Stan up and down, with a look of absolute disgust. 'Yes, they look like MI6 poofters, if ever I saw any.'

Reluctantly, very reluctantly, he went again to the Superintendent who, again, saw George alone. That hurt Sergeant Tooth. His investigation, and again he was excluded. 'There's something funny going on here all right. Perhaps I don't belong to the right golf club.'

The last of the Beswick locks was a pig of a lock. And, I thought, it was going to scupper us for the night. The lock, and the surrounding canal, was covered, quite literally, with hundreds, thousands possibly, of plastic food containers. They were everywhere. They floated and bobbed about on the surface of the water like a huge brood of ducklings.

'They should be banned,' I pronounced, with my usual tact and impartiality on matters that irritated me.

Apart from the mess, I didn't see any other obstacles. The gates opened. We started to enter, but when halfway in, the boat jammed between the doors. We tried to move backwards, but we didn't move. We tried to move forwards again, with the same result. It wasn't hard to see why one gate wouldn't open fully.

The lock was completely full of plastic containers, but even they wouldn't cause this problem. There was nothing else, that I could see, which refused to allow the gate to swing through its full arc.

I tried to prise us free with the mop. I couldn't. The boat hook, and boat pole, proved no better. Richard and Jo pulled with all their might on the arm above, but the gate wouldn't budge.

'There's a plank of wood wedged behind the door,' shouted Richard. 'Try and move it.'

I tried. It didn't move. We went through the whole gamut again. Nothing happened, apart from the fact that I became more irritable. I was by now resigned to a night stuck between the lock gates.

'Let me have a go.'

Richard was suddenly behind me, on the roof of the boat. He had come down the metal lock ladder. With all the force he could muster he rammed the boat pole between the gate and the boat, forcing the two apart. He ordered, 'Full ahead.'

Nothing happened. He forced the gate and boat further apart. There was a groan. Eventually there was a grinding noise as the metal hull grazed against the fully open gate. Gradually, with a great deal of grating and scraping, we were in.

We'd only done seven of these locks, and I was a nervous wreck already.

Sam ordered Ern to stay where he was, on the boat. Let no

one on, and stay awake for his return. Ern wanted to go
with him. He didn't fancy being left alone all night with
Fred for company. But it cut no ice. Sam wasn't going to
risk taking him along. And in any case he wanted May to
himself.

May arrived, late, in her BMW. She was small. A little
plump, but pretty, grossly over made-up, blonde, with a will
of her own. Sam apprised her of the job so far.

'I told you not to use those two amateurs. If I'd done it
with you, we wouldn't be in this mess. We'd be home, and
dry, with our feet up. Now you've got a body on the boat,
and we're chasing half the money, which you kindly
donated to someone else.'

'Don't be like that,' pleaded Sam.

'Don't be like that,' bleated May. 'Huh. I set it all up, and
then you mess it up!'

Sam decided to be diplomatic, and change the direction
of the conversation. 'Let's go and have a look for them.
They can't have got too far. Try out on the Ashton New
Road. We can check at the bottom of the Clayton Locks. We
can see up and down from the bridge.'

George was with the Superintendent an hour, during which
time the Superintendent spoke to the lock-keeper, and the
Chairman of the canal company. Eventually they emerged.
George was smiling. The Superintendent wasn't.

'Sergeant. Tell WPC Nonelly to take them back to where
she picked them up. All charges have been dropped.' He
didn't look at Sergeant Tooth.

'What! They were caught in the act! Bloody hooligans.'

'That will do, Sergeant. The canal company is not pressing any charges. Oh, and tell WPC Nonelly to collect a
chain, padlock and keys from the stores on the way out.
They are waiting for her. She will hand them to the lock-
keeper.'

'We're paying for their damage, out of police funds?'
Sergeant Tooth shrieked.

The Superintendent, still without looking at Sergeant
Tooth, turned on his heel and left.

'You heard, WPC Nonelly,' he snarled. 'Get this excre-
ment out of here, before we all get infected.'

Under the Ashton New Road. Then we started on the
Clayton Nine. There was some distance between the first
and second locks. To our right a small branch canal had
been built to service factories more directly. A swing bridge
carrying to towpath over it made it an attractive area to
explore. If only we had the time.

Now we could really see that we were going up in the
world. With each lock, the view around us opened up,
more and more. We looked out across the grey roofs of
Openshaw. Factories, chemical works, nestled among the
roofs of houses. Thousands of them. It was a beautiful,
warm, summer evening. The air was clear. We could see for
miles. An incredible view opened up before us. The whole
of south-east Manchester, down there below us. Whole
communities nestled under their grey slated roofs, villages
really, but all joined together, by one huge umbilical cord,
away into the distance to a blurred haze.

Worthwhile to just stop and look. But the clock kept our
nose to the grindstone. It was 7.30 now. A good two hours
to go. But what view would we have then?

May pulled up on the Ashton New Road, just short of the
canal bridge. They looked down towards Manchester.
Nothing in the city moved. Over the road, and they looked
up the bank of locks. There was a single boat working up
the bank.

'That's them, I'm sure of it, even at this distance. They're
shifting some, though,' said Sam.

'You sure it's them?'

'Yes. I'd recognise that girl working the locks anywhere.'

'Yes, you would, wouldn't you?'

'Let's go up to the Strawberry Duck and have a pint. We can watch them as they go past. You can see what we are up against.'

Both Brian's mum and Steve's dad had arrived. Neither could understand how their two boys, of exemplary character and behaviour, could possibly be inside a police station.

'They both say they found it lying along the canal bank, and were bringing it into you.'

Sergeant Tooth's eyes rose to the ceiling. The police were persecuting poor, innocent, children again. Hadn't they any criminals to catch? But he kept them waiting until Paul Boakes arrived.

He was a small, stooping man, in his fifties, with a hat at a rakish angle, and a cigarette permanently anchored to the right side of his lower lip.

'Just had your wallet handed in. Perhaps you would identify it for us, that's all.'

'That's all? And you sent a police car for me, Sergeant?'

'That's all,' Sergeant Tooth smiled.

'Very civil of you, Sergeant.' There was just a hint of an Irish accent. 'Let me have a look.'

He looked at the outside, and wondered whether to recognise it, or deny it. They were being very hospitable. Even offered him a cup of tea. And he did help them yesterday at the raid. In any case there was bound to be something inside which would irrevocably tie it to him.

'Yes, Sergeant. Well, I do declare. It is mine. Thank you so much for finding it for me.'

'Are the contents all there?'

He had a cursory look, but wasn't very thorough.

'Yes, Sergeant. Where did you find it?'

'Where did you lose it?'

'I'm not sure.'

'You were in the bank yesterday, on business. Did you have it then?'

'Oh, yes.'

'Did you have it this afternoon?'

'I'm not sure, Sergeant. I didn't go to the park today. And I haven't been along the canal since I was a kiddy. Dirty smelly place.'

Sergeant Tooth was about to blow, but not quite yet. He wanted to prove that he was ready for promotion to the CID. Keep cool. But it was hard, with this prat talking rubbish.

'Excuse me, Sergeant, but could I be excused?'

'Excused? Can't go home yet, lad.'

'No, I want to go to the little room.'

He crossed his legs tightly.

'The little room?'

'He wants to pee, Sarge,' advised WPC Nonelly, who had returned George and Stan, and delivered the chain. She was now helping Sergeant Tooth with his enquiries.

'Well, why doesn't he say so? Yes. No. Just a minute.'

'I can't wait too long. It's me bladder, see,' said Paul urgently.

Sergeant Tooth beckoned to WPC Nonelly, and whispered quietly to her. She nodded, and went out.

'You can go in a minute. She's just going to see if it's free. Did you lose it in the raid yesterday?' This time the enquiry was more forceful.

'Well, I may have done. I'm not sure.'

WPC Nonelly put her head around the door and nodded. 'OK now, sir,' she said.

Sergeant Tooth indicated with a gesture to Paul that he could retire. Paul got up, and followed the WPC. He hoped

she wasn't going to escort him into the loo. Equality of the
sexes was all right, but that would be going too far.

In the passage, they just happened to bump into, accidentally of course, Brian and Steve, who were with PC
Spriggs. There was no sign of recognition whatsoever on
any of their faces.

Paul went to the toilet on his own whilst WPC Nonelly
waited outside. Thank God for that he thought. If she'd
been there he wouldn't have been able to do it.

On returning to the interview room she shook her head
to Sergeant Tooth, and whispered something.

Wish they wouldn't keep whispering, thought Paul. It's
rude.

'Tell PC Spriggs he can let the lads go home. The owner
doesn't identify them,' Sergeant Tooth told WPC Nonelly.
'Thank them for being so public-spirited and bringing it
into us.'

She left without a word.

So that's why I was pushed into those kids, thought Paul.
I'd better be careful with this joker. 'No, Sergeant. I can't
rightly remember where I last had it,' he said. 'Strange, isn't
it? I didn't know I'd lost it until your officer kindly came for
me.'

'Now look here,' yelled Sergeant Tooth, who by now was
getting fed up with the fancy footwork. 'We've danced this
bloody fandango all around the station. Now I want some
proper answers. Get it?' he roared.

WPC Nonelly returned, nodding as she entered. She
again whispered to Sergeant Tooth.

Rude buggers, thought Paul.

'I think you were a look-out. Part of the set-up yesterday.
I don't believe your story so far, at all. So now let's cut the
crap. Do you get my drift? Or do I have to speak in plainer
English?'

'No. No, Sergeant.' Paul had got the message. 'Really,

Sergeant, I wasn't. But I know I wasn't quite frank with you.'

'You told me bloody lies.' Sergeant Tooth had a menacing expression.

'I did have my pocket picked by one of the gang.'

'Why didn't you say so before? Was it because you had some stolen credit cards in it, by any chance?'

'Stolen credit cards? Me, Sergeant?'

'Yes, you.'

'I've got a clean record, Sergeant, for all of my fifty years. How can you suggest such a thing, Sergeant?'

'You may have no previous record. But you know full well you had stolen credit cards, and were going to use them.'

'No, Sergeant, never. May God forgive you for saying such a thing,' he said coyly, crossing himself.

Sergeant Tooth's eyes again went heavenwards.

'You see, Sergeant, I didn't want any trouble, and I knew where I could get it back.'

Sergeant Tooth pricked up his ears, and leaned forward at his desk. 'You knew where you could get it back? Where?'

'The one who shot himself, Sargeant.'

'Yes?'

'I know who he is.'

'You do, do you? Why didn't you say before? Eh? You admit now to concealing information. I could string you up for this.'

'Look, Sergeant. You're a man of the world. You find my wallet, twenty-four hours after I lose it. There are now credit cards in it which don't belong to me. I didn't put them there, I'm sure you'll appreciate that.'

'Help me appreciate it a little better, if you don't mind. Then I might just understand what you are saying.'

'The man who shot himself,' said Paul confidentially, 'was Squadgy Fred.'

'Squadgy Fred? You must be joking. He's still inside.'

107

'No, Sarge,' said WPC Nonelly. 'He's out.'

'Is he now?' said Sergeant Tooth. 'It didn't take him long.'

'He had a mask on, Sergeant, but I'd know him anywhere. I didn't know the other two. But one was Squadgy Fred.'

'Where is he? We'd better bring him in.' Sergeant Tooth knew he was now getting somewhere.

'Shall I?' enquired WPC Nonelly.

'He's not at home. Nobody knows where he is. He went out yesterday morning. His wife said.'

'His wife! Mabel, that old slag he dosses with?'

'The same, Sergeant.'

'We'll find him, Sarge,' volunteered WPC Nonelly.

'Said he'd be in for his tea yesterday. He hasn't been seen since. And they were going to the pictures last night.'

'We'd better look for him,' confirmed Sergeant Tooth. 'You sure you don't know the other two?'

'No Sergeant. Cross my heart, and hope to die.'

'You bloody well will if this is wrong, I promise you. Right, get out, and take your wallet with you. But I'm having the credit cards.' He took out the credit cards, and threw the wallet at Paul. 'Now clear out. But if I should get evidence to link you to these cards, you'll be back. Got that?'

'Oh you won't, Sergeant, you won't. Thank you, Sergeant. Do I get a lift back home, Sergeant?.'

'Get out!' roared Sergeant Tooth.

Paul made a discreet exit.

The lock-keeper said nothing, but shook his head as George and Stan banged and crashed poor *Blue Belle* out of the lock, and went on their way.

He smiled. For he realised that although they would make the next two locks, they would certainly have to stop overnight, somewhere on the Aston Canal. He didn't proffer any advice to them. They knew it all anyway. His smile broadened.

He quickly slipped the new chain around the gates, and went in for his belated dinner.

9

It could have been Coronation Street: rows and rows of two-storey, time-worn, red brick terraced houses, in narrow streets, end on to the canal, greeted us on the northern flank as we rose higher and higher. Occasionally, over their grey slated roofs, or through the streets, between the rows, could be glimpsed Saddleworth Moor. Not so very far from the heart of this city. I stopped to think.

To the south the ground dropped away even faster, and one vast panoramic view dissolved into the haze. No time to stop, but it was magnificent.

The canal here is flanked on either side by wide, mown grass verges. The waters of the canal looked rather murky and, I thought, uninviting. Yet here, the locks were transformed into open air swimming pools. A group of young girls – Oh my God, girls! – in bathing costumes beside two of the locks were drying themselves down after their dip. There was no trouble, they simply ignored us. We were merely stopping them, momentarily, from diving back in.

The Strawberry Duck: an attractive name for a jovial little two-storey pub at the end of one of the terraces, built just like the other houses. It beckoned, invitingly. Richard pointed, for we'd discussed it as a possible stop. Outside stood a number of men with pint glasses, and a few women with smaller ones, making the most of a quiet drink out of doors, on a balmy summer evening.

'Five more locks and two swing bridges,' shouted a happy drinker, with a smile.

111

Richard grinned back, and nodded. Much as we would have liked to have joined them, we didn't stop. We were travelling into the unknown, and we had another hour and a half's work to go. Then we had to find a mooring for the night. By now we were tired, and hungry. We hadn't stopped all day, uphill all the way. Now with 20 locks under our belts.

May and Sam stood at the back of the crowd, glasses in hand.

'That's them,' said Sam. 'The bag is in the empty locker on this side of the cockpit.'

'Towpath is on the far side all the way now to Portland Basin. So I have to get over the boat to get it.'

'You've got to what?'

'I'm getting it tonight. I've got to sort this mess out, once and for all. I'm not leaving it to you lot any longer.'

'Yes, May.' Sam knew, after all these years, when not to argue.

'They've got the Cheshire Ring guide, you said. There are two recommended moorings, if I remember. Fairfield, or under the reservoir. I'll bet they take the second. But we'll have another drink. Then we'll track them to their next.'

'Yes, May. What will it be?'

'Christ. After all these years. You still don't know,' snapped May, as she thrust her empty glass at him.

'Yes, May.'

He came back with two glasses. May was intently watching *Colette* coming out of the next lock.

'No catches on the locker lids?'

'No, they're loose. Just placed on top.'

'And otherwise empty?'

'Yes. Was last night.'

'Better had be. And the bag is like the one in the car?'

'Exactly. Old leather shopping bag. Strong, but a bit tatty.

Like you said, nothing to draw attention to us.'

They watched *Colette* to the top of the rise, then she rounded a bend out of sight.

George and Stan found the boys back at the foot of the first lock, fishing again. The boys watched the wreckage of poor *Blue Belle* crash its way into the lower Ancoats lock. They didn't bother to follow. fishing was more interesting than watching that poor thing lose more paint and pieces of woodwork.

At the third lock, the girls were waiting. And they pounced. They wanted to get onto the boat. Two did, whilst George was warding off boarders on the other side. One took two packets of sandwiches, which were to have been their supper. The other departed with their mop.

'This boat's a shambles,' said the girl with the buck teeth, shaking her head.

'You little sods,' roared George.

Stan closed the gates behind *Blue Belle*, opened up the paddles on the front gate, and sat on the arm to wait for the lock to fill. As he daydreamed he was unaware that George, and *Blue Belle*, were floating backwards out of the lock, pushed by the force of the water, supposedly filling the lock.

The girls had, very kindly, opened the lower gates again. They stood on the iron of the bridge over the gates, as George floated back out of the lock. George fumed, fighting hard to stay within the lock. From the bridge the girls laughed, jeered and spat on him, as he gradually floated back.

It eventually dawned on Stan that the lock was filling up very slowly indeed. He looked around, and couldn't help smiling at George's predicament. But, of course, he knew full well that it would all be his fault in the end. He chased the girls away, and shepherded George back into the lock. He had to go full ahead, because water was still entering the

113

lock, fast, at the other end. A great deal more paint, and chips of wood, was lost in the process.

Stan closed one gate, ran over the bridge, and closed the other, only to see that the first gate was wide open again. Beside it stood six little grinning girls. Sweating hard, whilst George cussed and raved, Stan ran back to the first gate, closing it. Only to find that the other had been opened again.

This happened three times. Eventually the girls tired, turned, and left. This was no contest worthy of their participation. There was no serious opposition at all.

They ate the sandwiches, after sharing them equally. 'Ugh, pickle,' moaned one, throwing her ration into the canal. Their plastic containers followed very soon afterwards. They studied the mop for all of ten seconds. Pronounced it useless, and threw that in the canal also.

George and Stan had wasted a great deal of time, and dusk was closing in. They couldn't go much further.

The swing bridges made an interesting diversion. They, again, were key operated. The last two locks were now taken in their stride, and the six-hour ordeal of locking up was over. With relief, Richard and Jo clambered aboard, tired out, but content.

May and Sam looked down from the Fairfield bridge.

'They're going on. It'll be under the reservoir, as I thought. They haven't got time to go through the basin tonight.'

'Can we go home now for some grub? I'm starving.'

'Never knew you when you weren't. If you're not starving for one thing, you're starving for something else. On the way home I'm stopping at Mum's.'

'Oh, hell. Do we have to?'

'Yes, we certainly do. I'm getting rid of that bag in the car.

Hiding it away at her house. No one will think of looking for it there. If the police come knocking us up in the night, which they may well do thanks to your antics, there'll be nothing there for them to find.'

They got back into the car.

Stan was on his last legs, whilst George was literally worn out with worry. The girls had been the last straw. They moored, without any protest or acrimony, opposite an old mill half a mile below the Beswick locks.

Silenced reigned for some time as they sipped their mugs of coffee. They looked back over a hell of a day. George was in a far more amicable mood than usual. Perhaps it was that Stan was the only friend and ally he had, in this otherwise hostile world. Where friends and allies were precious.

Under the low bridge, carrying the road from the Audenshaw Reservoir, to Droylesden. A warehouse dominated the left bank, which led to the large winding hole, where narrowboats can be turned. Beyond some rather smart houses, with gardens extending down to the canal edge. On the right the towpath had wide green verges, and park benches. Recommended moorings indeed. A variety of trees masked the fence on the extremity of the towpath. Quiet, secluded, ideal.

We pulled in opposite a pleasant house, which had one drawback. A large dog was loose in the garden, and barked at everything. Richard cut the engines. Jo stepped ashore from the rear and I followed. We made fast. It was 9.35 p.m. exactly. Twelve hours, all but ten minutes. Without a let-up. The guide book was right. I stowed the lump hammer in the stern, where we had decided, for our ease, to keep it.

Jo clambered aboard into the cockpit. 'Those damn girls,' she exclaimed, finding spittle on the cockpit deck, and the cover of the outer locker.

It was getting dark, but she cleaned it up, lifting the cover as she did so. Her eyes were drawn to a bag inside the locker, a leather shopping bag.

'We piled our groceries here when we came aboard.' She lifted it. 'Heavy, must be vegetables, left out by mistake. Better store them in the vegetable box under the sink.'

She intended to mention it to Margery, but by this time Margery was in the bathroom, getting washed and tidied up for dinner. Jo pushed the bag into the vegetable box, behind the other items. She made a mental note to mention it later, then promptly forgot all about it.

From the bridge behind *Colette*, May and Sam looked down on the boat. May studied the towpath, access, and the lie of the land.

'There we are, just as I thought,' said May, with a smile, 'the left-hand cockpit locker, away from the towpath?'

'Yes.'

'And there are definitely no hooks or catches?'

'No.'

'Right. Now off to Mum. Home for a meal. Then back here for one a.m.'

'You sure? Can't we go to bed for a bit?'

'Bed? You'll be lucky. When I've got that bag, I'll take it to Mum's also. Then home to bed. I'm not having this messed up.'

'Wonder if Ern is OK by himself.'

'He's got Fred for company,' replied May, with obvious distaste, and distinct bad taste.

While they were eating their supper, the girls reappeared. They were walking up the towpath on their way home. It was long after their bedtimes, but who cared? They smiled, wicked little smiles, when they saw *Blue Belle* moored. They giggled amongst themselves. This was going to be fun.

Quietly they moved towards the boat.

George and Stan had almost finished their (very scratch) meal when, amid a great deal of shouting, the girls in unison grabbed the hand rail and started to rock the boat furiously. Thud, thud against the bank went the hull. Crash, bang, wallop went the utensils and tackle. Their almost empty plates fell to the floor, as coffee splashed over the rims of their mugs, splashing the objects already thrown to the deck.

'The buggers!' roared George.

He stormed off after the girls, who continued their quiet walk home. Unbeknown to George, the girls had also managed to untie the stern mooring rope.

'God, I do hate this place,' sighed George, as they set about to clean up the mess. Then they literally fell into their bunks.

'Shan't need much rocking to sleep,' said Stan.

'No. I've set the alarm for five.'

'What!' echoed Stan.

'We've got to catch 'em up. I want to be under way by six. I'll bet they won't be off early. They'll want to lie in, I expect. Anyway, that should give us about a four-hour start on them. I want them back in our sights. I hope they haven't made any move yet.'

'No.' Stan turned on his side, and went out like a light.

We had an excellent meal, and some good wines. Television was settling down to the Olympics again, so I slipped into bed, to study my wine bluffer's guide further, leaving the other three pole-vaulting.

What a day. It had been an eye-opener. Hard work, but we were intact, happy and content. No regrets now, having done it. This would certainly be the hardest day of the lot. The rest would just be plain sailing. I didn't manage to read a paragraph before my eyes closed.

*

Ern wondered where Sam and May were. They ought to be back by now. Tentatively, he entered the cabin. Fred was still there. He didn't much fancy being left alone with a corpse, even one he knew. Well, he knew him when he wasn't a corpse. But that didn't comfort him at all.

He turned to thoughts of May. A lovely girl. He had always fancied May. But she was a bit stand-offish with him. Perhaps she was shy. Pity, he thought, opening another can of lager. He could do with May, right now.

The canal was silent. There was no wind. Everything was quiet and still. The waning moon shone a few gleams of light, but very few, which was all to the good, for the work in hand. The car had been left some way up the road in front of some shops. Well out of the way, where it wouldn't disturb anyone. But it was, at the same time, easily accessible.

May was in a navy blue tracksuit, with a matching bala-clava round her neck which, once on the towpath, she lifted over her head. Only her face was showing. She had dark gloves on her hands, and lightweight black plimsolls on her feet. Too warm, one would have thought, for gloves and headgear, but May was not one for taking chances. She only worked to certainties. Sam was also in dark clothes, and he had his balaclava out again too.

They walked very quietly, taking each step carefully. They could hear the dog snuffling about, across the water. On the prowl, but there was no aggressive barking.

Colette was in complete darkness. They looked at each window very carefully before approaching. It was 2.05 a.m. The windows were of the louvre type, and were open, but the blinds were firmly drawn behind. From the forward cabin, a man's snores could be heard intermittently, but there was no sound whatsoever from either of the other

118

cabins. There was no radio, or television on. In fact, no noise at all except for the old man's snoring. There was a grunt – as he turned on his side, May thought. Then he also was silent.

They kept in the shadow of the trees on the extremity of the towpath, lest anyone should be disturbed by the sound of a foot on gravel, or a shadow passing a window, caught in a shaft of moonlight.

'If we're in trouble, jump the fence into the council store yard, and then out the other side, OK?' May snapped her orders, but they were no more than a whisper.

By now they were round at the front of *Colette*. They moved silently over the gravel footpath, and approached the boat from the front. The lounge was in the front, and that should be empty. The curtains were drawn. Sam knew exactly what he had to do. He stood beside the lounge, with May in front of the cockpit. He placed both his hands on the handrail which ran along the roof, gripping it firmly.

May nodded imperceptibly. Sam gave an upward pressure on the hand rail, to act as a counterbalance, as May stepped on board. There was no rocking of the boat as she stepped on. Sam's efforts were effective. Then he held it tightly so that there should be no rocking whatsoever from May's slight movements.

She made no noise as she stepped aboard and moved gently but swiftly across the cockpit. Then she felt for the lid over the locker on the canal side, and lifted the front edge upwards a fraction, with both hands, making sure it would not bang against the lounge wall, the hull, or even the lip over the edge of the bulwarks.

It slid out quietly, and with ease. She lowered it to rest on her feet, keeping a firm grip of it with her left hand. With her right she took a small torch from her pocket and bent forward so that the torch was actually inside the locker before she switched it on, ensuring that there could be no possible spillage of light on the water, which might have attracted the dog, or anyone else in the vicinity.

She switched it on. The locker was empty, except for an empty plastic sliced bread bag, and two empty beer cans. She looked in Sam's direction, but he could see nothing of her. Then she turned back to the locker again. It was still empty.

May replaced the lid, turned to her right, and with some precision removed the metal lid from the front locker. There was a barely perceptible sound of metal scraping against metal, but not enough to attract attention.

What the hell is she doing? thought Sam.

The locker contained only two gas cylinders, which were coupled to the gas supply of the boat. There was a small amount of bilge water, but otherwise, not even a discarded sweet wrapper.

Quietly she replaced the lid, to Sam's even greater surprise, as he could see what she was doing. She carefully lifted the lid of the locker on the towpath side.

Sam shook his head, and nodded towards the other side of the boat. May took no notice. She again shone her torch. This locker only contained the hosepipe for taking on water, which Sam had seen being used the previous morning.

May replaced the lid, and indicated that she was coming ashore. Sam took the strain, and held the boat rigid as she stepped ashore. He let go of the boat, which remained steady. He moved forward, away from the boat, following May.

They crossed the gravel path. As Sam did so, his foot accidentally slipped on a pebble, which was sent scuttling sideways, with a slight rattle. May and Sam froze. The dog, in the garden opposite, pricked up his ears, and started to bark.

They then moved quickly but quietly through the trees to

the fence and shimmied over it, into the council store yard. They ran diagonally across it, and over the fence on the far side, dropping down to the road. The dog soon stopped barking. It was only to be hoped that nobody had been disturbed.

Balaclavas off, they walked, respectably, along the road to the car. May said nothing. Sam was silent. He couldn't see whether she had the bag.

Once inside the car, all hell broke loose. May was in no mood for trifling now. She really let Sam have it.

'Either you got it wrong, or they've got it inside.'

'I didn't get it wrong, May. It was that boat, and it was that locker.'

'Then they've got it. Is it sealed inside?'

'Yes. It is all wrapped up inside the leather bag. Just like the other one.'

'Well, if it isn't obvious what it is, perhaps they don't yet know what they've got.'

'I don't expect so, May. If they'd found it, they'd have gone to the police.'

'Or taken it for themselves. Now, straight home. I want some sleep. We've only got about three hours.'

'Three hours?'

'We've got to be up early to load the car with supplies, because I'm bloody well coming with you.'

'You're coming?'

'I certainly am. I am not letting you lot out again on your own.'

'No, May.' Sam knew when to shut up.

'They open the Rochdale at nine a.m., and we'll be waiting. I'll take the boat. You two can operate the locks. And you'll do it like clockwork, at the double all the way.'

'Yes, May.' Sam knew when not to argue.

'They're six hours ahead of us, and by tomorrow evening, if we haven't caught them up, I'll kill you both!'

'Of course, May,' Sam knew when to be conciliatory.

'I'm going to tear their boat apart, from stern to stern, till I find it.'

'Definitely, May.' Sam knew when to agree.

'They are bound to leave the boat some time. Then I'll go through it with a fine-tooth comb, and they won't know I've been. I'll bring my work keys. Remind me.'

'Certainly, May,' Sam knew when her wrath was abating.

Ern was on to another can of lager. He dozed intermittently, dreaming of May. A lovely girl, how he fancied her. Oh, May. Pity she was so off-hand. But she'd get over that. He floated away again. Consciousness left him, and he was back into another wet dream. With May.

10

'What a disgusting mess!' May was furious. 'I left this boat spotless only forty-eight hours ago.'

Ern came to with a sudden jolt. His dream of lying beside the gentle, soft, ever-loving May was rudely shattered. Looming over him stood a harridan of immense proportions, breathing fire and smoke with every word she uttered.

'Look at it now!'

May had entered the living area, through the cockpit door, which was wide open, and had been all night. In a corner an expensively dressed couple on a large sofa were loftily discussing trivialities, of extreme urbanity, on breakfast television. May switched it off.

The table was littered with dirty plates and mugs. Overfull ashtrays spilled over onto the table, and then to the floor, mixed with baked beans, which had somehow fallen off their plates. Spoons, forks, knives, lay where they had fallen, grotesquely, as if in battle. Empty lager cans rolled about the floor.

Ern lay back on the sofa seat, one foot on the seat, the other at an obscure angle on to the floor. His mouth was open, and he was snoring loudly. There was a two-day stubble on his chin. In general he looked, and smelled, rather rancid.

His eyes opened wide and his jaw dropped as he jolted upright, still clutching a half-full can of lager, which slopped onto the floor as he did so. In front of him was the nymph of his dreams, transformed into a Gorgon.

'Get this cleaned up. And when I say spotless, I mean spotless.'

She walked through the filth of the kitchen, into the cabin. Ern jumped to his feet, spilling more lager on the floor. He trod on some baked beans, which caused him to slip back onto the sofa again, at the same time spilling even more lager.

May lifted the cover, and examined Fred intently. She already had ideas about what to do with him.

She went out onto the stern deck, and began the daily routine checks which, in the excitement yesterday, Sam had forgotten. May didn't forget. Sam came along the towpath, with two large boxes obscuring his view.

'Put it in the cockpit, and fetch the rest. This place is like a cesspit. I've given that dreamy sod half an hour to have it spotless. When you've done that you can help him.'

'Yes, May,' Sam meekly replied.

By 8.30 George and Stan had been locking up for two and a half hours. As The Strawberry Duck loomed on the horizon, Stan's attention was drawn to a smart little girl in a school uniform, who skipped gaily along, with her school bag on her arm. What a lovely girl, thought Stan as he watched her, waiting for the lock to fill. Such quiet, gentle innocence. The girl turned towards him and waved enthusiastically, as if to a well-loved friend. She grinned, and Stan couldn't help noticing the buck teeth. After a moment he grinned, and waved back. She winked at him and went on her way.

George was, of course, too busy to notice. He just wanted to catch up. He had laid his plans. He would be at the top by ten o'clock. A foray for groceries at Fairfield. Then hell for leather after them. He would have them in sight soon now. He had a gut feeling that this case was just about to take off.

*

Waiting for nine o'clock, *Hyacinth* lay before the first of the Rochdale Nine. Pavarotti was not singing now. He had long since gone home. There wasn't a soul about. The boat was spotless. May had seen to that. She had inspected every inch, and if any area was not up to her idea of perfection, Sam and Ern had cleaned it again. She dropped them off at the landing stage, each armed with a windlass, and key. They had the lock empty, and at the stroke of nine the gates were thrown open, and *Hyacinth* glided in.

They might just as well have been slaves building the pyramids. Sam and Ern perspired and ached as the slave driver kept to her word. They ran from lock to lock, as May brought *Hyacinth* along at almost top gear. She was going to do this stretch in less than two hours if it killed her – or, rather, them.

We had a leisurely breakfast, and were ready for the off by ten o'clock. No need to rush, the day was ours. The sun was already warm, and another beautifully clear sunny day greeted us. I had a walk to the main road, where a number of council workmen were waiting for transport. The garden opposite was beautiful in the full light of the day. But that damned dog still barked at almost everything that moved.

In the wide winding hole a number of black and white ducks enjoyed their morning bathe. We had seen, at times, a number of ducks along the canal. I couldn't help wondering how many dinners they provided.

Richard ran the routine daily maintainance checks. He pumped the bilges, screwed down the grease gun for the propeller shaft, started up … but something was wrong. Opening the plate over the propeller, he found, entwined in the blades, a large sheet of light blue plastic sheeting. With the aid of kitchen scissors, he eventually freed us. I laid the cut strips of plastic in a neat pile beside the towpath, next to the waste bin. We slipped our moorings, and glided into another unknown world.

At almost eleven May was underground, as her two bonds-men crawled towards the top lock. She pulled in tight to the pillar and the boat lay at rest, rubbing gently against the concrete. A few minutes elapsed before May emerged from the cabin, onto the stern deck, pulling Fred behind her. His bottom banged against each step, up to the stern deck, where she laid him, head over the side, facing the water, and almost in it. It was the side away from the towpath.

Looking carefully around, she checked all directions, to see that the coast was clear. It was gloomy and dank. Not a soul stirred. In fact they hadn't seen anyone on this length at all except the lock-keeper, who had extracted his dues from Sam. It was now or never. She bent down, and holding his feet, started to push him over the side.

'Hey! You can't chuck your litter in there.'

May jumped, and turned. In so doing she almost lost control of Fred. It was the lock-keeper, making a check across his domain.

'Don't you throw it in, or I'll prosecute you.'

She strained and heaved Fred back.

'Oh, it's not rubbish. It's my old man.'

'Well, it might be, but you can't get rid of him in there.'

'He had a skin full last night, and was spewing up over the side. I'm trying to keep hold of him.' She made a pretence of wrestling with his unruly legs.

'Don't let him be sick in the water, it will kill the fish.'

Fish! What bloody fish? thought May.

'Get him to bring it up in a bucket, like everyone else.'

'Yeah. I'll get him in again. He's better now.'

'You want any help?'

'No thanks. I'm all right now,' said May.

The lock-keeper went on his way, but she daren't go

126

through with it now. The body was bound to come to light sometime, and he might be able to identify the boat.

She grabbed Fred's legs, dragging him fully onto the stern again. She put her arms under his, clasped them across his chest, and pulled him back into the cabin.

The lock-keeper spoke to Sam, who was tired out, but didn't seem the worse for drink. They opened the gates, and called May in. She was a bit slow this time. She was normally ahead of them, pushing them to the limit, and over.

'My wife is a good navigator. She'll bring the boat in, spot on.' And she did.

'Your wife?' said the lock-keeper.

'Yes,' said Sam, as he set to close the gates.

She's got two husbands, and on the same boat. He doesn't even seem to care. Is this what women's lib means? Puzzled, the lock-keeper went on his way.

Blue Belle moored at Fairfield. George and Stan tidied up and went ashore. A sortie to the supermarket provided them with ample supplies. They knew now that this might not be just a two-minute job.

George was still being pleasant, which made Stan feel uneasy. It should have been more relaxing and enjoyable for Stan, but he couldn't fully relax as he wondered how long it would last. Inevitably George would revert to normal. The sooner the better, really, because he found himself waiting at every moment for a change. The waiting was unnerving.

'I reckon we can't be more than an hour or so behind now,' said George with an air of confidence.

'I hope you're right.'

Old, now long closed mills dominated the skyline, over Ashton-under-Lyne, as we completed our last mile of the

Ashton Canal. Portland Basin forms a large, wide pool. One could imagine it, once a hub of the canal transport system in the busy centre of the cotton trade, now quiet, and almost deserted. Warehouses no longer, but cleaned up and modernised to form a museum complex, the Tameside Heritage Centre.

Two boats were moored but we saw not a soul, except for a solitary middle-aged lady with her shopping bag on her arm, walking along the towpath towards the centre of Ashton-under-Lyne.

Our path took us to the right onto the Peak Forest Canal. Richard took a large sweeping arc to our left, and then right, through 270 degrees. He aimed our huge boat at what seemed to be a tiny entrance to the new canal, which is spanned at its mouth by a footbridge carrying the towpath. With consummate ease, we glided on to our fifth canal system in less than 48 hours. In the first few yards of the new canal system, there are no less than three bridges. Under the towpath footbridge, over the River Tame, which we were now to follow along its course for some time, and finally under the railway bridge.

Suddenly our whole world turned full circle. We rolled into open parkland, grassy banks rising to our left, broken by footpaths and little tracks. On our right, the towpath, dropping down to the river. The sheer contrast with our previous day's journey, made it almost unbelievable in its peaceful beauty. There were one or two bench seats, probably in use the previous day with families out for Sunday walks. But this was Monday morning, and there wasn't a soul about. A small, white-painted lifting bridge carried a vehicle track over the canal, which led down to a small farm nestling between the canal and the river. There wasn't a cloud, and the sun was bright in the sky, as we relaxed and glided through this peaceful idyll. To think that in the heyday of the canal, this was a colliery basin.

A man working in a boatyard said nothing, but swung out to us, as we passed, a long pole, with a leaflet in the cleft at the end, which he offered to us. The leaflet introduced us to timber-hulled craft. Very interesting, and very noble, but I must say I felt safer in a steel-hulled boat.

Strange to think that this quiet rural atmosphere isn't rural at all. We were still very much within the confines of Greater Manchester, and a short walk in either direction from the canal would prove it. But we didn't wish to prove it. We just let its beauty sink in. Occasional reminders of the past brought us back to reality. Along this 3 mile stretch, there are what is left of some nine cotton mills. Their chimneys no longer belch black smoke into this quiet little valley.

Still following the course of the River Tame, as it flows downstream with us. Through the small town of Hyde, where the M67 motorway crosses the canal, carrying traffic through some of the city's bottlenecks. Here the towpath is even diverted for a section, to ensure the privacy of Hyde Hall, once the home of an affluent mill owner.

The Tame left us at Woodley, as we ran through a tunnel in the hillside. Only 176 yards, and one can see straight through it. The canal emerged into a grassy cutting, and took us on to Romiley, where we moored to do some shopping; also to remind us what life was like ashore. Two days only, yet it already felt like weeks.

Whilst I didn't really know the town of Romiley very well, I had visited in the autumn, on a number of occasions, for the Annual Show. They had everything there, perched as it was on a hilltop from which the ground dropped gently away into a valley with rolling hills beyond. Richard had come with me on one occasion. It had poured with rain all day. We stopped at Jodrell Bank planetarium on the way home. On another occasion, my daughter Jane had bought herself a guinea pig there, and a cactus for Richard. She told the stall keeper that she wanted something prickly for a 'prickly boy'.

Idly browsing around one store, I found myself, quite by chance, in the ladies' lingerie department. Two ladies, quite oblivious to me, were busy browsing. They stopped at the bra counter.

'What size?' enquired the thin one.

'38DD,' replied her friend, scrutinising a black one.

'You lucky sod!' exclaimed the undernourished one, as I turned back quickly.

Yes! I thought, very true.

'There we are,' said George, 'That's their boat, moored the other side of the bridge.'

'No one about.'

'Pull in this side.'

Stan stepped ashore – George was getting better at this steering business – tied *Blue Belle* to the mooring ring, and walked towards the apparently deserted *Colette*.

There was no one about. All the curtains and blinds were drawn, and there were no sounds of anyone aboard. If there was anyone still in there, then surely there must be some noise, but Stan couldn't hear any.

The cockpit doors were tightly closed, and obviously bolted on the inside. He walked the length of the boat again. If anyone were to speak to him, he was just admiring the boat. In any case, he *was* admiring it. Much more comfortable, he had no doubt, than their poor little craft. But George had difficulty manoeuvering *Blue Belle*, so what on earth would he do with a 62 footer?

Then he noticed something interesting. From the stern deck, the doors leading down to the cabin were padlocked on the outside. So that if anyone was still in there – and he hoped they still were – they were locked in. Very thoughtfully, Stan walked back towards *Blue Belle*.

As he walked under the bridge, he heard voices behind him. He saw the old fogies and the young 'uns coming down off the bridge, laden with groceries, and chattering away.

He clambered aboard *Blue Belle* and explained his worries to George, who at first seemed somewhat concerned. Eventually he came to the conclusion that they would have to do that, to make it look authentic. In any case, if there were to be any trouble, the others could always get out by means of the cockpit, or the side hatch, which was only bolted on the inside. Stan was apparently reassured.

'I thought they'd make their drop at Castlefields, but this is much more cunning. They'll do it out here, in the quiet of the countryside. Very clever, coming all this way like tourists. It would put the average surveillance team right off.'

'Perhaps you're right.'

'Sure I am. But just to be certain, we'll make a move tonight.'

'Good idea.'

They laughed, and felt a lot better.

Colette loosed her moorings, and *Blue Belle* did likewise.

Emerging through the hill at Woodley, we had entered a new valley, this time following the valley of the river Goyt, but going upstream, not with the flow of the river.

These two pretty little rivers, the Goyt and the Tame, merge together in Stockport to form the mighty River Mersey – a name synonymous with boats, great ships, much larger than ours. From little acorns mighty oaks do grow. Looking at this little stream, you could hardly believe it.

From Romiley through the Hyde Bank Tunnel, into woods. Lush sweeping trees brushed down to the water, and provided intermittently a useful shade, but we were always on the move.

Out into the open, perched on an embankment. The valley below us became deeper and deeper, until finally we reached the Marple Aqueduct, which carries the canal high up over the steeply wooded ravine of the Goyt Valley, 100 feet below. Running almost parallel with us, but even higher, were the huge arches of the railway viaduct. A magnificent, majestic sight.

I was relieved. I didn't suffer from vertigo, as I had done on the Pontcysyllte Aqueduct, which is 20 feet higher than this, but that is 1,000 feet long. This is nothing like that huge deep expanse.

Saved from my embarrassment, we entered a heavily wooded glade, under the railway, and swung right into a large, enchanting pool surrounded by neat grassy banks, rising to our right on the inside of the bend, and falling down towards the Goyt Valley on our left. Trees surrounded us, huge oaks, which must have been standing there long before the canal was built. Ahead of us, surrounded by a huge sandstone arch, were huge wooden gates leading to an enchanted castle. I stopped, blinked, but I was still in this far-off Never-Never Land of Merlin and magic. I was enchanted, truly enchanted.

The medieval entrance was truly an entrance, but not to King Arthur's castle. The stone arch formed the bridge over the canal, and the huge castle gates behind were no more than lock gates. The first of the Marple flight. An architectural masterpiece, so beautifully designed and executed, it lifts the canal over 200 feet, by means of a wonderful flight of 16 locks. From the magical woodland setting at the bottom, right up into the centre of this lovely town, crossing, or rather slipping under, two busy roads as it does so.

Well-cut grassy banks, surrounded by shady trees, transformed the lower slopes into a pleasant parkland, and playground area. There were mothers with children, boys, and girls, with their fishing rods, and two large family groups picnicking. We were now in the thick of boat country again. Since Manchester they had slowly increased in numbers, but this was now certainly boating country. There were boats going up, as other boats came down. Sixteen locks, but in this situation it was not arduous work.

There was also, sometimes, an added bonus. When there was a boat in the lock ahead, coming down as we were going up, the locking crews changed places, each leaving their gates open for the other so that each boat could emerge from its lock at the same time, pass in the pound between, and go straight into the lock above, or below, as the case maybe. Which was already open, and ready to receive them.

Passing through the pound between the fourth and fifth locks we heard a train approaching. It was obviously on the line which crossed the viaduct, which was higher than us over the Goyt Valley, and beneath which we had passed before entering the lower pool. But where was it going? Its roar grew louder as it approached, but just as suddenly the noise ceased, only to be brought back to us a short time later on the opposite side of the canal. The noise receded as the train travelled away towards Sheffield. Half a mile before, we were below the railway; now we were above it, and rising fast.

We left the pleasing parkland behind us and glided under the road that led to Glossop. Rising in lock nine we found ourselves in suburbia. A policeman and a policewoman were walking along the road towards the towpath, which was set in a large open grassy area, beyond which smart houses basked in the afternoon sun. Ahead of us was a wide pound, on the left bank of which stood an old warehouse, now tastefully transformed into a suite of offices.

'Good afternoon, sir. No more trouble?' It was WPC Nonelly, escorted by PC Jones.

'Oh, hello. None at all, thanks.'

'Nice holiday?' she enquired.

'Wonderful. This really is a magnificent trip.'

'We should be so lucky!' said PC Jones despondently. WPC Nonelly, I noticed, looked at him sharply.

'Glad you're enjoying it,' he said, this time with a smile, realising that he had better try and show a better image.

'Did you find anything?' I enquired.

'No, only the drunk,' replied WPC Nonelly.

With that the lock gates opened and we were on our way. Beyond the warehouses over the next three locks, pretty well-kept gardens flanked the left-hand bank, as the leafy, shaded towpath ran along the other. Under the busy town centre road, the scenery changed again. A row of small terraced houses faced the canal beyond the towpath, with only a small service road in front of them. The last four locks came quickly, one upon the other, as the rise got steeper. Nearing the top, a small inlet of canal sweeps off to the left, actually into the heart of the garden, of a house perched right at the top of the canal bank. The site of a former dry dock, once a workplace, now an imaginative creation.

We looked behind us at the wonderful view far out across the Goyt Valley. To think we had climbed all the way, thanks to the art of the canal builders of old. How lucky we are that this art still flourishes. The vandalism of the powers that were 40 years ago has been reversed in time, before the canals were lost forever.

Out of the top lock, a sharp right under a tight bridge, and we joined the Macclesfield Canal, leaving behind us the Peak Forest, which continues on a spur to Whalley Bridge.

Just beyond the bridge we pulled in for water, and deposited our rubbish. Whilst the tank was filling Richard was busy setting his camera on timer, and taking pictures of our party in different poses, draped over the boat.

Inevitably another boater, thinking that we were merely playing at the watering point, ordered us very brusquely to move. Then he realised that we were in fact watering, as well as playing about.

WPC Nonelly and PC Jones crossed the road and, looking down the lower part of the flight, saw George and Stan, busily working their way up.

'Christ! Let's go,' she said. 'Before I have a heart attack.'

11

The Strawberry Duck was nearby, but May refused all requests for a refreshment stop. The lads clearly thought they deserved one, but May certainly didn't.

'The stingy bastard,' exclaimed Ern, taking care that he was out of earshot of May.

'Eh! That's my wife you're talking about,' rebuked Sam.

'Yeah. Sorry.' But with a shrug of his shoulders, indicating that he wasn't really.

'But I know what you mean. When she sets her mind to something there is no stopping her.'

They turned reluctantly to their work again. To obviate any waiting time on her part, May had organised her lads on a one-jump-ahead basis. There were no other boats about, so it was easy. As soon as one lock was ready for *Hyacinth* to enter, one of the lads ran ahead to prepare the next lock so that it was empty, with its gates open. May could simply sail straight out of one lock, across the pound, into the next. Not a moment wasted.

They were making very good time indeed. May drove *Hyacinth* flat out whenever she had a chance of doing so. The lads, if you could still call them lads, had to work flat out all day, except for a short rest after leaving the city centre. This was, however, no more than a very few minutes' sit-down with a drink.

The toll was really telling. They worked on, their clothes soaking in perspiration, aching all over, feeling pain in muscles they never knew they had. Their complete lack of

137

exercise, too much beer and too many fags, gave them the appearance of worn-out geriatrics, certainly not the would-be Olympians, to which they aspired.

Before they reached the top of the flight, Sam's chest was feeling tight. Neither of them had very much breath left in them. They were indeed a very sorry sight.

As they finally clambered aboard, May very magnanimously said, 'Well done. We'll catch them up tonight. Have a lager.'

'Be easier if we followed them by car,' moaned Ern.

'Cheeky sod,' retorted May sharply. 'If you hadn't buggered this whole operation we wouldn't be here now.'

All thoughts of generosity on her part were stifled by Ern's thoughtless remark. True though it might be.

Sam asked to be allowed to sit down, until he got his breath back.

'All right, you two make the tea, and sandwiches.'

They went below. May opened the throttle, and the wake from *Hyacinth* left huge waves running along both banks. She was in her element, and going to make up even more time.

Sam sat on a seat in the lounge. His breathing was heavy and laboured. He closed his eyes, but the occasional twitch of his cheek indicated that he was in some pain.

After a short sit-down, Ern set about making the tea and sandwiches.

'You all right?' he enquired of Sam.

Sam opened his eyes and winced. 'Got hellish indigestion,' he replied, and closed his eyes again.

The old Goyt Mill greeted us on the outskirts of High Lane, striking red brick work, with lines of cream bricks blending in very attractively. Then out into open country again. To our left, through a mass of trees and unkempt undergrowth, the ruins of Windlehurst Hall stood out starkly.

Cracked uneven walls, covered with ivy, gave a gloomy air of abandoned desolation. Another relic of past glories. High Lane, the last outpost of Greater Manchester, after 28 miles of water through the capital of the north.

We moored opposite a small open field, bordered on the far side by some modern housing. Two closed-up boats were moored alongside the field. A small brood of ducks chattered and darted around them. Another field, with trees overhanging the towpath beside us, made a nice shady prospect.

Stan, as a precaution, was trotting along the towpath again, into High Lane, keeping a keen eye open for his quarry. George felt that this appeared a likely overnight resting place for the pursued.

'George. George.'

Crackle … Crackle.

'George!'

'Yes.'

'You're right. I'm at bridge ten. They are moored down here.'

'Good. I'm bringing the boat up to you. We'll moor there. This seems just the spot for a drop. Are they all there?'

'Yes … Well, the old 'uns, and the young 'uns. No sign of anybody else.'

'Well, keep a sharp eye out.'

Stan put his phone down. I hope this is it. I just want to get this over with and go home!

'OK, action stations!' shouted May.

'What's up?' enquired Sam, whose head emerged through the back hatch. He was still feeling tired, but seemed otherwise back to normal. Well, as normal as he was ever likely to be.

Ern followed him out on to the stern deck. He also had
had a doze, and although only just waking up, was certainly
refreshed.

'There,' said May, nodding ahead.

'Bloody hell,' exclaimed Ern, and his jaw dropped.

'Oh hell. No, May. Give it a rest. We can't do the Marple
flight as well, we're knackered.' Sam spoke from his
heart.

'Just this. There's only sixteen.'

'Jesus. Sixteen!' moaned Ern.

'It's pretty scenery. You'll enjoy it. Collect your tools, and
off you go.'

They obeyed, but were slower this time, and the one-
jump-ahead principle didn't always work as there were
other boats to be considered. Although May wasn't for
considering anyone. Sam was certainly feeling the strain,
but he carried on. He wasn't going to argue.

Having been deprived of my birthday dinner, I determined
to have it tonight, whatever happened. A reconnaissance of
the town was vital, and, after a cup of coffee, I set off.

'Get rid of those empty wine bottles. You forgot them
when you put out the rubbish at Marple,' said Margery,
handing me a large plastic Co-op carrier bag of bottles.

'We can't have drunk all of these,' I protested.

'You have.'

'Suppose there isn't one?'

'There will be. You'll find it.'

With my carrier bag firmly gripped in my hand, I set off
with a sprightly step. I intended to find just the right place
for my celebration dinner. The canalside pub was not
serving evening meals. Nor did it have a bottle bank. But
undeterred, I started to explore the canal beyond the
bridge. I had plenty of time, and who knows what I would
find. It was a pleasant cutting, flanked with trees. An old

wharf on the towpath side had been turned into private moorings.

I was about to turn back when my attention was drawn to a lady on a moored boat, in the cutting beyond the old wharf. There was something familiar about her. I stopped. She smiled in my direction. There wasn't anybody else about. Perhaps she was smiling at me. I didn't know why she should be smiling at me. Whilst she was vaguely familiar, I couldn't place her at all. In fact I was sure I didn't know her. I looked around. No one else in sight. She smiled again, quite definitely at me, this time giving a little affected wave.

I didn't know what to do. I was covered in confusion. Suppose I didn't know her? I pulled myself together and walked slowly towards her.

She was very familiar. Long, slender bare legs, open-toed sandals, through which scarlet toenails peeped. Red shorts and … Suddenly it hit me. Yes, I did recognise her … her ample – nay, very ample – bosom, inadequately covered with a silk scarf, tied across the valley, and barely covering the essentials. Oh yes, I knew her, she was familiar all right. I'd recognise those … er … anywhere. We had seen her moored at High Walton, adjacent to the barbecue party. She doesn't know me, I thought. So why is she paying me all this attention? I looked around again. Still no one else about.

She raised a flute of white wine towards me with her right hand, continuing to wave with her left, all the time smiling as if I was a long-lost friend. My instinct was to run. But from what? What was the harm? She was merely a pleasant, sociable young lady. It would be rude of me simply to ignore her. I approached slowly.

'Hello. I'm Rose.'

'Er … Nice day, isn't it?'

'Lovely,' she replied. 'I was just having a glass of wine. Would you care to join me? Pity to drink alone.'

141

'Oh, I couldn't do that. I'm just …'

'Vouvray. Well chilled. Do come and tell me about your holiday on the canal. You are on holiday, aren't you?'

'Er, yes …'

'I thought so. It's such a lovely spot, isn't it? I'm always so happy here.'

'I've got a job to do. I'd … er … better not stop.' I started to move off.

'Nonsense, one drink won't hurt. I know just what you need. I'm sure I can help.'

'Do you really? It's the bottle bank.'

'Of course it is. I know perfectly well what you want.'

So helpful too, I thought.

'Do come aboard.' She ushered me onto the stern deck and then led me down into the cabin. It was a little dark, but a warm red light gave it a warm glow.

The curtains were closed, but the cabin was huge. It contained an extra-large double bed. Curiously, there was a mirror on the ceiling. Funny place for a mirror, I mused. A large picture graced the wall above the head of the bed. Picture? Photograph, of her … on this bed … in the nude. I faltered, looking hard at it again. Perhaps some people decorated their boats like this, but it was new to me. Her full, very ample bosom was shown in full-colour detail. But the picture left nothing else to the imagination either. I've definitely got to get out of here, I thought.

'The wine is in the lounge.' Rose ushered me on. With her bosom in my back, I couldn't help but be projected forward, into a palatial lounge.

Again the curtains were drawn, and the room was lit only by a warm suffused red glow. Large red plush sofas ranged round the walls. Beside the cockpit doors, shut and curtained, stood a small bar. From this, Rose dispensed me a large glass of white wine.

'Do sit down,' she said quietly, ushering me, again with

her bosom, over to the sofa. 'Try this. I buy it myself direct from the importers.'

I sat down, resting my large carrier bag of empty bottles on the floor.

'Please excuse me, just a moment. Then we can have a chat. I'd like that.' With that she disappeared.

The lounge was rather out of this world, but not at all unattractive. I tried to open the curtains, but found the windows firmly boarded up. What an odd situation. There was no table. Why no table? Tables were usual, in fact necessary. This was a dining area after all. Where did she eat? I took a sip of wine. Very good, I thought. Admirable vintage.

Then I noticed it again. There was a mirror on this ceiling also. And pictures! Again of Rose, nude. There was something decidedly odd about this boat. What on earth was I doing here? Thoughts darted through my mind, but nevertheless I got up to examine the pictures more closely. There was, after all, no one else present ushering me on, or pushing me on with her bosom. I had to admit they were a very good likeness, but not quite as explicit as the one in the cabin. She really did photograph well.

In the opposite corner to the bar, adjacent to the cockpit, was a large television set. Suddenly it started to flicker. I sat down again. It was covered in white dots, and it made a terrible crackling noise. Nice of her, I thought. But I don't really want to see the Olympics again.

'George. George!'
Crackle, crackle.
'George!'
'Yes?'
'I think you're right. I've just followed the old geezer. He's acting very odd.'
'What's he doing?'
'He's got a heavy Co-op carrier bag, and he's gone down

143

the canal with it. I've followed him to a boat way down here. He's gone on board, with a flashy blonde.'

'Where did he meet her?'

'She was on the boat, waiting for him.'

'Where is he now?'

'He's gone inside with her.'

'And the bag?'

'And the bag!'

'Looks like a drop all right. Keep your eyes skinned.'

'Wait …'

'Yes?'

'She's come out again. She's looking all around. Now she's hanging out her knickers on the washing line. They're red, with black lace edging.'

'I don't want to know about her knickers.'

'They're quite something. So thin you can see right through them.'

'Never mind her knickers!'

'She's looking around again. Why is she always looking around like that? Now she's gone inside again, closing the door.'

'We've got 'em. I don't think we'll pounce just yet. Keep an eye on her, and we'll get the pick-up if someone comes for it, or follows her, whichever comes first.'

Sam was in a very poor way when they came back on board, bitterly complaining of his indigestion.

'Sit down for a bit, you'll feel better. Ern will make us a nice cup of tea, won't you, Ern?'

'Yes, May,' Ern sighed.

He put on the kettle, while Sam slumped on the settee. His eyes closed. His breathing was uneven.

May, in her element again, was full steam ahead, waving as Sam had done to irritated protesters. At Windlehurst Hall, she pulled into the side, away from the towpath. The boat grounded itself on gravel as she steered in among the overhanging trees and undergrowth.

'What the hell's that?' asked Sam, wakened from his uneven sleep, but feeling somewhat better.

'She's run aground,' replied Ern with a smile. 'Never thought May would get caught running aground.'

'Right you two. Off your backsides.'

'Give us a rest,' said Sam, and lay back again, closing his eyes.

'Just one more job. This is the place to land Fred.'

'I'd forgotten Fred. Been walking past him all day, and I'd forgotten all about him.' Ern seemed genuinely concerned that, in the excitement of the day, he had quite forgotten Fred.

'Come on, now. Slip him ashore. We can't be far off catching them up now.'

'I'm fed up with the locks!' snapped Sam.

'There aren't any before Bosley. And they won't even reach them tomorrow.'

Reluctantly, Ern started to move. Sam followed. He felt awful, and looked terrible. He almost stumbled, but neither May, nor Ern, saw him. His indigestion was getting much worse.

May pulled the cover off Fred, who now lay in a more composed state than he ever had in life. Ern pulled his legs off the bunk, turning him sideways. Sam tucked his arms under Fred's, and clasped them together round his chest.

Sideways, once again, they carried Fred out towards the steps up to the stern deck. Ern walked up slowly backwards. Sam, following with the heavier head end of Fred, was labouring hard under the weight. Climbing onto the third step, he tripped. Fred's body hurtled forwards onto the stern deck, with Sam on top of him. Ern was forced back against the rudder arm.

145

'Come on, Sam.' May took hold of Fred's shoulders, and turned him round through 90 degrees.

'Sorry, May,' said Sam quietly, as he staggered up the steps, taking Fred from her.

There was a gap of some 2 feet between the boat and dry land. Ern dangled Fred's legs over the side of the stern deck, jumped ashore, and then picked him up again. He then dragged Fred ashore, with Sam and May holding his shoulders, laying his head down carefully over the side of the boat. Ern pulled him ashore.

When Fred's body was only just ashore, Ern tried to jump back onto the boat.

'Don't be daft,' exclaimed May, 'you can't leave him there, on the bank, in full view of every passing boat.' So saying, she pushed Sam ashore. He stumbled as he landed.

Ern, without much assistance from Sam, pulled Fred's body about 20 yards in from the canal bank, then deposited him in heavy undergrowth. Sam bent down, and laid him out tidily as he had two nights earlier.

'Now tidy up the bracken where he's been dragged, so that it doesn't show anything.'

The lads did as they were bidden. Ern jumped aboard.

'There's a bonfire or something over there.' Ern pointed towards the ruin.

May looked carefully, 'Appears to be nothing serious, but let's move quickly.'

Sam couldn't make it back on his own. May helped him aboard, realising for the first time that he really wasn't feeling too well.

'What's up, love?' she enquired, with genuine feeling.

'I've got terrible indigestion, and now I've got this awful pain in my chest. It's so tight it could burst.'

'Come on, love,' May said, helping him down the steps.

'I want to puke.'

She took him to the bathroom, and then laid him down on the empty bunk opposite where Fred had lain.

'Ern, make him a cup of tea, while I get the boat off.' With that she went up on to the stern deck, poled *Hyacinth* off the gravel, and went full ahead.

The crackling of the television set stopped and a picture appeared on the screen. I couldn't make it out at first.

'What is it? What's happening?'

The strains of a Strauss waltz filled the lounge, but what was the film? I went cold and gulped hard. I suddenly realised that it was a couple. A naked couple. In the height of intercourse. Doing it in time to the *Blue Danube*. One two three. One two three. It was mind-boggling in its simple complexity. My jaw dropped in wonderment, as the full impact hit me. Dah dah dah dah di di dum dum. Dah dah dah dah tit tit bum bum.

They really were doing it in time with the music. Perhaps this was how Strauss got his idea for the *Blue Danube*. 'Blue' was right. Where did this nice young lady get this film? It couldn't be legal!

'You like the film?' said Rose, who had entered silently, and unnoticed as I had been so engrossed in the performance. Luckily she didn't wait for a reply.

'That is me, you know. I made it on holiday in Aberystwyth last year. He was a rugby player, ever so versatile. Very powerful in the scrum. Always had his eye on the ball.' The ball! 'His touch-down was perfect.'

I was sweating profusely. I must get out of this! 'I ... er ...' I stuttered.

'This is the Menu,' whispered Rose. She slipped an elaborate leather-bound folder into my hands. The type usually seen in the most exclusive restaurants.

Menu! I'm certainly not bringing the family here to eat. I opened it gingerly. My eyes nearly popped out of my head.

It contained delicate line-drawn prints of couples, in all sorts of unimaginable positions, doing sometimes unrepeatable things to each other. Beside each were price tags in pounds, euros and dollars. They were carefully divided according to specialties:

'Hors d'oeuvres … Entree … Main Course … Sweet Trolley … Wine provided – Coffee extra …

Coffee extra! My eyes bulged.

A note at the bottom read:

'All courses are subject to VAT and 10% service charge.'

Service charge!

'Bloody hell. A floating knocking shop!' I exclaimed.

I looked up at Rose, who had now lost her red shorts and brief scarf. She wore only red stockings, with matching suspender belt and red briefs. Very brief. Her bare, ample – very ample – breasts hung out towards me, as she leaned over me.

'I'm here,' she whispered, 'just as you like me.'

I tried desperately to shout 'Help!' as she swung her huge chest in my face, almost stifling me. Fighting for breath, I managed to extricate myself.

'Another glass of wine?' she simpered.

'Er … No, thanks. I …'

'Now, then. What would you like?' she enquired, stroking my knee. 'Don't be shy with Rose, now will you.'

'Oh my God!' I screamed, clutching my left groin. 'It's my hernia. It's playing me up.'

'Can I help?' she enquired, pushing herself upon me.

'No!' I yelled. 'I've forgotten my truss. Ow!'

'Never mind, Rose will look after you,' she said in a gentle soothing voice. 'It will all be all right.'

She leaned forward towards me, searching for the belt of my trousers, catching, as she did so, her foot on the bag of empty bottles on the floor and losing her balance momentarily.

I dodged around her and ran out into the cabin, to find that she had bolted the hatch on to the stern deck, top and bottom. I undid the bottom bolt, but as I was reaching up for the top bolt, Rose was upon me again, clutching at my belt buckle, which she quickly had undone.

'Don't worry. Rose will look after you. Help your little problem,' she whispered quietly.

'I haven't any problems!'

'You'll have the experience of a lifetime. My customers are always satisfied. I'll show you my testimonials, if you would like.'

'Click' went the top bolt, and I fell out onto the stern deck, my trousers around my ankles.

'Sod it!' said Rose, as she realised that her quarry had escaped.

I hitched up my trousers, and ran.

Who should be standing on the towpath, but Richard.

'What the hell do you think you are doing?'

'It's a knocking shop,' I spluttered. 'It's a floating knocking shop.'

'Of course it is,' he replied. 'What did you think it was?'

'You knew?'

'Of course I knew. I was just about to come in and get you out.'

'How did you know?'

'Sometimes I wonder who the parent is in this relationship. What Mother will say, I dread to think!'

'You won't tell her?'

'Of course I won't tell her. I expect she'd die of laughter anyway.'

'He's come out, George, and the young bloke was waiting for him.'

'Well done,' said George, who was, strangely, still in an affable mood. 'Did he leave the bag?'

'Yes.'

'Splendid.'

'Hang on. She's just coming out again, glass in hand. Looking around. Now she's taking her knickers down again. Why is she doing that? They couldn't possibly have dried in that time.'

'You seem to be obsessed with her knickers. The bag is still aboard. So we wait and see if someone comes to collect it, or where she takes it.'

'What about tea?' enquired Stan. 'I'm getting damned hungry.'

'Moan, moan, bloody moan. Can't you keep quiet for a minute? Always thinking of yourself. Now keep a careful watch. Can you see both boats?'

'Yes!' said Stan, making a raspberry noise and switching off. You mean sod!

12

'You did get rid of the bottles, then,' said Margery, who was changed and ready to go out. She sat in the cockpit reading a paper. I went into the bathroom to cover my confusion.

'George, George.'
Crackle. Crackle ...
'George!'
'Yes!'
'They have gone up town, all dressed up. I've been back to their boat. It's big enough to carry another four, but I can't hear a thing from inside.'
'They're professionals, you wouldn't.'
'Hold on. A man in a raincoat, with his collar turned up, is going towards the blonde's boat. Imagine a raincoat in this heat. She's waving.'
'Good. It's the pick-up.'
'She's waving furiously. All covered in smiles.'
'Good.'
'He's gone aboard. Big chap. She's gone inside with him. No, she's come straight out again. Now she's hanging her red knickers on the line again. Why is she doing that again? Perhaps she realised they weren't dry.'
'You really are a fool.'
'Why?'
'We've got 'em.'
'How?'

151

'It's a signal. She uses her flaming knickers as a signal. Do not disturb.'

'I see.'

'They're a clever lot, this bunch. A clever lot.'

'What do we do now?'

'I'll be along. We'll go in a minute.'

Sergeant Tooth and PC Spriggs pulled into the car park of the Bull's Head on the A6, to find that PC Jones and WPC Nonelly had beaten them to it.

'Where's the contact?' enquired Sergeant Tooth.

'We've only just arrived,' said WPC Nonelly. 'We haven't seen anyone yet.'

A voice behind then said, 'Oh, there you are, Sergeant.'

Sergeant Tooth and his team turned to see George, who had just come up from the towpath.

'Struth! Not you again!' exclaimed Sergeant Tooth.

'We tried hard to avoid them only half an hour ago at Marple,' said WPC Nonelly, 'and now they are here!'

'You are the support team?' enquired George.

'What do you mean? We've been sent here,' Sergeant Tooth explained, 'to back up the Drug Squad. Not you mate. But I'll tell you one thing, if I have any trouble from you, I'll book you before you can turn around. Now get going.'

'I am the Drug Squad,' George said proudly. 'We're on a Covert Special Operation.'

'So covert, I notice, that I've nicked you already for misdemeanors, twice in two days. Now here you are again, as bold as brass, for the third day running, making the place untidy.' To his subordinate he snapped, through gritted teeth. 'All right! Shove him in your car. I've got him this time. Hoax phone calls, wasting police time, for a start. Where is your accomplice?'

They moved in to arrest George, but he suddenly

produced his identity card, in the nick of time.

'We are following a load of drugs, as part of a country-wide operation. We believe that a drop has been made here tonight, and the courier has just arrived to pick it up. My colleague is keeping close surveillance. I need your back-up, as I am going in for the arrest.'

'I don't believe this,' said Sergeant Tooth. 'I must be bloody dreaming.'

'Follow me,' ordered George, moving off towards the canal.

'I know how you feel,' commiserated WPC Nonelly, patting Sergeant Tooth affectionately on the back.

'MI6 poofters I could accept for this useless lot. But Drug Squad? Proper police work? It can't be true.'

'He has shown you his ID, Sarge. We've been called out to assist him, so we must go.' She patted his hand. 'Keep calm. We don't want you getting into any trouble. It'll be all right, you'll see.'

'But that stupid sod couldn't tie his own shoelaces,' he protested. 'Him being in charge of an investigation beggars belief.'

'I know,' she said, almost taking his hand.

It seemed that Sergeant Tooth was about to bang his head against the pub wall. However, encouraged by WPC Nonelly, he resisted, and pulled himself together.

'Aren't you coming?' enquired George from the top of the embankment.

'Right,' said Sergeant Tooth, pulling his head up, and throwing his chest out. 'You're in charge. What are your instructions?'

'Down to the canal,' said George. 'I'll do what is necessary. I just need your back-up in case of any trouble.'

'We should have been properly briefed,' complained Sergeant Tooth. George wondered what more was needed, but said nothing.

'OK, off we go,' he said haughtily.

As they went down to the towpath, George thought that perhaps he ought to explain the position fully. He preceeded, rather pompously, to give a full explanation of the operation. It even sounded vaguely plausible.

'Perhaps I've misjudged him,' whispered Sergeant Tooth under his breath.

'We'll see,' replied WPC Nonelly, with a knowing look.

They reached Stan in his hideaway.

'Any developments?'

'None,' replied Stan. 'He's still in there with her, and the package.'

'All right. We're going in,' said George with an air of authority.

'We really are?' enquired Stan, almost in disbelief.

'Yes.'

'Thank God for that, I can be home in a proper bed tonight.'

The stern doors were bolted on the inside, but they weren't very strong. A splitting of wood, and the hatch doors were open. George and Stan rushed down the steps, quickly followed by Sergeant Tooth and WPC Nonelly, more slowly followed by PCs Jones and Spriggs.

They all stood in the cabin dumbfounded at the sight before them. The cabin was still lit by a warm rosy glow, but now there was an added attraction. If indeed, an attraction it was. Psychedelic lighting, a myriad of colours, flowed, ran, positively oozed, over the ceiling, down the walls, running across the floor, everywhere.

This was atmosphere, but the sight which gripped their attention, and held them literally spellbound, was of a massive pair of hairy, naked buttocks, which heaved and plunged, up and down, thrusting with considerable intensity, whilst a pair of shapely legs clasped those monstrous buttocks, holding them in a vice-like grip.

Both parties were floating endlessly on cloud nine, in a state of sheer ecstasy. Rose, her massive bosom, or rather one of them, was much in evidence. Her cries and moans mingled with her stallion's grunts, and heavy breathing, whilst the strains of the 'Blue Danube' wafted into the cabin from the lounge. They were moving in time with the music. Dah dah dah dah di di dum dum. Dah dah dah dah tit tit bum, bum.

'Bloody hell,' exclaimed Stan.

The rest stood boggled-eyed, their mission forgotten, completely overwhelmed by this magnificent sight. WPC Nonelly moved closer to get a better view. She didn't want to miss anything of this spectacle.

So quick and quiet had been their entry, so loud the music, so intense the love-making, and so engrossed were the participants in their activities, that it took them some time to realise that something was wrong. And that their very private activity was not quite as private as they had thought, or intended.

'Now that's what I call outstanding,' said WPC Nonelly under her breath, surveying the owner of the massive hairy buttocks as he went about his task with energy and vigour.

Slowly it dawned on the couple that they were not alone.

'Sod it!' said Rose, realising that something was wrong, without knowing what.

The man slipped off, his back to the audience.

Rose turned, saw the assembled company and smiled. 'Hello,' she said, with considerable affability, and no pretence at modesty, or covering herself. 'I'm Rose.'

She surveyed the group, whose mouths were, for the most part, open, as their Adam's apples gulped. They were struck dumb at such a magnificent sight.

'Look,' she said, 'your friends have come to join us.'

It was then, and only then, that Sergeant Tooth paid

155

any real attention to Rose's stallion, whose attributes WPC
Nonelly had so longingly admired. He suddenly went cold
when he realised that it was none other than their Superintendent. The activity had been so riveting that no one had
bothered to look at faces. Now their jaws dropped even
further.

Rose, seeing WPC Nonelly, smiled. 'Oh, you've come for
an orgy have you? That would be nice.'

WPC Nonelly, suddenly, realising her vulnerable position,
replied smartly, 'No we bloody haven't.'

At this the others also came to.

'This is a drugs raid,' said George. 'Stay where you are.'

'I'm not going anywhere.' Rose stretched herself, raising
the blood pressure even higher.

'I have reason to believe,' he gulped, finding it difficult to
concentrate, 'that a delivery of dangerous drugs was made
to you, at these premises, a short while ago.'

Stan managed for a moment to take his eyes off Rose,
and went through into the lounge, more to see if there was
any other activity than anything else. There wasn't, to his
obvious disappointment.

'It's here,' he shouted, and brought the large, heavy,
Co-op carrier bag through into the cabin. He placed it very
carefully on the floor.

'Oh, that silly old bugger,' sighed Rose, seeing the carrier
bag. 'He came round here all smiles, wanting it, then got
cold feet and ran off.'

'I'm not surprised,' said WPC Nonelly under her breath,
looking at Rose.

The others weren't so certain. At the right moment
they would not be averse to an encounter with Rose. They
couldn't keep their eyes off her.

'Those tits,' sighed PC Jones.

WPC Nonelly looked at her partner with disgust. 'You
shit,' she whispered in his ear. But his eyes still bulged.

George gleefully took the carrier bag, and carefully emptied the contents on the floor.

'Empty wine bottles!' shrieked Sergeant Tooth. 'What sort of bloody joke is this?'

He was livid with George, embarrassed that WPC Nonelly, such a nice young girl, should see this wanton exhibition, and disturbed that this might hamper his chances of promotion with his Superintendent.

'You call us out on a so-called special mission to seize a bag of empty wine bottles!' he fumed. 'I'll have you for this. You are nicked.'

The Superintendent wrapped a sheet around himself, and after carefully composing himself, asked George for a full explanation. He was, of course, the only person present who was aware of the covert operation being carried out by the Drug Squad. The explanation completed, he asked George if he had a search warrant. He hadn't. The Superintendent looked angrily at Sergeant Tooth.

'We were merely instructed to report here. To give whatever support was required of us by the Drug Squad. We had no idea where we were going, or what we were going to be called upon to do. When I met this gentleman' – indicating George, who winced at the word 'gentleman' – 'I realised that he had your full confidence and support, and we have merely followed instructions. I naturally assumed that he had the appropriate warrant, as we would have done, had it been our case.'

He looked at George, who didn't know where to look. But wouldn't have minded looking at Rose.

'Rose,' the Superintendent enquired firmly. 'Do you have any drugs?'

'Don't be daft, Ian, I make a good living as it is. I don't need drugs. You know that well enough.' She was hurt at the suggestion.

She then got up, still quite naked, but not bothering to

hide herself. Unlike the Superintendent. Rose wasn't one to bear grudges. But she felt this episode could well be turned to her advantage.

'I give a ten per cent discount to policemen, and police-women,' she said, looking at WPC Nonelly, who snarled, 'You'll be lucky' under her breath.

Rose then pressed her card into each warm clammy hand, also a photograph. The same photograph, Sergeant Tooth realised, as the one he had found in the stolen wallet.

Once outside, Sergeant Tooth gave George the dressing-down of his life. George sheepishly explained that *Colette* was carrying drugs, and he was following it, waiting for the drop.

'What!' exclaimed Sergeant Tooth. 'That old fart? Don't be so bloody stupid. You really ought to be locked up for your own protection.' Then he pointed south and added venomously, 'The boundary of Greater Manchester, my jurisdiction, finishes two miles down the canal. So keep going and don't, whatever you do, come back!'

Sergeant Tooth turned sharply on the final word, and surrounded by his satellites, moved away from George and Stan, who looked a very desolate pair.

He then gathered his brood around him, and gave a very strict injunction. 'You didn't see the Superintendent. Right?'

'No, Sarge. We didn't see him at all,' they agreed. Their thoughts were, anyway, all on Rose. Those tits.

WPC Nonelly's thoughts were elsewhere. She had noted, with considerable admiration, the Superintendent's endowment.

Hyacinth reduced speed through High Lane.

'Stay below, and out of sight,' ordered May, when she spotted *Colette*. 'They're here. We'll pass them, then slip around the corner to moor.'

She steered sedately under the bridge, only to be confronted by a group of policemen, and a policewoman, talking amicably on the towpath.

She gave fresh orders. 'Police in force. Duck well down
out of sight. I'm going on.'

She put on her dark glasses and didn't look directly at the
policemen as she passed. They were so dejected and miserable they didn't even look up at her.

Below, Sam couldn't move anyway. The pains in his
chest were increasing, and his breathing becoming more
uneven.

'May! Come to Sam. He's in a bad way,' whispered Ern up
the steps of the stern deck. 'I'll take over up here when the
coast is clear.'

'OK.'

He went up to the stern deck and took over the steering.
'I think it's a heart attack,' he whispered quietly to May.

'Can't be.' Her brow furrowed.

'I'm sure it is. My Dad had one. Better get him to
hospital.'

She went below, but soon returned. 'Turn into the boatyard just down on the left. I'll ring for an ambulance.'

'Best thing. I'm sure I'm right.'

'I'm afraid you might be. This is all we need!'

'You must do it. He's my best mate.'

'He's my husband!'

Sergeant Tooth had no sooner reached the car park than
his phone rang again: orders to take his team to investigate
a report of a death.

'Wish it was those two,' PC Jones said with feeling.

They arrived by road, at the ruined Windlehurst Hall,
within minutes. They were greeted by three boys aged about
ten years. They were vaguely dressed in an indefinable
uniform, of indescribably scruffy appearance. They eagerly

stood to attention and saluted as Sergeant Tooth approached. He pleased them by saluting back.

'We've found a stiff,' said one boy, obviously the leader.

'I see,' said Sergeant Tooth. 'And what are you doing here?'

'We're camping.'

'What? Here? In these ruins?'

'Yes.'

'They're dangerous.'

'They're great fun.'

'Who's in charge?'

They pointed to the boy who did all the answering and was certainly the leader.

'Where is your Scout Master?'

'He's ... er ... Just gone away for a few minutes.'

'Are you really Scouts?' enquired WPC Nonelly.

The boys finally confessed that they weren't really Scouts, and that there was no Scout Leader. They had found that if they dressed in Scout uniform people let them do things, or go to places from which they would otherwise be chased away.

'Right, then. Where's the body?' enquired Sergeant Tooth, not believing for a moment that there really was one.

'How did you come to find it? The ... er ... body,' asked Sergeant Tooth.

'Well, we made our camp fire. Had our tea. Then went on a hunting game for him,' pointing at the smallest boy. 'As he was running away from us, he fell over it.'

With that he, and his troop, ran off ahead, as Sergeant Tooth and his team fought their way through the under-growth. About 20 yards from the canal bank, the boys stopped, and lined up beside the body of Fred.

'He's dead,' volunteered another boy, 'I gave him the kiss of life, but he didn't wake up.'

Investigation revealed that he was indeed dead.

'WPC Nonelly, take these boys to your car. Get full details from them. Then take them all home.'

'We don't want to go home. This is great,' complained the smallest boy.

'Well, you're going,' said Sergeant Tooth, ushering WPC Nonelly and her troop off. 'PC Jones.'

'Yes, Sarge.'

'Go with her, and see that they behave.'

He turned to the boys and saluted. 'Well done, lads.'

They were delighted at his approval. They lined up, saluted, and then went off with WPC Nonelly and PC Jones.

PC Spriggs eyed the body very carefully. 'You know, Sarge. This fits the description of the body we didn't find at Thelwall on Saturday.'

'My thoughts entirely. There is something funny going on here.'

He called in the CID. 'Suspicious death. Looks as though he's been dead for some days. All very suspicious. Fits a reported death on Saturday when we couldn't find the body. We'll wait until you come.'

He turned to PC Spriggs. 'This is very odd. We find the body miles away, two days later. And what is more, the man who reported the body, and the other one who was hanging about it, are both moored just down the road.'

'He's been dragged here from a boat, Sarge, look at the marks.'

'And they've both got boats.'

'The blood is there, just where he said.'

'Stay here, and wait for the CID. I'm going to collar the old faggot who saw Saturday's mysterious body. See if he can identify it.'

It was still light when we got back. We opened a bottle of wine, and sat back to watch the Olympics. All except me. I decided to stay in the lounge, and read a little more of my new wine book.

There was a tap, tap on the cockpit door. Sergeant Tooth poked his head around the door.

'Sorry to interrupt sir, madam, but I have a delicate matter, sir.'

'Anything to help, officer.' I thought eagerness to help was the best policy.

'You remember, sir, we couldn't find your body on Saturday. I mean the body you discovered.'

'Yes.'

'Well I think we may have found it.'

'Really? So there was a body after all.'

'I wonder if you would kindly come and try and identify it for us.'

'Over to Thelwall?'

'No, sir. The body has been found close by. It isn't far. It won't take long.'

'I didn't know who it was, officer.'

'No. But I hope that you can tell us if this definitely is the body you found on Saturday.'

'Over here? That's very odd,' I said, rising to leave.

'Very odd, sir. I quite agree.'

'I'll come with you,' said Richard, getting up and finishing his glass. On the way to the police car he whispered to me, 'Keep your mouth shut.'

It didn't take us more that a few minutes to find ourselves back at Windlehurst Hall. This time on land, and taking a closer look. The CID hadn't arrived by the time we got there.

'Well, sir. What do you think?' enquired Sergeant Tooth.

I looked down, wondering what I would find. The body was lying on its back, as it had been before. The hands crossed over the chest, just as they had been on Saturday.

'He was lying just like that,' I said. 'Yes, officer, I'm sure that is the same man. But what is he doing here?'

'That's what we would like to know, sir.'

'It was dark, Dad. You only had a torch. Are you really sure?'

'Yes. The bloodstain. That's him all right. I did look him over very carefully with my torch.'

The CID arrived, and set to work with a keen urgency.

'Who's he?' enquired Inspector Cleaver.

'Holidaying on the canal. Reported the body on the towpath at Thelwall on Saturday. No trace when we got there. It now seems that this may be the same one.'

'Thelwall to High Lane. That's a bit odd isn't it? We'll see when the doctor puts the time of death, when he arrives.'

'I know who he is,' said Sergeant Tooth, with a smug, knowing look.

'Do you now?' Inspector Cleaver was all ears.

'Yes, I've been looking for him for the bank raid on Saturday.'

'Indeed. Who is he?' Inspector Cleaver was impressed.

'Squadgy Fred.'

'What is this then? Love among thieves?'

'I have a witness who says that Squadgy Fred shot himself during the raid.'

'If it is, where has he been for two days? And how did he get here?'

'Somehow it's all tied up with the damned canal, but I don't know how yet.'

'Looks as if we've got a messy one.'

''Fraid so,' said Sergeant Tooth. 'I'll take a statement from this gentleman' – indicating me – 'and then take him back. Unless you want to talk to him.'

'No. That's OK.'

'I've also got two strange suspects, down here on the canal. When I've returned these gentlemen. I'll pick up the other two. You can see them down at the station when you get in.'

'You've been working fast, Sergeant.'

'My nose is twitching. There is something funny going on, along this bloody canal. I've spent more time here in the last three days than anywhere else. Nothing adds up at present, but I'm sure there is a connection somewhere.'

Sergeant Tooth returned us, and he was most polite. It appeared he had always been interested in boats. Had in mind getting one of his own. I offered to show him ours.

'Very kind of you, sir,' he said.

He thought the lounge spacious, the galley very functional and compact. Nice large bathroom. Two comfortable double beds, two single bunks in the rear cabin, very useful for extra luggage.

'Lovely boat, sir. Thank you for all your help. Goodnight, sir, madam.'

He disappeared, and we had to tell Margery and Jo all the gory details. Well, I did. Richard, very laid back as usual, watched the Olympics.

'No one there but the four of them,' Sergeant Tooth advised PC Spriggs. 'I don't know what those two queer blokes think they are up to. They insist that there are another four blokes on that boat, and there quite definitely aren't. Only two more bunks, anyway.'

'I expect you can put a small hammock above the single bunks. Intended for children, I suppose.'

'Well, children, or not, there is no one extra on that boat. Those bunks are piled high with their cases and luggage.' Sergeant Tooth seemed well satisfied.

'Now for those other two. God, they make me puke!'

They walked purposefully along the towpath towards *Bluebell*. Stan was at last trying to eat his supper. What little George had left him.

'Well, you really buggered that up for me.' George was

still furious. 'I might have known you couldn't be left alone to do that single job properly.'

Back to normal, thought Stan. I know where I am now! He just ignored George's rantings.

'Come with us please, gentlemen,' said Sergeant Tooth, loudly banging on the side of the boat.

'I haven't had my supper yet,' whined Stan.

'Neither have I,' snapped Sergeant Tooth irritably.

They came ashore quietly.

'I want to see the Superintendent,' said George trying to show some authority.

'You have already seen more of him than you are entitled to.'

'I protest at all this harassment.' George was very indignant, but it cut no ice with Sergeant Tooth.

'We've just found a body near here. A body which has been identified as the one which your friend was skulking around suspiciously on the towpath at Thelwall on Saturday. So come on. Or do I have to put the cuffs on?'

13

Hyacinth moved slowly out of the cutting into quiet, gentle, wooded country. Ern was taking it very gently indeed. He was making sure Sam would not be disturbed in the slightest. All fast, erratic or bumpy movements were to be avoided at all costs. The boat moved, but at a snail's pace, gliding peacefully through the smooth waters.

May, strangely calm, appeared beside him. She said nothing for some time, but squeezed his hand. She stood, quietly looking down at the waters of the canal, as it rippled slightly alongside the boat.

'He's gone,' she said, putting her hand upon his shoulder, as if seeking comfort. Ern was visibly shaken, not only by her quiet message, but the fact that May was actually touching him with a gesture, however brief, of affection.

'Can't possibly be. Get a doctor.'

He put his arm around her waist, and held her protectively. She did not object, and he thought, for a moment, that he could see a tear in her eye. It was only fleeting, but he was sure it was there. Perhaps there was a gentler streak underneath after all.

'No, it's too late.'

'Struth. Are you sure?'

'Quite sure. We can't help him now.' She sat on the seat beside him, and buried her head in her hands.

'Sorry, May.'

'Thanks, Ern. You've been a great pal to him.' She looked up and the slightest flicker of a smile momentarily crossed

167

her cheek. 'To both of us, in fact.'

Ern gulped. He hadn't thought she had even noticed him. But she clearly had. He felt slightly elated, despite the loss of his friend. She had really noticed him, and showed, in her moment of loss, some slight – ever so slight – affection for him.

'Pull in Ern, please. I must stop and think.'

He steered towards the towpath.

'Not the towpath. Pull in the other side.'

He swung the tiller gently the other way.

'Yes, by those boats.'

They were just ahead on their left, among some trees. Three moored boats; they were not new boats, and all of them were shut up and unattended. Unattended for some time it appeared, for one of them, they saw as they neared, had sunk down onto the canal bed. Through the torn curtains at its windows, the still waters of the canal could be seen almost filling the cabin, lapping on the outside at its window sills.

Ern reverently steered his craft to the bank and quietly moored, without *Hyacinth* being so much as rocked or jolted in the slightest. He went below and brewed a pot of tea, and carried it up on a tray. The sun was now fading, but it was still not too cool to be outside.

May looked up, and smiled wanly. 'This is kind,' she said as she sat beside him.

When they had put their cups down, she took his hand. 'Thank you, Ern. You're a nice kind lad,' May said, still looking down.

Ern was overcome by May's unusual gentleness, this show of affection. So she could be affectionate; or was it simply a reaction at the loss of Sam? Whatever, he appreciated it, and squeezed her hand. She squeezed back.

'When I've had another cup of tea, I'll go and tidy him up.'

168

Half an hour went by without a word passing between them.

'I'll go down now,' she said quietly. 'I'm over the shock.'

'Can I help?'

'No, I'll do it.'

'Call if you want me.'

'Thanks.' Again a wan smile, as she went below to the cabin.

Ern stayed a few minutes, and then went round the boat to the galley, and washed up. Having tidied round he went back to the stern and sat down. He watched a mother duck gather her brood as dusk started to fall. He thought about May. Perhaps she might, eventually, see him as an ardent admirer.

Her steps, up and out of the cabin, were more self-assured. May had washed and changed. She had her hand-bag on her arm.

'All right?' Ern enquired.

'Yes. I've laid him out. He looks very peaceful. He's on the same bunk as Fred was. I've covered him with a sheet. I'll slip into town, and do some phoning. I've got plenty to arrange.'

'Can I help? Come with you?'

'No. I'll be all right. Thanks.'

'Do you want me to take you over to the towpath?'

'There's a footpath just here, behind us.' She indicated over her shoulder.

'Oh. I didn't know.'

'I've been around here before. We're only on the edge of town anyway. I can soon get to a phone.'

'Be careful.'

'I will.'

Another wan smile and a quick kiss on the cheek, which nearly bowled him over with delight. She jumped ashore, and, without looking back, was gone.

Guilt was uppermost in Ern's thoughts. The loss of an old friend was taking second place to the lust for his wife. He went below into the cabin and looked at the shrouded figure, where a few hours before Fred had lain.

'Sorry, Sam,' with a lump in his throat, was all that he could say.

He lifted the sheet off the face, and for a moment looked down on his old friend. Gone, left him in a moment. What was he going to do now? He was the sole survivor. He was in charge. Although, after a few moments, he realised May was in charge. Very much in charge. But could she now cope with this obviously very sad loss as well? He would certainly have to take over and mastermind the operation from now on.

At the station Sergeant Tooth sat behind his desk, WPC Nonelly at his side. George and Stan sat opposite him looking very dejected and dishevelled. Like two naughty schoolboys caught out by Teacher.

'Now then, let's try again!' He pulled himself up with an air of authority. 'What is the real story?'

'We've told you already. There isn't any more,' said George. 'We're on the drugs surveillance stake-out. That's all.'

Sergeant Tooth became rather angry. 'Don't give me any more of that damned bullshit,' he roared. Then, realising what he had said, he turned to WPC Nonelly. 'Sorry.' He was always very conscious that she was a nicely brought-up young lady and that her parents were very respectable.

'It's all right, Sarge. I've heard worse in the canteen.'

'Well you shouldn't have done.' He knew, unfortunately, that it was probably true, but he didn't like it all the same. The truth was that he rather fancied WPC Nonelly, but it didn't do to say, or even think it.

George listened to the interchange, but said nothing.

'Well?' shouted Sergeant Tooth.

'Well what, Sergeant?' George tentatively enquired.

'What the hell are you two up to?'

'I've already explained all that. There isn't anything else to say.'

'I'm losing my patience with you two.' Sergeant Tooth drummed his fingers on the top of his desk with irritation. 'I require a full and proper answer, and if I don't get one soon I'm banging you up until I do.'

'I want to speak to the Superintendent.'

'You're not speaking to anyone but me.'

'I insist.'

'You are not in any position to insist.' There was no reply. 'Well?'

'I insist on speaking to the Superintendent.'

'We've been through all that. Who is your superior? If you won't tell me what this is all about, I shall speak to him.'

'I can't do that. It would be more than my life is worth.'

'Lock 'em up. See if they change their minds in a couple of hours.'

'You can't do that!'

'Can't I?'

'Right,' snapped WPC Nonelly. 'On your feet, you two gits. At the double, and down to the cells with you.' She was quite vicious. 'And there you will stay until you show the Sergeant some respect. One, two, one, two, one, two, one, two.'

With that she literally marched them out, at the double. Sergeant Tooth sat back in his chair, aghast at such an approach from such a nice girl. What would her parents say? He hoped they wouldn't blame him. His musings were interrupted by PCs Jones and Spriggs.

'We've seen Squadgy Fred's wife. She's very upset about her old man,' PC Jones reported.

'Husband,' corrected PC Spriggs.

'Yes, husband. She now says he's been associating lately with Sweaty Sam. They were banged up together some time ago in Strangeways, but of late, she says, they've been very close. We've been to Sam's house but he's not there. Nor's his wife.'

'May not at home either?' Sergeant Tooth mused. Nice girl, May. In fact, he rather fancied her himself. I wonder where she is? Not that she's ever been involved in Sam's antics. Never could see what she saw in him, he thought.

'We've also seen that poxy Boakes bloke,' added PC Spriggs.

'Language, please.'

'Sorry, Sarge. He doesn't recognise Sam. Says he doesn't know him.'

They were about to leave when WPC Nonelly reappeared, her face lit up like a Christmas tree.

'They'll talk now,' she said. 'Didn't take me long to make them see reason.'

Sergeant Tooth wondered what third degree she had put them through to get such quick results: the thumbscrews or the rack. 'Send 'em up,' he ordered.

She left, followed by PC Jones and Spriggs. Within less than a minute, or so it seemed, they were back at the double, standing to attention before Sergeant Tooth. Such a transformation he had never seen. WPC Nonelly stood beside George, slightly in front of him, and at right angles towards him.

'Right,' she snapped. 'Tell the Sergeant who he is to tele-phone.'

'Couldn't I phone him?' George enquired nervously.

The roar of her 'No!' made him jump rigidly upright. 'Name and phone number.'

'Ponsonby-Smythe!' and he gave the number, a London number. An 0207 number.

'Ponsonby-Smythe! What sort of poncy name is that?' the Sergeant enquired.

'Roderick Ponsonby-Smythe.'

'And who is he?'

'My Field Service Administration Officer. No one knows the controller,' he whispered, 'he's known only as S. We can only go through our Field Service Administration Officer.'

'Sounds worse than M16. What does S mean?'

'It's his secret code name.'

'I can think of some good names for him beginning with S, Sarge,' interrupted WPC Nonelly.

'That will do, Constable,' admonished Sergeant Tooth. Perhaps he had got the wrong impression of this young lady. She was getting coarse, and more like a gauleiter every moment.

'Sorry,' snapped WPC Nonelly. He could swear he heard a clicking of her heels.

'Excuse me, Sergeant,' George enquired sheepishly. 'Could my assistant wait outside?'

'Why?'

'He shouldn't be hearing all this.'

'Why not?'

'He's not the right grade. It is confidential.'

'Don't talk bloody silly,' again snapped WPC Nonelly.

'Oh, sorry, Sarge.'

'Certainly not. He stays right where he is. Now let's see.' Sergeant Tooth picked up the phone and dialled.

'Field Service Administration Officer,' a voice at the other end replied.

'Is that Roderick Ponsonby-Smythe?'

'We never use names for security reasons. I am the Field Service Administration Officer. Who is that?'

'Look, I've got two of your men here on, potentially, very serious charges, and I don't intend to ponce around all night. Are you Roderick Ponsonby-Smythe?'

'Er, yes. What is this all about?'

'I want S. And what is his proper name?'

George was nearly having heart failure. Stan appeared interested to know something of the structure above him.

'I can't disclose that. It's top security.'

'Look here, your security has more holes than my old mum's colander.'

'I'm sorry, what is it that you want?'

'I want the name of your boss, and I want to speak to him. So make it snappy.'

'I'm sorry, but S never speaks to anyone.'

'Right!' roared Sergeant Tooth into the phone, and to all parties present. 'WPC Nonelly, take them down to the cells and lock them up, until our friend here, Roderick Ponsonby-Smythe, comes to his senses.'

'There is no need to adopt that tone with me. He couldn't speak with you anyway. He's dining at the Savoy with the Under-Secretary.'

'I don't care if he is having fish and chips with Madonna at Harry Ramsden's. Your men stay banged up until he phones me.' He gave his phone number, added 'Good-night', and slammed down the receiver. 'OK, WPC Nonelly, they are all yours.'

'Do we have to go with her?' pleaded George.

'Most men would be very pleased with the opportunity of going with her.'

'Thanks, Sarge.' WPC Nonelly marched them out.

So many strings, and none of them tied up. Sergeant Tooth was worn out, but pleased that he had put his foot down with those M16 poofters.

'This is Smith & Spindrift, Accountants. We are unable to facilitate a reply at the moment, but if you would care to leave a message after the tone ...' Pause. Beep.

'Come on, Les, answer the phone. I know you're in there listening to the calls. Les, stop buggering about. Les, answer me, Les ...'

'Sorry, love, the battery of my calculator is on the blink, and I was having to use mental arithmetic.'

'No messing about, Les. I've had a hell of a day.'

'Sorry! Glad you phoned though. I've missed you. I hope you are coming around tonight. I need you.'

'Les, listen. Sam has died,' May said quietly.

'Struth, I am sorry.' There was a silence. 'Dead?'

'Yes.'

May explained briefly the tragic events of the day. Les now listened with rapt attention, and arranged to pick her up at High Lane.

I was very concerned about the body. Who was he, poor devil? Why had he been brought here? For what purpose? By whom? Worst of all, who had killed him, and why was he still around ... us? A few more glasses of wine were very soothing.

Poor Jo kept going over it, and was obviously worried. 'Let's shut all the doors and windows now.'

'Too hot,' said Richard, very laid back as usual, as he got down to the discus and javelin with a can of lager.

Margery looked at me, worried that I had been upset. Or was it that she thought I had already drunk too much wine?

I saw no future in the Olympics, and there was no chance of the film on the other channel, so I went quietly to my bed, and a further study of my wine book. I looked out before I finally turned in. It was a beautiful clear night. The moon was high and glinted across the water.

Richard was not as disinterested as he appeared, for he said to Margery when he thought I was out of earshot, 'He's getting all worked up over it.'

'I know,' she replied quietly.

175

I went off to sleep, with Why here? Why us? nagging in my subconscious.

Les picked up May in his rather tatty BMW.

'You could afford a better car, for a start,' said May.

'All in good time. Sorry, love, we will have to try and sort things out.'

'Yes,' said May. 'I wasn't ready for this.'

'It solves some problems, but makes more, I'm afraid.'

'We've got some work to do tonight.'

'I'm afraid I've got some more bad news.'

May started and looked at him. 'What?'

'They've found Fred,' Les said quietly.

'Oh hell. That does it. I thought we would have some leeway. So now we've got to get rid of Sam, until everything is tidied up.'

'Sorry, love.'

May gave a careful résumé of the up-to-date position, advising that the main heavy bag was still somewhere on board *Colette*. Les appeared to know about the whole operation. The first job was to call upon May's mother to collect the light bag from where May had hidden it, in the coal house in the back yard.

'You only use me as a bloody convenience,' her mother said as she lit another cigarette. 'I should have thought, at my age, I was due for some respect.' She poured another Guinness, and changed channel on her television. She wanted something raunchy.

Looking at Les, she said, 'Bit of a devil when you have to flaunt your fancy man in front of me. Where's Sam? Inside again, I suppose.'

May went out into the back yard and Les followed. She opened the door of the coal house. She had left the bag beside a small pile of slack in the back left-hand corner of the otherwise empty coal house. Now it was full of coal. They scrambled over the coal, but could find no bag. They were going to have to dig for it. Having crawled over the 3 foot high pile of coal, May started to dig with her bare hands. Les was behind her, giving encouragement and using a small coal shovel. He couldn't afford to get his hands dirty – after all, accountants weren't expected to do dirty jobs.

'The bitch.' There was real venom in May's words as she threw more coal up against the opposite wall, with renewed fury. 'She's done it on purpose.'

'She hasn't.' Les tried to defuse the situation.

'You don't know the awkward sod. You have to be prepared for anything to be her daughter.'

After a hard 15 minutes, May had excavated a deep hole in the back left-hand corner of the coal house, and there was no bag.

'I'll kill the bitch.'

'No you won't. You'll only antagonise her and make it even worse.'

But tact was not her strong point. 'What the hell is all this?' May stormed at her mother.

'I always get my coal in the summer, when it's cheap, you know that,' she replied.

May did know that, but had forgotten. She had never bought coal herself.

Maude lit another cigarette and changed channels again. 'John Breeze always looks after me. He brought me ten, hundredweight bags.'

'You mean ten, fifty-kilo bags,' corrected Les, trying hard to lighten the proceedings, but failing miserably.

'Bloody know-all.' Maude gave him a withering look and blew smoke at him.

He backed away. He wasn't going to tangle with her.

'You stupid bugger,' fumed May, 'I left a bag in there.'

'I know you did, with Sam. I'm not daft, you know.' She took another drink of Guinness.

'Where is it? Have you buried it, you old bugger?'

'If that's the way you talk to your poor old mum, you can bloody well dig through all the coal and see if it is there.'

Les realised May was going to get nowhere by being belligerent. He looked at May and shook his head.

'May's a bit upset today,' he said quietly. 'Inclined to be overexcited. I'm sorry if she has upset you.'

'Well, she did.'

'How about getting yourself a nice bottle of whisky tomorrow,' he said smoothly, slipping her a £20 note.

'You're a slimy bugger I must say, but if you'll slip to the off-licence on the corner, and get me three bottles of Teacher's, I'll tell you where it is,' Maude said, quickly slipping the £20 note down the front of her blouse to ensure its safety.

Les had no alternative. He came back at the double with three bottles of Teacher's under his arm.

After sampling a glass to ensure that it was genuine, Maude confided, 'It is on top of the cistern in the outside bog.'

They arrived, late, at Les's flat over his office in Hulme. It was at first glance all rather seedy and run-down – the area and the office – but his flat was immaculate and expensively furnished.

He wanted May, but she pushed him off. 'Not now. Check the bag first.'

Les opened the tatty old bag and emptied the contents of the bank's canvas bag inside it.

'Christ, these are just used cheques. The stupid sods.'

'Oh, hell,' sighed May, wondering what the other bag would hold.

'I could kill 'em. These are quite useless. I'll have to burn them straight away. We can't have any incriminating evidence around, can we?'

'Poor old Sam,' May sighed. 'All this for nothing.'

178

'For us.'

'The other bag was so heavy they had to drop it off. Now I must make sure I get it back.'

'The stupid sods, though. A bag of old cheques!'

'We've got to get away to Spain anyway, and we can live in luxury for the rest of our lives. But I'll not be beaten by that lot!'

'Every little bit helps. But I did well on BCCI and Barlow Clowes. Oh, we can live in comfort on the Costas all right, rest assured of that!'

'Sam has amassed a good fortune over the years that you are holding for me, remember.'

'Yes,' agreed Les. 'Credit where it is due. Sam has done you proud.'

'Never mind all the other accounts you are holding for others – mostly inside for a long time.'

Les grinned. 'Come now.' He made another pass at May.

'Not now, you randy sod. Take me back now. I've got to keep Ern in a good mood, and somehow I must get rid of Sam myself. I'll move him to the boat next door. Ern is so far gone he will never notice.'

Ern didn't feel like much, but thought he must eat something. After going through the provisions twice, he settled for beefburgers.

For the second night in three days he was having to spend it alone on a boat, in a remote corner of the canal system, with only the corpse of a dead friend for company. Admittedly a different corpse, but a corpse never the less.

He was beginning to get a little edgy, and thought he heard slight sounds from the cabin, a small creak, a slight movement of the boat. Perhaps Sam wasn't dead after all. The whole thing was a mistake. But silence fell again, and the silence was deafening. Until he thought he heard a slight sound from the cabin again. Yes, definite this time.

He started to sweat profusely, a cold sweat that sent a shiver down his spine. He listened intently, but nothing happened. Nothing but silence and stillness again.

He took a forkful of his supper, which didn't taste very good. A seventh can was opened to swill the mess down, but even that didn't help. He belched loudly twice and decided to call it a day, by throwing all his food in the bin. He had another drink from his can, and thought it best to clean up before May came back. The cans were carefully stowed in the bin, the crockery and china washed and the table wiped. He used an air freshener, which May had brought with her. Everything neat and tidy, he sat down to finish his can. What the hell was he going to do?

The boat started to rock gently. 'My God!' the movement was quite definite. 'He is alive!' There were very definite movements now. These could not be put down to his imagination. He came out in a cold sweat again. The boat rocked gently on its moorings. Sounds from the cabin. Only faint, but quite distinct.

What do I say to him? He stood up to face his friend … apparition … whatever it was. His jaw dropped when he saw the door handle move very slightly. His hands were clammy and shaking, and the door started to open gently. Ern's eyes were popping out his head, which was starting to swim.

The door swung open. And there in the doorway…

'What's up? Have you seen a ghost?' enquired May.

'Thank God,' sighed Ern as he sank back into his seat.

She bent forward and kissed him on his cheek. 'You are a fool,' she said gently. 'Get washed, while I get some supper together and a bottle of wine. Then it's off to bed. We've got plenty to do tomorrow.'

'There's only your bed,' Ern said awkwardly. 'I don't fancy going in there with Sam. Can I stay in the lounge?'

'You really are a softy,' she smiled kindly at him. 'We both need each other's company tonight.' She took his hand and kissed his cheek. 'Off you go.'

Ern was in his element. A lovely supper with the girl of his dreams. May plied him with plenty of wine and a number of double whiskies, escorting him happily to bed. He was on cloud nine, but almost as soon as his head touched the pillow he was out like a light.

14

I awoke early to hear a light footfall on the towpath and looked towards the window, which was just above the side of our large double bed. The events of the previous day flooded into my mind. It was all true. It had happened, it was not a nightmare at all. I was wide awake now, looking intently at the window blind. The small louvres behind were open. There was no movement of the blind, and the steps did not falter. I listened. They kept on along the towpath and eventually faded away.

A near thing. I breathed again. But then, I wondered, how many feet had trodden the towpath during my slumbers? Why should these footsteps have been any more sinister than those which had passed in the darkness of night, which I hadn't heard? Of course, I hadn't heard the others to have worried about them. But these I had heard, and they were therefore sinister. And how sinister they had sounded, as I lay halfway between sleep and consciousness.

The ducks were alive and well. I could hear them, busy about their ablutions, and their breakfast. I got up and put the kettle on. It was seven o'clock. I opened the side hatch and the lounge doors, and stood in the cockpit. The scene was idyllic. The sun was well up, and it was a bright, brisk morning, but not quite as warm as previous mornings. I could see the ducks now, as they darted hither and thither, the young ones bobbing about like little corks. We had seen so many ducks on our trip so far that I couldn't help wondering, how many disappeared for the pot.

Whilst Margery prepared breakfast, I slipped along the towpath and over the bridge to the newsagents. I was back within a few minutes, laid the breakfast, and sat down with the newspaper awaiting the youngsters. They had started the trip as early risers, but were rising later by the day, and today was Tuesday. Margaret toyed with yesterday's crossword, which had, as yet, eluded her.

When the Captain had oiled and greased everything that needed oiling and greasing, we cast off fore and aft, and set off into the unknown. What new adventures, we wondered, awaited us today?

Under the bridge and through the cutting. Rose's boat, still moored against the towpath, was all shut up and deserted, except for a very brief pair of knickers which fluttered in the light breeze. I looked the other way, but out of the corner of my eye I saw Richard lean towards Jo and say something. She smiled. So she knew. He'd told her.

Although the sun was out, it was a cooler morning, and for the first time we needed our jumpers once we got underway, but they were soon thrown off as the morning warmed us.

Beyond the shade of some trees on our left some boats were moored. They all, bar one, seemed to have been lying there neglected and decaying for some time. One was even sitting on the canal bed, its cabin awash. Fancy leaving a boat just to rot like that! I gazed at the dismal sight as we passed. Through a gap in the torn curtains I could see something. Could I see a face? Not a body floating in the water!

'Look,' I said to Richard. He turned and looked, but we were almost past.

'Look at what?' he replied calmly.

'Was that a face in the water? In the cabin? Stop a minute.'

184

'Oh my God! He's seeing more bodies. There isn't a body. There is nothing there,' he said, taking a keener look, but without reducing speed. 'You're seeing things Dad. Forget it. I have. There is nothing for us to worry about. Yesterday was yesterday. It was nothing to do with us. Put it out of your mind.' And, as he did when he was happy, he started to sing.

Perhaps I had been wrong. Yes, I must have been. Richard and Jo hadn't seen anything. But, just suppose I was right, and I had seen a face in the water, floating about in the derelict cabin. What then?

We were, by now, well past it. Over the railway and across the border. No passports were needed, but we were out of Greater Manchester, and ahead of us lay the Cheshire Plain. The Cage, a small hill, rose from the flat landscape on our left, at the lower end of which sits in state Lyme Hall, the eighteenth-century mansion which had been the home of the Legh family for 600 years, and still incorporates part of the original Elizabethan house.

The village of Higher Poynton stood out clearly on our right, while on the opposite bank lay the remains of the old Mount Vernon coal wharf, now private moorings, but in its heyday this had been the hub, the heart of a large, prosperous, busy mining area. Now gone forever. Time had moved on, and we glided by into the future.

Then another left turn under a bridge. Strange, how so many canal bridges seem to be built over bends in the canal, making navigation more difficult. Richard took all 62 feet of us through so easily, with only inches to spare on either side. Our paintwork remained intact. This bridge, like others in the area, was flat-decked, not as picturesque as normal canal bridges, but designed for ease of raising, if there was subsidence from the local mining activities.

Once through the bridge, the evidence of subsidence was only too clear. We sailed into a shallow pool, where the canal widens. Seemingly, a breach in the canal bank had occurred, and had just been left, widening the canal at this point. Presumably it was cheaper to acquire land than to pay for the costly work of rebuilding and supporting the canal wall.

Ern had slept heavily. He woke late to find the sun very high, and came to slowly. He was happy. He slowly remembered that he was in bed with May. May, that apparition of loveliness who he had longed for, for so very long. And he was in bed with her. He put out a hand towards her, but encountered no soft flesh, as he had expected. He slowly turned his head and found that he was alone in bed. Her side of the bed, his hand told him, was cold. She had not recently gone from him.

She must be getting breakfast, but there was no smell of food. No movement on the boat, or the slightest hint of any noise. Where was she? What was she doing? Was she soon going to come back to bed? He hoped for another amorous encounter, like that of last night … but try as he might he could not recall their lovemaking. They must have done it, so why couldn't he remember? He must remember! It was so important to him.

But still he couldn't. He remembered clearly the wonderful supper she had cooked for him, with plenty of wine. He remembered, if hazily, arms around each other going into the cabin, undressing and sitting on the bed. May had undressed and sat on the bed as well. But after that, a blank! He must have done it though, so why couldn't he remember? He had wanted it badly, May wanted it, and she always got what she wanted. So they quite surely made love. Fancy doing May, fabulous May, and not remembering. She'd kill him if she thought he'd forgotten her. So he started to imagine, as he had done so many times before, making love to May. It was a wonderful experience, even though she was not there. It must have happened, or he could not have imagined it in such detail.

Probably another hour, or more, went by, before he finally decided to investigate. For he could not smell, hear, or feel anyone else on the boat. Strange. Where was she? On the table in the lounge he found the answer. He slowly read May's note:

Dear Ern,
Hope you had a good rest, and I didn't disturb
you when I got up. Have a good breakfast, there is plenty in the fridge.
I have gone to make the arrangements for poor
Sam. I have tidied him up, and he looks very peaceful.
Please, whatever you do, don't touch him any more. I don't want him disturbed again. Let him rest, he deserves it.
Keep on to them. I don't expect them to get any further than the Fools Nook Inn today. I'll see you there this evening.
Thanks for last night. I shall always remember.
Love
May XXX

So there was something to remember! May could remember it. Why couldn't he? It really didn't make much sense. All that he could remember was a slight swaying movement of the boat during the night, which he had put down to the effect of all he had drunk the previous evening. There was nothing for it. He had to resign himself to the fact that he certainly had done it with May. But how could anything so beautiful have possibly been forgotten?

He went into the rear cabin. It was still and quiet, almost chilly with the curtains drawn. Sam lay on the bunk where Fred had lain, completely covered by a sheet. Ern didn't go too close. He stayed, looking at Sam for some minutes, shuddered, crossed himself, and went out, quietly closing the door. He resolved to go around the side of the boat in future, rather than use this cabin as a walkway. It wouldn't seem right with Sam there. Strangely, he and Sam had had no such thoughts when Fred had lain there, but now he was by himself, alone on the boat with the body of Sam. He hoped May would soon get things organised, and Sam could be taken away. He would feel happier when he had gone. She would be waiting to pick him up at Fool's Nook, so he should hasten there.

He had a good breakfast, and set out in hot pursuit, but first moving over to the towpath side, mooring, and walking towards the town. *Colette* was gone, as he had expected. Back on board he was now in pursuit with a vengeance. He daren't lose them.

During the night Sergeant Tooth had received a very important phone call from S, but he had remained singularly unimpressed. Eventually S explained the nature of their covert operation. It was agreed that S would send his Field Service Administration Officer. None other than Roderick Ponsonby-Smythe, in person. He would be in Manchester by mid-morning, take custody of George and Stan, and control of the operation himself to ensure that there would be no further problems.

Field Service Administration Officer Roderick Ponsonby-Smythe duly arrived, parking his MGB GT in the space reserved for the Chief Superintendent, only reluctantly moving it to the visitor's area at the behest of WPC Nonelly. He tried to flatter her, but received such a withering reply that he moved his car instantly.

Sergeant Tooth was even less impressed with him in person than he had been on the phone the previous evening. Roderick was gushing, and Sergeant Tooth didn't like gushers. He was tall and slim, with a long face, blue eyes and short, smartly groomed mousy hair. He was immaculately dressed in grey flannels with a gold buttoned double-breasted blue blazer, and silk neck square – old school, college or regiment, Sergeant Tooth didn't care which. But to make the spectacle completely bizarre, he wore a blue sailor's cap at a jaunty angle.

'Are you a sailor, or going on your bloody holidays, lad?' enquired Sergeant Tooth.

'Well, if I've got to take command of the boat, I thought I ought to look the part. Less conspicuous, you see.'

WPC Nonelly's eyes went heavenwards.

The other two are idiots, this one is a prat, thought Sergeant Tooth, who tried valiantly to restrain himself, but finally realised that he simply could not manage it.

'You're not commanding a bloody frigate, you know. Their tub is a heap of scrap barely able to float.'

'Oh,' replied Roderick, nervously taking off his cap.

On the strict understanding that George and Stan were taken post haste off his patch, he released them into Roderick's custody. All three drove away in Roderick's two-seater sports car.

Roderick couldn't believe his eyes when he saw poor *Blue Belle*. She was, presumably, once proud but was now a seriously demolished wreck. What had he come to take command of, and skipper? He'd die of shame. It really wouldn't do at all. It would have to be changed; there was no doubt about that. He couldn't get another boat here, but he would change it at the next available opportunity.

'It was the only one available when we needed it,' pleaded George shyly. 'We couldn't afford a better one on our allowance scale anyway. But there is now damage, not of our doing, to be put right at the Department's expense. Vandals it was.'

'Yes, vandals,' agreed Stan.

Roderick sighed, realising the trouble he was going to

have with these two. Discipline, that's what they needed.

George and Stan knew their place in the scheme of things. They set off formally, with Roderick at the tiller, Stan standing at ease in the bows, and George in the stern, in what Roderick considered to be true naval fashion.

Not only did *Blue Belle* look a sorry sight, but she was now made to look ridiculous. Stan in his by now completely filthy shell suit was not exactly the figure to grace the bows of any boat, whilst George was equally scruffy in the stern.

Roderick's steering, he soon realised, left a lot to be desired, but it also dawned on him that instead of being inconspicuous in their operation, literally everybody stopped to see this quaint apparition as it passed. Old-age pensioners stopped and stared. All had certainly seen service in the last war, for they stood to attention and saluted. They seemed to think it a great joke. Some youths on the bridge jeered with derision.

'Tell Her Majesty to come out and give us a wave.'

'You don't half look a ponce, mate.'

'Life on the ocean wave.'

'I've seen better pedalos at New Brighton.'

This wouldn't do at all. When he thought no one was looking, Roderick bent down and threw his hat through the hatch into the cabin. As he did he inadvertently turned the steering wheel sharply, and *Blue Belle* veered sharply to one side. Stan in the bows managed to keep his balance – just – but George fell off the stern, with a yell for help before he submerged.

In his panic Roderick accelerated instead of stopping, and turned the steering wheel so that the boat was heading straight for the bank at full speed. Seconds before impact, Stan had the presence of mind to jump. He landed safely on the bank.

The youths had come down from the bridge on to the towpath opposite to enjoy the spectacle thoroughly.

'Did you forget to take on the pilot?'

'Better switch your radar on, mate!'

'Up yours!' Accompanied by obscene gestures.

George crawled aboard, and it was now his turn to hang out his clothes to dry. Roderick manoeuvered the bows around, out into the stream, and Stan jumped aboard the stern as it came close to the bank.

Strict naval discipline was immediately abandoned in favour of a less formal approach, and the steering was handed to Stan. Furthermore, at the first boatyard they left the battered *Blue Belle*, and took charge of a much larger and more up-market boat, *Turandot*. Roderick, all smiles, couldn't help humming Puccini.

The manager of the boatyard made an issue of pointing out the clauses regarding damage to be paid for by the hirer. He then rang his insurance company to increase the cover on *Turandot*.

They now had a cabin each; or rather, Roderick had one cabin whilst George and Stan shared the other. But there was a separate galley, and a lounge with television. They loaded plenty of stores, including wine. Stan was pleased. They had now to make up lost time, and were half a day behind.

Across our right beam the Cheshire Plain spread out below us in detail, away into the hazy distance, an intricate patchwork quilt. Close at hand was an airfield, with a surprising number of planes on the ground – Woodford Aerodrome. It seemed strange to find an airfield here, and it came upon us unexpectedly. Yet, at the height of the Second World War it was from this airfield, in the dark days of 1941, that the famous Lancaster Bomber made its inaugural flight. Some years later, after the war, the Shackleton reconnaissance plane also flew for the first time from here. It took me back, and I looked upon the airfield in awe. This was history. I wondered if the people I saw there realised what had gone before.

The trees in full leaf made a canopy over the canal, which was pierced, jewel-like, by the sun's sharp arrows. Tranquil and peaceful, we glided gently through a dream.

Beyond the towpath the dismantled railway line has been turned into a route for walkers and cyclists. Middlewood Way runs some 11 miles from Bollington towards Manchester. Some walkers joined the towpath at one point, for a change of scene. They left it again 2 miles further on to continue their trek.

Emerging from our leafy canopy the high red brick walls of Clarence Mill come into view. Towering above us were five rows of rectangular windows, one above the other in precise symmetry, each window broken into four panes, two long ones at the bottom with two smaller ones above. The mill was flat-roofed, with a cornice at each corner. In the centre along the front of the building adjacent to the canal is a magnificent square tower rising well above the roof level, surmounted by a small steeple. This was not just a workaday factory, but a building of some elegance. Beyond, over its roof, rose a newer red brick chimney. There was some pipework going on just beyond the building, which caused Richard to take a second look. Huge 15 inch pipes, but their purpose, I knew not.

A gentle turn to the right and we were on the Bollington Aqueduct. Nestling among the hills, an old mill town. The canal high above weaves its way on high, literally looking down upon a quaint little town, Bollington, a joy to the eye. We floated high over the River Dean, and the rooftops and chimneys of this quiet town. From high on the aqueduct we had a magnificent view of the Cheshire Plain to our right, sweeping back towards the edge of Manchester itself, at Alderley Edge. All the time the canal was winding its way along the edge of the Pennines.

Lunchtime, and we chose a place for exploration, and a little essential shopping. We moored alongside a steep flight of steps leading from the towpath down into the town, way below us. I could hardly believe my eyes: just ahead, bordering the towpath, was another magnificent mill, the Adelphi Mill, more ornate than the nearby Clarence Mill. This is no longer a mill, and in its heyday this was not merely a functional mill, but built with such architectural finesse that it represented more a baronial hall than a workplace. It fits in so beautifully with its surroundings, but it seems strange to think what it was built for.

On the way down the steps we stopped at the Discovery Centre, full of information, before descending further into the town. Warm terraced stone houses, quaint unspoiled shops. Still a gem. How long, I wondered, before it's discovered and turned into a tourist trap?

We decided to lunch al fresco, sitting in the cockpit of *Colette*, surrounded by magnificent views. I felt I could stay here longer, and the rest of the crew were of the same mind. Some day I shall come back and have another look at Bollington. But we had done only 4½ miles, and needed to keep up our average to complete the ring within a week.

Ern was taking *Hyacinth* flat out, as both Sam and May had done their turn. He had made it with May, and now she was as surely his, as bacon and eggs is for breakfast. He was on top of the world. Sorry about Sam, but if he didn't go into the cabin he could put him from the forefront of his mind. He tore along the embankment, over the aqueduct, where he thought it prudent to reduce speed as he was coming towards habitation, and a boatyard.

Then panic struck. He felt a cold shiver run down his back, and he perspired profusely. To stop would attract more attention than carrying on, but how could he carry on with *Colette* moored no more than 20 yards in front of him? The turning point was ahead of *Colette*, so he would be even more conspicuous turning, than just going straight past.

Nothing for it. He pulled his dark glasses out of his shirt pocket, slumped down as far as he could and steered with his left hand, whilst his right hand was open across his fore-head and cheek. At the same time he leaned towards his right, so that he couldn't be recognised by the occupants of the boat he was supposed to be shadowing.

There was no one about the boat; perhaps they had gone ashore. But as his stern came level with *Colette*'s cockpit, he saw that they were all sitting in the sun, having lunch. But no one seemed to give him even a glance. He kept his head down, and kept straight on.

What a fool he had been not keeping a proper look-out. Now he was in front of the boat he was supposed to be following. What would May say? She would be furious. There was only one thing, he would carry on as ordered to the Fools Nook Inn at Oakgrove, moor quietly, and await them – and May. He only hoped that *Colette* would catch him up before she did, or she'd kill him. Literally kill him.

It was a lovely sunny day, and as he had the day off, Rex Turner decided to walk with Millie along the path out of High Lane. But Millie didn't want to walk. She was so excited that she ran on ahead, then back to Rex, occasion-ally stopping beside the canal to look at her reflection in the still dark water, admiring her beauty. Then with a wag of her tail she would be off again with all the energy of a young Russell Beagle cross.

Rex always enjoyed his walks across the field beside the canal. Quiet, peaceful, and with no one to worry him, he could evade the frantic scurry of life for a moment, and think. Think his own quiet thoughts, which were so much more pleasant on a warm June morning. How did Mary Webb put it?

Face to face with the sunflower,
Cheek to cheek with the rose,
We follow a secret highway
Hardly a traveller knows.

They crossed over the railway tunnel which had burrowed its way under the canal, and emerged just beyond, then they were in among the cool shade of the trees. Millie was still dashing hither and thither. What could be more idyllic for a day off work?

Just ahead were some moored boats, three of them. They had been there for some years without any attention. One had sunk right down onto the canal bed. When he had first seen it, Rex had thought it an appalling waste, but by now he was used to seeing it lying there.

Millie ran up to it, and stopped to admire her beautiful reflection again, but her tail didn't wag. Instead she put her head on one side, and gazed as if uncertain of herself. Which was unusual for Millie, who was usually very certain of herself. As Rex approached she started to bark at the boat. But there was nothing, no one, near the boat. It was lying on the canal bed, just as it had for a long time now, its curtains torn and rotting and the cabin half-filled with water. Suddenly Rex came back to reality. Through the torn curtains he could see a face, still and motionless, with unblinking open eyes, staring out at him and Millie.

15

The bows of *Turandot* cut the waters of the canal like a knife as it sped south. It reduced speed approaching Bollington, as it had done when nearing other craft or habitation.

Rodney Ponsonby-Smythe – 'Call me Rod' – had learned fast. He had had to. Recruited when a subaltern in the Guards, as a Field Service Administration Officer in security, his duties were to administer the operators on the ground, although he had never been on the ground himself, to know what he was administrating. He now realised very quickly that for his own survival, he had to depend on George and Stan. He couldn't operate the boat, so he had given 'his team' full rein, and they responded to the responsibility magnificently.

The gap, he was sure, was closing. They would soon, under his supervision, be carrying out surveillance of the suspects on *Colette*.

He didn't know why it was, but her attitude had hardened. The once nice, shy, demure young lady was turning, in front of his eyes, into a coarse lout. He couldn't understand how it had happened. Sergeant Tooth mused over his cup of tea. He still fancied WPC Nonelly, and had hoped that one day he might see more of her outside work, but she was now almost overconfident. She questioned his instructions, even answered back; and Sergeant Tooth didn't like people who answered back.

'Have they determined the cause of death yet?' he enquired.

'Not yet. What was he doing there though?' she replied.

'He was dumped. That's what. But why, and by whom? And I let two prime suspects go this morning. They were within a mile of the body. They must be in it somewhere. Why are we suddenly getting all these problems on the canal? Normally it's as peaceful as the grave. Must be a boat involved, but which one, and why? Why, why?'

'There weren't any obvious marks on him, Sarge. Perhaps it was natural causes.'

'Like Squadgy Fred shooting himself.'

PC Spriggs put his head around the door and grinned. 'Just arrived, Sarge,' he said, giving Sergeant Tooth a report. 'Natural causes. Massive coronary.'

'Stuck in that sunken boat, no wonder he had a heart attack,' interjected WPC Nonelly. 'I would.'

'You might,' retorted Sergeant Tooth. 'Go on.'

'Strange thing is, he died yesterday afternoon, and it was only some hours after he died that he was dumped in the sunken boat,' continued PC Spriggs. 'He's …'

'Oh I know who he is all right,' cut in Sergeant Tooth. 'Sweaty Sam. He was with Squadgy Fred on that bank raid on Saturday. So who is the mysterious third person? Why were they both found dead on the canal?'

'Perhaps they used it as a getaway,' suggested PC Jones.

'How on earth could they have used the canal for their getaway? The canal doesn't go through Wilmslow,' interrupted WPC Nonelly curtly. 'It doesn't go anywhere.'

'Sorry.' PC Jones wished he'd said nothing.

'Good lad, I think you've got it,' said Sergeant Tooth. 'They hop on the canal at the nearest point, and get lost. They know we would never think of looking there. Fred dies from his wounds and they dump him, then Sam has a heart attack and he is dumped. So who is the joker who is left, and where is he going?'

'One problem,' cut in WPC Nonelly, 'why was the body moved from Thelwall, and found near High Lane? Doesn't make sense.'

''Course it does,' corrected Sergeant Tooth irritably. 'They knew that doddery old fart had seen the body, before they had time to get away. So they took the body back again. We didn't believe the old fool had seen a body, now did we?'

'Brilliant, Sarge,' complimented PC Jones. 'And he said there had been a boat where there wasn't one.'

'Yes. The boat must now be going south. Macclesfield, Congleton … But where are they making for? Stoke-on-Trent?'

They were disturbed by the telephone ringing.

'Sergeant Tooth,' he snapped. He grunted and put the phone down. 'Still no sign of May! Now I wonder where the hell she is?'

'Perhaps she's the third man,' suggested WPC Nonelly.

'Don't talk so daft.' Sergeant Tooth was now getting annoyed with her, or was it with himself for fancying this woman, and not really getting anywhere?

'Now I just wonder if our friends, whom we set free this morning, have been hoodwinking us all the time, and they are really following this lot for some strange reason. Not the holiday boat, as they maintain.'

'Wow, that does make sense Sarge,' agreed PC Spriggs.

'OK, make haste. Find *Blue Belle*. And smartly. I'll see the Super so that we can liaise with our neighbours. We've got 'em. I can feel it.' Sergeant Tooth was elated.

Bridges on the Macclesfield Canal are little gems. Extremely beautiful, remarkably interesting, and surprisingly utilitarian. Built of large sandstone blocks, they have, where the towpath crosses from one side of the canal to the other, a very original design. They are called 'snake bridges', and they live up to their name beautifully.

With these bridges, when the towpath deviates from one side to the other, the barge horses of old did not have to be unhitched from their barges on one side, cross over the bridge to be rehitched the other side of it. If the towpath was on the left-hand side of the canal, but moved over to the right-hand side after the bridge, the horse, still hitched to its narrowboat, would mount the bridge on the left side, and turn to its right over the top of the bridge as the boat approached it. Then coming down from the bridge on the right-hand side, the horse would curl back on itself, always turning to the right, just like a curled snake's tail, coming down on the opposite side of the canel. Thus, the horse completed a circle, by winding around to its right. It would step out on to the towpath again, under the bridge, and carry straight on along the towpath. The craft would simply continue its uninterrupted journey. No stopping, no unhitching, one complete steady movement.

Beautiful in design, so simple in operation. Sheer genius. Would that there were still towing horses on the canal, that I could see it, just once.

We slipped through the outskirts of Hurdsfield and entered the 'Silk Town', Macclesfield, the centre of silk weaving for over 200 years. Mainly Victorian, the Paradise Mill, now closed down, is still used by a few independent contemporary weavers. Strange to think that the work of millions of Chinese silkworms, for centuries, travelled all the way across the world to be turned into delicate finery for the gentry.

The canal skirts through the southern edge of the town only, but widens near the town centre into a large basin dominated by the huge Hovis Mill. The canal played a great part in the transporting of grain to, and flour from, this vast mill. At water level there is a large archway for boats to enter and load or unload their cargo. Milling moved from here to Manchester, however, for easier access of North American grain to be delivered via the Manchester Ship Canal.

Out of town again, through a cutting, over the aqueduct above the River Bollin, and magnificent countryside greeted us again. Fields, with grazing sheep, down to the water's edge. Wire fences and well-cut hedges bordered the towpath on the other side. Ahead of us, Tegg's Nose rose majestically from the fields, its gentle slopes ringed at the base by a circle of trees.

Margery took the helm, whilst Richard and Jo sat quietly in the cockpit with a can of lager each. I made a pot of tea, and sat in the stern taking in the tranquility of it all, at the same time supervising the careful running of the boat.

The remains of a twisted ancient wood to our right clung for survival to the edge of an ancient peat bog, Danes Moss. A little further along a strange old raft-cum-pontoon bridge, pulled to the side, linked a cottage on the towpath side with the main road on the other. The road ran parallel with the canal; behind it wooded slopes rose above us.

At Oakgrove, our destination for the night, we found our way barred by an electrically operated swing bridge, which carries a side road over the canal. It proved simple to operate when we read the instructions, but it is always fun to try and work it out for yourself first. The British Waterways sanitary key opened the bridge for us, much to the annoyance of a middle-aged lady with glasses who obviously felt that her car had the prior right of way. We didn't hurry, but eventually swung the bridge back, and let her go on her way. I could swear I heard 'Damned tourists!' as her foot went down on her accelerator, as if she were at the start of the Grand Prix.

We bore to our right and entered a cool, leafy glade. A

wooded embankment rose on our left, whilst to our right, beyond the towpath, the ground dropped very sharply. We were on a narrow shelf cut along the hillside. There was also another shelf up above us carrying the roadway.

There was already another boat, moored and shut up in our leafy wooded glade. We pulled in some way ahead of it and made ourselves secure fore and aft. It was 5 p.m. and we had covered 13 miles. We settled down for a quiet rest, before tidying up for a visit to the Fools Nook.

Ern, from the closed up boat, watched *Colette* moor ahead of him. May had anticipated their movements well, and this had saved his bacon. He certainly wasn't going to tell her that he had got there first.

He quietly prepared himself a sandwich and had a can of lager. Afterwards he carefully washed and shaved. May was coming, and he must look his best. Whatever happened, he was going to remember tonight.

Some time after seven we walked leisurely back to the electric swing bridge, and crossed it into Oakgrove. It proved to be no more than a handful of houses bordering the main Macclesfield to Leek road, where any thought of reducing speed in a built-up area, however small, seemed to be quite unheard of. We took our lives in our hands and crossed to the Fools Nook Inn unscathed. So far so good.

The beer of repute had to be well sampled, and we sat outside in the courtyard. I watched as a large car pulled into the car park, not close to the pub, but at the farthest extremity. An attractive, slightly plump lady got out, but instead of entering the pub she crossed the main road and turned towards the canal.

It became chilly, so we went home early for a light supper. On our return we noticed that there was another larger boat moored behind the other. Both were shut up, and gave

202

the appearance of being empty. All the curtains were drawn and there were no lights on either. Everyone was in the pub, I had little doubt.

Margery in the galley looked in the cupboard under the sink for salad, only to find a tatty old leather bag. It smelled musty and looked awful.

'What on earth is this?' she enquired, holding it disdainfully at arm's length.

'I thought it was yours.' Jo was embarrassed. 'I found it in a locker in the cockpit. The one with the loose seat. I thought it had fallen in accidentally when we were loading the boat.'

'Can't tell what it is.' Margery shook it vigorously. 'But it's very heavy and smells awful. Some of their boat stuff, I suppose. Better put it back where you found it.'

Jo agreed. 'Funny old thing, isn't it?' she mused.

'Heavier than the money bags at work,' she added, as she came back, having accomplished her mission and carefully made the seat in the cockpit safe.

'The stupid sods have come back!' whined May, who had arrived shortly before the occupants of *Colette* returned to their boat.

'Only been gone an hour and a half,' replied Ern. 'I expected them to make a night of it. I would.'

'You might. I must say I would have expected them to eat out. After all they are supposed to be on holiday.'

'But they did have fish and chips for lunch.'

'How the hell do you know that?'

'Oh … er … I … You told me to keep a careful watch of them, and I did.'

'You have indeed been a studious lad. Perhaps you will get your reward.'

I hope so, thought Ern longingly.

She looked at him quizzically, but said no more. Ern

breathed a long sigh of relief. He thought he had given the game away over the chips, and was about to be crucified.

'Well. We can't tear the boat apart tonight, with them in it. This is far too public a place to take them head on. So we'll have to wait.'

Ern was delighted. They could now settle down for a good night. One that he would, this time, remember.

'I expect they'll make for Scholar Green tomorrow on their schedule. They've also got the Bosley flight to contend with, so I guess it will be a light lunch and dinner out tomorrow night.'

'There are chip shops in Congleton, I think.'

'Well, you make sure they don't buy any, OK?'

'Yes,' replied Ern meekly, but he had no idea how he could possibly accomplish that.

'Right.' May turned, and went alone into the cabin to see Sam, returning a few minutes later.

'If we can't get the bag tomorrow, we'll have to go in with a heavy hand later.'

Ern just smiled. This was going to be his moment together with May. He had been looking forward to it all day.

'Well, I'm off now. Leave Sam in peace.'

'Aren't you going to stay?' enquired Ern pleadingly. 'I hoped …'

'No time, I'm afraid. Nothing to stay for, anyway. See you soon.'

'But I can't operate all those locks on my own.'

''Course you can. Just keep your head down.' She gave him a quick peck on the cheek. 'Cheerio.' And she was gone.

Ern was desperately disappointed. He had hoped for another night with May. Now he would have to wait until tomorrow. She would surely stay then.

What if she didn't? He recalled the Polaroid of the lovely

Rose in the wallet he had nicked in the bank raid, which unfortunately had now been pinched from him, but he had memorised her address on the back. He enjoyed thinking about the lovely woman in that picture. He would keep her in mind, but surely May was his now, after last night. He knew that for certain.

On the way back to her car, May noticed that there were lights on the boat behind *Hyacinth*, but all the curtains were drawn and she could see nothing inside.

Suddenly she was alerted. What was that slight rustle among the long grasses at the side of the towpath, where it dropped away to the field below? She was fully aware now, every sense was engaged. She quickened her step. There it was again. Quite definite this time. She turned quickly to face whoever it was, but there was nothing there. No one. She continued her brisk walk back to her car, but keeping a careful eye over her shoulder.

Once in the car she locked all her doors and drove speedily away. It had unnerved her a little, but she composed herself as she drove back into town.

Les was uneasy. She could see that as soon as she was in his flat above his seedy office. The flat was well appointed, and used by Les when he had dinners to attend in town, or had to work late, which was quite often. Well, that was what he told his wife Sylvia.

'What's up?' she enquired.

'Nothing,' he replied.

She looked questioningly at him and tried again.

'You'll have to get that bag quickly.'

'Why so urgent?' she enquired. 'I'm trying again tomorrow.'

'We're flying out on Saturday afternoon,' explained Les.

'So soon? I can't possibly get everything done in that time!'

'Got to!' he said. 'I've just had a tip-off. The liquidators have found my name. They don't know anything yet, but they'll soon start putting two and two together. Then I'll be up to my neck in the dung heap. We daren't leave it any longer.'

'I thought you said it was all secure.'

'I thought it was. But just in case, I've been quietly liquidating all the funds I've been holding for you, and the others, and have been transferring the proceeds into Swiss bank accounts for us. We were going next month, anyway. This will just bring it all a bit nearer.'

'What about David in your office? You sure he doesn't know anything?'

'He hasn't a clue.'

'He's your son, for God's sake!'

'He's too tied to Sylvia's apron strings to think for himself. No, he hasn't got a clue.'

'And the dumb blonde downstairs?'

'Trixie.'

'What a stupid bloody name.' May didn't like her, and showed it. She was no threat to her, she knew that Les had more taste, but she disliked her nevertheless. 'You'd think she was a poodle. Yes, Trixie.'

'No. She knows nothing. Don't worry about it. I've got all Sam's savings, and it's all for you. It's quite substantial; you could live well on that for the rest of your life. Now come on.' He lunged forward and grabbed himself an ample handful of her left breast.

He said no more, and she seemed quite content as she gradually lost control.

Wednesday proved another beautiful morning. I was up and about early, but not before the sun had already shed a lattice-work pattern across the still waters as it pierced the canopy of trees. The two boats behind us were still, and had their curtains drawn. We had seen no sign of life in either.

206

Perhaps they were shut up and temporarily unoccupied.

Margery and I breakfasted alone, and left the youngsters abed. They were just about stirring when we decided to walk on to the toll house and wait for them at the watering point just above the top lock. There was ragwort and willowherb among the grasses at the water's edge. I stopped to take a photograph of this wonderful tranquility. Across to our right we could just see the top of the large telescope dish at Jodrell Bank.

Tied up at the watering point was a large boat. Inside, a group of handicapped children were at breakfast. A happier, livelier bunch it would have been hard to find. A few years ago this just would not have happened, but now it all seemed so natural. And were they responding to it.

We stood by the bridge, just below the top lock, and took in the magnificent scenery. Cloudless skies, and a view for miles all around us. The boat moved off from the watering point northwards, just as *Colette* came into view. She slipped in to take on water. Richard and Jo seemed full of beans.

'You know you asked if you should leave the side hatch open, before you went?'

'Yes,' I confirmed.

'Well, I caught a strange bloke leaning in through the hatch as I was going to the kitchen. So I brought the lid down on his fingers. I don't think he'll do it again in a hurry. I'm sure he'd have been in given half the chance.'

'I didn't see anybody about,' I replied. 'I didn't see another soul on that stretch the whole time we were there.'

'Spooky,' said Jo.

Richard and Jo jumped ashore with their windlasses to operate the top lock. Margery navigated. After the first lock they jumped aboard, as there was a fair distance to the second.

The Bosley flight of 12 locks falls 100 feet in less than a mile. It has been truly described as the most superbly engineered, magnificently located flight of locks in the country. I can easily believe it. It is breathtaking in its beauty and the ease of operation. Wide, well-cut grass verges flank the canal on both sides, bordered by hedges, like gliding through beautifully manicured lawns. All around us a flat plain was dotted with oak trees. But there just directly ahead of us we saw the gentle slopes of The Cloud, a hill which dominated the skyline.

From the second lock Richard and Jo stayed ashore. There was no one in front going down, and we met no one coming up. They prepared each lock for us. When we were in one lock, Jo went ahead to prepare the next, whilst Richard stayed with us to let us out, and close the paddles and gates. By the time we were ready to emerge from one lock, the next was ready for us to enter. All went swingingly, locks came and went.

The engineering here is cleverly organised, with side pounds retaining half the water for use when the lock is next required. The intention was to halve the flow of water downstream as the locks were lowered. But seemingly this was beyond the capabilities of the canal users to operate properly, and the system sadly is no longer used.

I went ashore to inspect these works of art. It was fascinating to see how it had all been so carefully laid out.

We entered the penultimate lock, number 11, whilst Jo went ahead to lock 12, which she found contained a boat just rising to the top, about to emerge. It was not a hired boat as it carried containers of plants. It was, presumably, operated by the owner. Jo stood by the lock, politely opened the gate for it as there was no one ashore with the boat, and suggested to the helmsman that he stay in the lock until we were ready to emerge, so that both boats could leave their respective locks at the same time, cross the pound and enter the open lock vacated by the other. This works so easily and well, being to the advantage of both boat users.

We had never experienced any difficulty. Until now!

Unfortunately on this occasion Jo was given short shrift, and was virtually told that we should have gone back to let him pass. Whether he meant go back from the lock we were in, or back up the whole ten locks, he didn't make clear. In any case, as a boat owner as opposed to a hire boat user, he knew it all, and certainly wasn't going to take any notice of a young chit of a girl.

Instead of waiting in his lock, as any normal person would, he, knowing it all, moved out into the pound before we were ready to emerge. He didn't even thank Jo for opening the upper gate for him. He was seemingly doing everything himself, although he had with him his wife, or lady friend, who stayed out of his way and smiled at Jo. She waved a glass of wine in her hand.

The pound is a large one, and these locks are not in line; in fact he had to turn through 90 degrees to his left. This pound used to contain a large transshipment wharf, hence its size, and the old Leek–Macclesfield railway line used to cross the wharf.

Apart from the main route through the pound the old wharf area is badly overgrown with reeds and bulrushes, and he was gradually veering towards them. When we eventually emerged he was well in amongst the bulrushes and scowled at us as we passed. The lady, a slim attractive brunette in shorts, with a glass in her hand, was still keeping well out of his way. She grinned and tried to placate us, thereby hoping to detract from the stupid, macho attitude of her friend, who clearly couldn't ask, or even accept, help from a woman. He knew it all, and with every attempt he made, he was getting in a worse mess.

We entered the lock he had vacated, and as we went down within the lock, my last glimpse was of him with his boat pole desperately trying to free himself. I couldn't help hoping that another boat would come along, and seeing him playing in the shallows, take the lock that was open for him. I wondered what his temper would be like then. The brunette, still with a glass of wine, was last seen sitting quietly in the stern.

Open countryside greeted us on either hand, and now over to our left stood The Cloud, a gently rolling wooded hill rising 700 feet above the canal. High up its slopes light green fields were interspersed among the darker green of the woodland. In the past it was quarried for gritstone, of which the beautiful Bosley locks were built, almost as beautiful as Chatsworth, which was also built from the Cloud's stone.

We pulled in for a quiet lunch, the exertions of the day now over. No more locks for 10 miles, and we were not proposing to go beyond that. But somehow it was all so beautiful it had hardly been an exertion.

May drove quietly home, but was disturbed to see a police car parked in close proximity. She had the presence of mind to drive on, parking around the corner, and gaining access to her home via the garden of the neighbour behind her, and then through her back door. The neighbour didn't mind, she had helped them out before when Sam had been in trouble. She assumed it was the same again.

There was a message on the answering machine, asking her to contact Les, but that was from last night. There were others from the police, requesting she contact them.

Hell! They must have found Sam sooner than she'd expected, and she thought she had been so clever. Now she would have to avoid them until Saturday. Three days!

She started packing in earnest, meticulous, as she always was. The house was now hers, so she would arrange for it to be let out furnished. Those possessions she couldn't take with her were to be locked in a private garage, until they could be sent for. She would make some provision for her mother, but it must be discreet. Though why she should bother she didn't know, for Maude was such an ungrateful old woman, and complained whatever one did for her. Anyway, provide for her she must, and decided to call on her after dark.

The doorbell rang. She stiffened. Through the net curtains, she saw it was a policeman, and didn't move until he had gone. He came back again, and again. She phoned Les.

'The police keep calling here. They must have found Sam.'

'Every damned thing at once. Well, just pack and make sure they don't see you.'

'I shan't, don't worry. The car is parked around the corner, and I can sneak in and out around the back, just as I please.'

'What about the neighbours? Don't let them see you.'

'If they do they won't let on. Is everything all right at your end?'

'The villa's all set up. No need to worry.'

'You're sure?'

'A discreet villa in the Algarve. Own swimming pool, so you needn't bring your bathing costume.'

'You'll be lucky.'

'I hope so.'

Ern, nursing a bandaged finger, was soon in pursuit of his quarry. He waited above the top lock of the flight until *Colette* was entering the second lock, before starting his descent. He moved slowly, as he had to moor his boat before he could open the lock ahead, and then moor again on the lower side, to allow him to close it again.

Precious minutes, which seemed like hours, were running away from him. His fingers ached. He was again all alone, except for poor old Sam lying quietly in the cabin. He still went around rather than through the cabin.

He envisaged May lying in bed whilst he was flogging his guts out for her. Was she worth it? She was. He knew she was. But he would feel better if only he could remember what it had been like making love to her. Anything as wonderful as that should stand out in his mind, his senses, forever, surrounded by flashing lights. He tried to imagine it, but it didn't help. He could, however, recall in detail the Polaroid of Rose.

He became aware of a large boat behind him at the fourth lock, pushing him, obviously anxious to be speeding ahead. Held up behind him at the fifth he could feel the impatience. A long pound stretched between the fifth and the sixth locks, and the large boat was thundering down the pound behind him, before he had *Hyacinth* properly moored. He opened the lock, and had almost reached his craft again, when the huge *Turandot*, with three crew aboard, passed by him.

The Captain, singing an aria from *Madam Butterfly*, doffed his cap and shouted to Ern, 'Sorry old chap. We're on official business, you know. I hope you don't mind us taking your water.'

Ern's jaw dropped. 'You buggers!' he shouted back, but his voice was drowned out by the Captain, who was loudly continuing his aria, as *Turandot* slid into the lock he had opened for *Hyacinth*.

'Bit off, that,' Stan breathed out of the side of his mouth to George. Although with Rodney singing at the top of his voice, there was no chance of him being overheard.

'Shut up. He's in charge. Field Officer grade, remember.'

George went on to prepare the lock ahead, leaving Stan to see *Turandot* through the lock. He stayed behind afterwards, refilled the lock again and opened it for Ern. He closed the gate behind *Hyacinth* and opened the lower paddles for him to empty the lock.

'Sorry,' he said, 'but orders is orders, and we are in a desperate hurry.'

Ern felt better after that gesture, and found afterwards that all the locks were left full for him, with the upper gate open, to enable him to steer straight in without having to disembark or moor. In the end he was pleased. They had been more of a help than a hindrance. He now had only half the job to do at each lock.

Turandot emerged from the eleventh lock, intending to run straight across into the already open final twelfth lock. Rodney noticed a boat stranded among the bulrushes with an irate, almost apoplectic man madly trying to ease himself loose with his boat pole. He was shouting at a brunette, who was still sitting in the stern with a wine glass in her hand, ignoring him.

'I say,' said Rodney, considering an offer of help. 'Are you stuck?'

''Course I'm bloody well stuck, what does it look like, you stupid inebriated git,' he roared back, scuppering what little likelihood of an offer of help there might have been.

'Roddy!' exclaimed the brunette, standing up and smiling.

'Gosh,' said Roddy, wide-eyed. 'Lucinda, what are you doing here?'

'Wish I knew,' she sighed. 'I can't think why I ever agreed to come with him!'

'Are you stuck?' enquired Roddy, although it was really quite obvious, and so doing he stopped the boat.

'Yes,' said Lucinda. 'Stuck here and stuck with him!'

'I am sorry,' replied Roddy with feeling. 'But we are in a most awful hurry Lucinda. I'll … er … look you up when I get back.'

'He'll get the flamin' thing stuck,' sighed Stan.

'That's his business. He's in charge.' George was quite indifferent.

213

'Will you two silly buggers shut up and do something!' roared the apoplectic, as he fumed and stormed in frustrated and quite ineffective rage.

'That's it. Stay there, Roddy,' cried Lucinda. 'I'm coming.'

She tried to jump from one boat to the other, but landed waist-deep among the bulrushes, between the two. Roddy put out his hand to help pull her aboard.

'He'll get our damned boat stuck as well, and I suppose we'll have to get it off the bottom.' George now realised that it could affect him.

'Look. He's pulling that tart on to our boat.' Stan was becoming interested. 'Struth, we could do with her.'

They were paying so little attention that they hadn't noticed *Hyacinth* slip out of the penultimate lock into the open bottom lock, which was waiting for *Turandot.*

George suddenly came to. 'You cheeky sod!' he shouted, as he ran from the side of the pound, where he and Stan had been watching Roddy's amorous antics in rescuing the brunette, up to the lock.

'Going down,' said Ern, with a nod as *Hyacinth* started to drop within the lock.

Stan opened the lower gates for him, closed them behind him, and refilled the lock for *Turandot.* By which time the brunette was aboard and Roddy was trying to pole himself off the bulrushes. This time, however, with the brunette's help.

'Don't you ever come back,' stormed the apopleptic, who was by now jumping up and down with rage and frustration, shaking his fist.

'Don't worry. I shan't. I'll send Daddy's chauffeur for my things. Don't lose any!' she shouted back as she stood on the deck, her shirt and shorts dripping with dirty water from the canal.

'We're stuck too, well stuck. Go and stand in the bows,' she ordered.

With that Lucinda took the boat pole, and with Roddy's weight in the bows helping to give the stern a lift she put the engine into gear, fast forward, and gently eased *Turandot* off the mud with the pole. Lucinda reduced the thrust, and took over the controls.

Rodney ran back to her. 'That was brilliant, Lucinda.'

George and Stan on the bank clapped in admiration.

'Hmmm,' she replied to Rodney. 'You're just about as useless as he is.' Looking back over her shoulder. 'I could have got him off easily if he'd let me.'

'Bitch!' roared the apoplectic.

Rodney took her cold wet hand, 'Your tiny hand is frozen,' he sang.

'I'm not surprised. My knickers are soaked and I haven't got a spare pair.'

'You cow,' fumed the apoplectic. 'I don't ever want to see you again,' and with that he rammed his boat pole so hard into the mud that he got it stuck.

'Don't worry. You won't.' She gave him a wave.

'He's a rather coarse fellow,' said Roddy. 'Not very good with his boat either, is he?'

'No. He's not much good at anything,' sighed Lucinda. 'The only thing he can get up is his blood pressure.'

16

We could easily have stayed in this peaceful glade all afternoon, but we had another 7 miles before our proposed overnight stop. Through two brief cuttings, then a 90 degree left turn and we entered a long straight stretch almost 2 miles in length. The outskirts of Buglawton rose to our right above the canal, and ahead we could see no less than eight bridges, including a railway bridge. In the centre of the straight was a half-mile cutting. No variation at all, just dead straight. A number of boats were moored at the ends of gardens bordering the canal. One, I noticed, was lying on the canal bed, its cabin awash with water.

'No bodies?' enquired Richard, winking at Jo.

'Can't see any,' I replied disappointedly.

It became so boring, just going straight, that Richard left me at the helm, and went to get a can of lager, joining Jo in the cockpit. He happily started singing again.

At the end of the straight we bore slightly right, whilst to our left the site of another old transshipment basin. Through another cutting, and we entered Congleton. We passed under the main road through the town, followed quickly by the railway bridge, and moored beside a busy walkway towpath.

We took our time walking back along the towpath to the footbridge into the town, which runs beneath the main road bridge. Coming down to ground level the other side I noticed, under the bridge, a man in a bright shell suit, with dark glasses, animatedly talking into a mobile telephone.

He kept turning his back towards us, as if he didn't want to see us.

'What in hell's name is that?' I said loudly pointing out this strange apparition to Richard.

'Shut up. It's a policeman,' he replied under his breath.

'What?' I took another keen look.

'Don't do that. He'll see you,' he said, again under his breath. 'He's in plain clothes, and doesn't want to be recognised.'

'Plain clothes! But he sticks out like a sore thumb.' I took another look in bewilderment.

'Don't!' He was now very insistent.

We walked on.

Stan, running ahead along the towpath, had seen *Colette* moor and reported back. To keep better surveillance he had moved to the other side of the canal, and was standing under the main road bridge. His phone bleeped. He put it to his ear.

Crackle … Crackle …

'Rod here.'

'Yup.'

Crackle … Crackle …

'I say, could you do me a favour?'

'Yup.'

'We have this boat in our sights now, and I wonder if …'

'Bloody hell. They're here. Coming across the bridge. I must go.'

'No, hang on, it's urgent.'

'Urgent! It's essential they don't see me.'

'You're in mufti, plain clothes, aren't you?'

'Yes, but I don't want them to see me.'

'They won't think there's anything to worry about if you're in mufti. They won't even notice you.'

'God, they're coming down. Going into the town!'

'Don't panic, old chap. You'll be all right. Act normal. I just want you to go shopping as well. So you can follow them and see what they get up to, OK?'

'What do you want me to get? I can't move now, anyway.'

'Poor Lucinda here hasn't brought any clothes. She's living in my T-shirt, but she hasn't any knickers. Would you be a good chap, and get her, say, five pairs of panties?'

'No bloody fear. Me go and buy ladies' knickers? Not on your Nellie! Not in my job description.'

Crackle ... Crackle ...

'Good chap. Five pairs, normal woman's size. Oh, and get her a toothbrush. Over and out.'

Crackle ... Crackle ...

'Hey.'

Crackle ... Crackle ...

They had passed him whilst he was phoning. He had had his back to them. No one could have possibly recognised him, or thought there was anything in the least untoward. After all, he was in plain clothes. Stan reassured himself, and felt better. Except for his shopping commission. He waited for a safe distance to open up, and followed them into Hightown.

After leaving the lower lock, Ern, for the second time in two days, found himself passing by his quarry *Colette* and its occupants, who were lunching. There was nothing now to be done except to move post haste to Scholar Green, and wait for their arrival. They seemed to be having a good sit-down lunch, and it was therefore unlikely that they would be getting fish and chips in Congleton.

May, he knew, would kill him if he had got it wrong. But he was merely following orders. She was going to meet him at Scholar Green, so it would be her own fault. However, he knew that was no real consolation. For she'd kill him even if it was her own mistake.

*

'No sighting of *Blue Belle* anywhere, Sarge,' reported PC Jones.

'Well it can't have vanished. Keep looking,' ordered Sergeant Tooth. 'It can't have got far.'

'OK, Sarge. We'll get 'em.' He turned and left.

Sergeant Tooth mused for a moment, and wondered where they could possibly have vanished to! His nose was itchy. A sure sign that something was in the wind. But what? There must be a reason, so he decided to see what, if anything, was happening in the information room. In the corridor he came upon WPC Nonelly, with a cup of strong tea in her hand.

'Not out picking bluebells?' he enquired.

'Just off again, Sarge, as soon as I've taken the Super his tea.' She walked on.

Time was when she brought me my tea. Changing her affections, she is. But he won't be interested in her. Far too skinny, especially when he's used to Rose's superb endowments, he thought as he went on his way.

In the operations room there was nothing of any interest. On his way back PC Spriggs, rushing urgently, bumped into him.

'Sorry, Sarge.'

'Is everybody in here having tea, instead of finding *Blue Belle*?'

'Sighted, Sarge. That's what I've come to tell you. Just in. Found almost wrecked in a boatyard. They've taken a new boat with a funny name.'

'They all have funny names, haven't you noticed?'

'"Ture-an-dot", or something.'

'"Tur-an-doh", it's pronounced. An opera by Puccini.'

'Eh … who's he?'

'An Italian ice cream man from Salford I expect.' Then getting down to business, 'Put a call out all round to find the new boat.'

'Already done, Sarge. Trouble is, it's getting late now. I don't suppose we'll manage to find them tonight.'

'Keep trying. Well done, lad.' A smile crept across his face, and his nose itched.

In the supermarket, Margery and Jo did the grocery shopping. Richard, with his eye to the essentials of life, collected a huge pack of cans of lager.

I just happened to be lingering near the ladies lingerie section, when I noticed the strange man in the shell suit, still wearing his dark glasses. He was buying a pile of ladies' knickers. He also had a toothbrush in his hand. I had thought him odd before, but this only confirmed my worst suspicions. Fancy any man wearing a shell suit, let alone a pink one. The mind boggled!

A brief stop only, then it was all aboard again, and off through the lower edges of Congleton. We travelled over an aqueduct taking the road beneath us, past the old Congleton Wharf, complete with a large but now decaying warehouse. Then out again, close by the golf course.

Coming into view over the left bank rose Mow Cop, with its castellated ruined folly. Wilbraham's Folly, built in 1754, was intended to be seen by the local squire from his house, Rode Hall, some 2 miles away across the Cheshire Plain. It became famous, however, in the early nineteenth century when Hugh Bourne held his primitive Methodist Revivalist meetings in the open there, and the 'Ranters', as they became known, were born.

Below it was Ramsdell Hall, built in the mid-eighteenth century, bordering the canal, its beautifully manicured lawns sweeping down to the canal's edge. A majestic red brick hall sits proudly just off the canal. One could almost look through its windows. In fact the canal is part of the setting of this lovely house, for it acts as a 'ha ha', as the ground to our right drops steeply beyond the towpath to fields below.

221

Across the fields was another beautiful house, but very much older, the late fifteenth-century Little Moreton Hall. One of the finest half-timbered buildings in the country. The top of the house is surmounted by a long, leaning, sagging gallery, with floors that slope in more than one direction. Heavily underpinned now, it has been described as looking like some vast, unstable doll's house. Giant goldfish swim in the moat, whilst to the rear there is a lovely formal knot garden. I have visited it a number of times, and I'm always eager to go back again to see if it is still as beautiful as I had imagined. It always is.

At the end of the cutting, under the shade of the Ranters' meeting place, we moored, tying up to rings set into the towpath. This spot was just before the lock-keeper's cottage, and the final 'stop' lock on the Macclesfield canal. There was, we noticed, a boat already moored behind us, shut up and presumably unoccupied.

Inside, Ern smiled to himself with satisfaction as he saw *Colette*, through a chink in the curtains, moor just in front of him. He had got it right again. May would be pleased, and there would be no problems tonight. Of that he was certain. She was bound to stay tonight, and he was determined that it was definitely going to be a night to remember!

Carefully choosing and laying out a change of clothes, he went for a shower. His finger still hurt, but he had asked for it by sticking his neck out. He must be more careful in future. In fact, when all this was over, he would get a job and go straight. The trials of the last few days had proved to him that this sort of life just wasn't worth it. Perhaps, in the fullness of time, he and May might yet get together.

When he had returned from his shopping, Stan was surprised to note the low-key, happy atmosphere aboard. He had expected to see the bimbo bursting out of a tight

T-shirt, with just a brief towel about her waist. But he found no such thing. Lucinda looked every bit a woman of the world, hair swept back, wearing a light blue sweat shirt and a pair of light grey slacks, slightly too big but not enough to really notice.

'You're a gem,' she said with a smile, as he stepped aboard, and handed her his package. He was rewarded by a kiss on the cheek.

When Stan had gone below for a cup of tea, and Lucinda was alone in the stern with Rodney, she got back to her enquiries.

'All right, it's top secret surveillance. It can't be spies, now. So what is it then? Drugs?'

The bluntness of the question shook him. He stammered and tried to cover up, but only made his confusion worse.

'OK, drugs!' She was sure that he had, in his confusion, confirmed her suspicions.

'Oh, no. I … er … didn't say that.'

'You didn't have to. Oh Roddy you are a prat. A nice one, but a prat nevertheless,' she grinned. 'I'll bet you were never able to conceal a comic from your mum. What the hell you're doing in this security nonsense is beyond me.'

'Oh. I say,' he stammered.

'OK. You're following those drug barons, and keeping them under surveillance,' she looked at him, but he didn't answer. Instead George poked his head through the after cabin hatch.

'They're off again,' he said with some urgency.

'Good,' replied Rodney, pleased to be relieved from his interrogation. 'Ask Stan to slip ashore and keep in eye contact with them.'

'Rubbish,' cut in Lucinda. 'We can keep an eye on them from here. No need for that poor devil to keep trotting along the towpath.'

George and Stan stared.

JOHN OLIVER

'Don't waste time, boys. Let go fore and aft,' she ordered, taking complete control, and starting up the engine.

The boys did her bidding immediately, whilst Roddy just stared open-mouthed.

'Close your mouth, Rod. You're not catching flies.'

She pulled out, and caught up with *Colette*, keeping a safe distance. She had them clearly in her sights, increasing or decreasing her distance according to the terrain. Momentarily out of sight on bends, but never for long.

'You know how to sail this thing,' smiled Roddy.

'Of course. Been used to canals all my life. Mummy and Daddy often took us as children. Not been on this stretch before, though.'

'How exciting,' beamed Rodney in admiration and considerable relief. 'None of us has ever been on a boat before.'

'That has been plainly obvious. Clive there just wanted a bimbo on board. So I obliged. I could have got him off the mud, but his macho attitude wouldn't allow him to think that a woman could possibly be any help. So I let him get on with it. I had got the rest of the week free, so I just drank his wine and sat out in the sun.'

She certainly knew what she was doing and the confidence of the whole ship's company soared as a result.

'So it is drugs.' Lucinda resumed her interrogation. 'Are we just to follow? Or do we check them out?'

'I shouldn't really say. But we are following them to find their contacts, and then have them apprehended.'

'I don't know much about them, but they seem very unlikely suspects to me. They look just like a family on holiday.'

'Ah, but there are two others at least hiding on board.'

'What?' she looked at him in disbelief. 'Two others at least? Well, I suppose it is a large boat, but it doesn't seem likely.'

Rodney hadn't really thought. He had been trained to do exactly what he was told, in true military fashion, and take it as gospel.

'I'll sus it out,' she said.

'You won't do anything silly?' Rodney enquired anxiously.

'Wouldn't dream of it, old son,' she grinned. 'Let's have a look at the map.'

She pored over it for some minutes.

'Scholar Green for the night at this rate I expect.'

'Do you think so?'

'Well, they won't get into the Harecastle Tunnel tonight, and they won't start on the Red Bull flight the other way. Scholar Green – it has to be.'

Rodney was full of admiration.

'I expect we can get a good meal there.' Lucinda was looking forward to a good meal.

'Can't leave the boat.' Roddy was emphatic.

'Rubbish!' sighed Lucinda in desperation. 'You've got portable phones. Leave someone keeping an eye open, whilst the others go for a meal. If you are called away before you've finished, I'll eat your meal for you, because I'm as hungry as a horse.'

He tried to protest, but she ignored him.

'Now take this for a minute,' she said, handing him the helm. 'Whilst I go and put some pants on.'

She went to her improvised line to see if her washed clothes were drying, and then down into the cabin. Rodney had a large smile on his face as he started to sing another aria.

May left the A34 in Scholar Green, turned into a small side road, and parked her car outside a new bungalow beside the footpath leading down to the lock-keeper's cottage on the canal.

She had had a remarkably good day packing, and was

225

surprised at what she had achieved. She had also been into her bank and made arrangements for monies to be transferred, on a regular basis, to her mother. More than the old witch is worth, she thought. But she is my mum.

Colette was moored 200 yards up from the watering point. *Hyacinth*, therefore, should be somewhere behind it. May turned left along the towpath, apparently paying no attention to *Colette* as she passed. There was activity inside, and the shower was being used. The old couple were having a cup of tea in the lounge, reading newspapers. The stern doors were open, and on one hung a padlock. She was certain she could pick it.

When boarding *Hyacinth*, which was just on the bend behind *Colette*, she noticed another boat moored behind *Hyacinth*, further round the bend. Familiar, she thought. *Turandot*. Yes, moored behind us last night. The same three boats together, again? Coincidence, or not? She must keep an eye on this. Probably it was nothing, but it couldn't be ignored. She hadn't kept out of trouble so long by not paying attention to detail.

'Nothing to report,' said Ern, who was looking as bright and smart as a new pin, as she came down into the cabin. 'I think they are preparing to go out for a meal. They only had a very light lunch at the bottom of the Bosley flight. No one has been on, no one came off. No sign of the bag.'

'Good,' she replied. 'Who are the lot behind?'

'What lot behind?'

May closed her eyes. 'Give me strength. No wonder this operation is such a mess. *Turandot*, the boat that was right behind you last night, is here again tonight. The three of you – together!'

'Who are they?' enquired Ern going through the boat, past Sam, and looking out through the stern.

'That's what I am asking you!' She was getting annoyed,

but seeing his bandaged finger she restrained herself. 'What's that?'

'Oh, I hurt it this morning, that's all. Had a look at the boat in front. Thought it was empty. The young bloke slammed the hatch shut and caught my finger.'

'Did he recognise you?'

'No. I don't think so. No.'

May bit her lip, and said no more on the subject. 'Make us a cup of tea love. I'm parched.' She was trying to keep Ern sweet.

'They're going now, all smart and tidy,' reported George. 'And they're not taking anything with them.'

'Now Rodney is taking me out for a meal, so we can keep an eye on them whilst they are out. You two' – to George and Stan – 'keep an eye on their boat while we're gone. Then we can change over, and you can go for a meal. OK?' She did not defer to Rodney, but was certainly giving the orders.

'I'm not sure …' he said quietly, but she ushered him out.

'This way,' she said. 'Don't go down there past their boat. We'll take the track up from the cutting behind us.'

With that, she marched Rodney off.

George commented, 'At last we seem to have a comptroller who knows what she is doing.'

'OK, all systems go.' May, now in a black tracksuit, black woolly hat, gloves and plimsolls, was ready.

'I want you to stand out on the towpath, and fiddle with the stern mooring rope, to cover me as I slip off from the bows. Just in case there is anyone behind, watching them, or us!' Ern hadn't thought of that. 'Make it a good show, attract their attention. The same when I'm coming back, please.'

Ern did her proud. So much so that in the boat behind, Stan commented, 'He's making a hell of a meal of tying up his mooring ropes. Anyone would think there was a typhoon coming.'

May, doubled up, ran quickly down the towpath and slipped onto the stern deck of *Colette*. Crouching low, careful to ensure that her head was below the cabin roof, she took out her skeleton keys. It seemed an age, but in no more than two minutes, three at the outside, the lock clicked open. She deftly slipped it off, opened one of the rear doors, and slipped inside, closing the door carefully behind her. All very clean and tidy. Wish ours was like this, she thought.

Cases, boxes and luggage were stacked on the two bunks on either side of the rear cabin. She opened, and went carefully through each in turn, putting everything back exactly where it was. May, if anything, was very good at her job, and she prided herself that people did not realise that anyone had been through their most private possessions, until they discovered that their valuables were missing.

Next, the lockers and wardrobes. Then the en suite facilities. Nothing, however small, was missed. On to the two occupied cabins, with the same care, precision, and attention to detail. She worked swiftly, and diligently, but it all took time.

After a quiet drink, the Bleeding Wolf provided an excellent dinner. We felt it was no more that we deserved. It had been another good day, and we were all in good form.

From a corner of the dining room, Lucinda kept an eye on all that went on.

'They don't look like drug traffickers to me,' she said. 'Do they to you?'

'That's the cleverness of them,' assured Rodney.

'They're a family on holiday. Who said they were into drugs?'

'They're a dangerous group, and they've been targeted. There are at least two more, who never come off the boat. In fact we haven't seen them since they went on board on Saturday.'

'What?' Lucinda couldn't believe her ears.

'Yes. It really is big stuff, Lucinda.'

'Bollocks.' She took another mouthful of lobster, whilst he looked offended.

When we had finished our meal, Margery and I decided to go for a walk, leaving Richard and Jo having a quiet drink together in the bar.

'OK,' said Lucinda. 'You hop it back and send the others off for their meal. I've got work to do.'

'What work? What are you going to do?'

'Never you mind. What you don't know you can't worry about.'

Rodney left reluctantly after paying the bill, and giving Lucinda a £20 note to pay for her drink.

May finished the galley. She had had every item out and scrutinised it.

'The buggers!' she said aloud, and started to go through the lounge, but found there nothing but newspapers and books. She looked at her watch. She had been over an hour and a quarter. There was only one place she hadn't tried. She shut up the cabin, and started to lift the metal plate over the engine housing. This was the place they had hidden it. She was certain. No one would think of looking here, in the engine well.

The lid was heavy, and there was a little grating sound as she lifted it carefully and placed it beside her. She put her torch inside the engine housing before switching it on.

*

'He's out there again testing his moorings,' said George. 'He's a queer bloke all right. What's that behind him?' His voice was suddenly urgent.

'Where?'

'Something, someone, on the towpath behind him.'

'I can't see anything.'

'There's a person, hunched up. Or is it a dog?'

'A dog maybe. Can't be anything else.' Stan looked out carefully. 'Nothing there as far as I can see. Apart from him.'

'I was sure I saw some movement beyond him, but it wasn't on that boat anyway. Whatever it was.'

'I hope they come back soon.' Stan stretched. 'I'm starving.'

There was a movement on the boat and Rodney stepped aboard.

'Nothing doing,' reported George.

'Apart from the chap on the boat in front fiddling with his mooring ropes all the time,' added Stan.

'All right. I'll take over now. Go and get yourselves something to eat, and have a drink on me.' He handed George a £10 note.

'Where's Lucinda?' Stan enquired.

'Stayed on, chatting to someone.'

'Is anyone sitting here?' Lucinda enquired, putting her hand on the back of an armchair in the lounge bar.

'No,' smiled Jo, drawing her own glass nearer to herself as Lucinda sat down in the chair beside her.

'Nice countryside, isn't it? You live near here?' Lucinda asked in all innocence.

'No. We're on the canal.'

'Oh, are you? What a coincidence! So am I.'

They were sharing reminiscences. Where they had been.

What they had done. Where they were going. Lucinda had the complete background.

May was livid. There was no containing her. She cursed the occupants of *Colette* for being such a cunning bunch of two-timing crooks. She cursed Ern for always being in the way, and never getting anything right. She cursed Fred for lousing up the whole operation from the outset. Finally she cursed poor old Sam for recruiting such a useless bunch of has-beens, who were better off in jail out of the way.

'That does it. I've played it easy with them up to now. Tomorrow night we'll go in and really do them over until we find where they have hidden our cash.'

'The bank's money, actually,' stammered Ern, who had been shocked by her outburst, and was trying desperately to lighten the situation.

'*Our* bloody money, you fool. It has cost us a lot to get it. We've paid for it all right.' Ern thought she was going to burst into tears.

'Shall I make a nice cup of tea?' He tried desperately to quieten her.

'No, I won't have any flaming tea. I've got to plan tomorrow thanks to you.'

She looked carefully at the map. 'It seems they're on the Cheshire Ring. There are about twenty-six locks down to Wheelock. That's eight miles. Meet me at eight-thirty sharp in Ettiley Heath. If by any chance they go the other way, they could be in the middle of Stoke-on-Trent. Ring me with precise details as soon as they are moored. But I don't think that's likely. I'm sure they're on the Ring.'

'Yes, I've got it. You sure you're not stopping?' he enquired gently.

'No. I'm off,' was her curt reply.

'What about Sam? Aren't you going to see him? When will you be moving him?'

May changed her tune suddenly, remembering she had a part to play. 'Yes. I'll just go and see him.' She turned towards the cabin door.

'He's very peaceful. I haven't disturbed him.'

'No.' She disappeared into the cabin and closed the door.

On her return she was almost tearful. 'Sorry, Ern,' she whispered. She gave him a peck on the cheek, and was gone.

'I knew it was all bollocks!' Lucinda announced to Rodney upon her return. 'You're just wasting your time.'

17

Thursday dawned with another bright sunny morning. The Ranters above were silent, and we hadn't been disturbed by the railway. It had been a quiet, peaceful night without a single worry.

I strolled down along the cutting, passed the old lock-keeper's cottage, still in occupation, and took a long look at the stop lock. There was now only one lock, of just 6 inches, but one could clearly see where there had once been a second. Seemingly when the canals were built, the owners of the Macclesfield did not trust the Trent & Mersey's operators, lest they should drain their waters downwards. And *vice versa*, lest the Macclesfield should steal the Trent & Mersey's waters upwards. I had naively thought that they were all gentlemen in those days, but it seems that knavery was as rife then as it is now.

We sat over a leisurely breakfast for we knew it was going to be a fairly hard day. In total 26 locks to work, with the stop lock.

'Oh look, it's Lucinda.' Jo smiled and waved, obviously pleased to see her friend.

She walked down the cutting towards us. She had ironed her blouse and shorts, and looked very chic.

'So this is where you are,' she smiled. 'We're just round the corner.' She pointed back up the canal, where the bows of a boat were just visible.

Jo went out into the cockpit to greet her.

'We met her last night in the pub,' explained Richard. 'She's a good laugh.'

'This is Lucinda.' Jo introduced us amid the dirty crockery.

Lucinda looked around the lounge admiringly. 'This is lovely. It's a super boat. I wouldn't mind one like it.'

'It's brill,' enthused Jo. 'You don't mind if I show her round, do you?'

'Not in the slightest. We'll do the washing up.' Margery looked at me and started to clear the cups and plates.

'I'm afraid the beds aren't made yet,' apologised Jo.

'Speak for yourself,' cut in Margery.

'Whoops.' Jo ducked her head into her shoulders. 'Well, ours isn't … yet!'

Lucinda was taken on a comprehensive tour of *Colette*, shown every detail, from oven, sink, lights, fridge and toaster to cupboards, drawers and closets. Jo was very thorough with her tour, and Lucinda took it all in. She loved the decorations, the detailed map of the Cheshire Ring on the wall, the large comfy double beds, day and night blinds to all the windows.

'We're going down the Red Bull flight,' she advised.

'So are we!' rejoined Richard, without much relish, as he greased the propeller shaft.

'Oh good. We'll see you then.' She looked anxiously at her watch. 'Heavens, half past nine. Rodney will kill me. He wants to be off early, and I said I wouldn't stay long.'

Richard started the engine. 'We're just off.'

She said her farewells, and walked off beside the cut with a light step.

'Where have you been?' enquired Rodney anxiously, as she stepped on board.

'They are just off,' she announced. 'But you are wasting your time.'

'You shouldn't have done that, you know. We are only supposed to be keeping surveillance. But I suppose it doesn't really matter in your case, you're not part of the Firm.'

'Do stop patronising me, and talking rubbish. The Firm indeed. A gang of would-be spies, who couldn't keep an eye on the Houses of Parliament without them being nicked.'

'I say, do be careful, old girl.'

'I am not an "old girl", as you call me. But I can tell you that you have, so far, wasted five days following a family group from Shropshire. Parents, son and daughter-in-law, who set out last Saturday, on holiday touring the Cheshire Ring. What is more, they are due back at Acton Bridge in two days. Saturday morning at ten a.m. to be precise. I have been all over the boat. There are not two mafia men, at least, on board. There is no luggage for the two mafia men, or perhaps they slipped quietly overboard with their luggage, without my noticing. Oh, and there are no signs of drugs anywhere.'

'None?'

'None!' Lucinda was emphatic. 'I have got Jo's address and telephone number.'

'Good girl.' Rodney bucked up at this news. 'Give them to me, and I'll have them checked out.'

'No fear. Have you stake out those poor people in their own homes, and start harassing them there? I am keeping that safely to myself. I shall get in touch with Jo when they are home again, but certainly not you and your lot.'

Stan appeared in the cockpit doorway. 'They're off. We'll follow when they're gone through this first lock. It isn't very deep.'

'Stop lock,' corrected Lucinda. Rodney and Stan looked at her, but dared not ask what she meant.

'Queer bloke in front is off as well, just as he was yesterday,' commented George.

'As he was yesterday?' exclaimed Lucinda. 'You mean that you, and that boat between us, are both trailing after those poor people.'

'Well, yes. It was there yesterday. Followed them down the Bosley locks,' agreed Rodney.

'Set off as soon as it was gone yesterday, and it has done the same today,' confirmed Stan.

'You prize pillocks.' Lucinda was clearly annoyed. 'Why are you both following that boat? What is the intention of the people in the boat in front?'

'I don't think there is one,' Rodney assured her.

'Yes,' agreed Stan. 'But a woman went on board for a short time at Fools Nook, and again for about two hours last night. He seems to be on his own this morning.'

'You find that you are not the only boat shadowing them, and haven't tried to find out anything about them?' Lucinda just couldn't believe what she was hearing.

'Never occurred to us.' Rodney now realised that they ought to have put two and two together.

'Poor bloke's got a bad finger. He was looking in their boat when they shut the hatch on him.' Stan was anxious to tell all he knew. 'That's why I helped him yesterday.'

'I don't believe I'm hearing this,' Lucinda sighed. 'You even saw him snooping round their boat. Then you helped him because of his bad hand, and you got nothing out of him.'

'Sorry.' Rodney was feeling very inadequate.

'Sorry!' Lucinda shook her head. 'I was going to suggest that we just cruised on for the rest of the week. But with this joker in front, and the mysterious lady who calls each evening, perhaps we have got something to watch after all.'

'Perhaps you have,' agreed Rodney.

'If he follows them down the Red Bull flight, as I think he will, we are going to help this poor man, with his injured finger, in and out of the locks, all the way down. OK?'

'If you say so.' Rodney was not going to argue.

'Who is the best helmsman of you three?'

'George.' Stan jumped in straight away; the others agreed.

'Right. George, take the helm. You, Rodney and Stan, see to the locking. I'll go and chat to the man with the poorly finger.'

'But I'm the Field Service ...' Rodney was anxious about his status.

'Shut up Rodney,' she snapped. 'Anchors away!'

The crew jumped to her command.

He hadn't slept very well. The case seemed an absolute shambles. He got to the station early to see if there were any more developments, but there were none. Sergeant Tooth was, however, even more worried by mid-morning, with no reported sighting of *Turandot*. The operations room had nothing. Deep in thought, on his way back to his office, he saw WPC Nonelly, with another cup of tea.

'For me?' he enquired.

'This is for the Super,' she replied. 'But I'll get you one if you like.'

'No need. I've just had one. But get your skates on, you've got work to do.'

'Yes, Sarge. I'm off.'

He hadn't been long at his desk when PC Jones pushed his head around the door.

'Got 'em, Sarge,' he said eagerly. 'Sighted from the bridge at Hall Green.'

'Good lad. Well done. We've got 'em now.' Then he thought for a moment. 'Any news of May yet? I can't think where she's got to.'

'Not yet, Sarge. We're still making regular calls at her house.'

'Good lad.' Sergeant Tooth pulled out his map. 'The A34.

No, they may be past there by the time we arrive. No, let's say the A50.' He picked up the canal map. 'Yes, that's it. Bridge 135. Tell the local police to meet us on the canal there, midway between the Lawton and the Thurlwood locks. I'm getting to know a lot about the canal system, last week I didn't know it existed.' He smiled with obvious satisfaction. 'They won't be able to go anywhere then, will they? Good lad. Off you go.'

Still smiling and full of the joys of summer, he went upstairs to advise the Superintendent of progress. The Superintendent's door was slightly open, so instead of knocking, he pushed it wider and poked his head in. He said nothing, but his eyes widened.

The Superintendent and WPC Nonelly were in each other's arms, kissing passionately. WPC Nonelly's standard uniform skirt was pulled up to her waist, and the Superintendent had his hands on her bottom. She wasn't wearing standard issue black tights, but black stockings, suspenders and very tiny pink briefs He took it all in for nearly half a minute, as the Superintendent eased his hands inside her pink briefs, they were so engrossed they never noticed him. He quietly pulled the door to again but did not shut it.

So that was the way the wind blew. He realised now how slow he had been, when she had been so attentive to him, bringing him cups of tea regularly. And she had a very nice bottom too.

On opening the office door of Smith & Spindrift, May was confronted by the dumb blonde, Trixie, who gave a sickly smile.

'What name shall I say is calling?' she whimpered.

'Same as last time,' May snapped. She couldn't stand the insipid, dreaming look of the girl.

Trixie didn't pursue the formalities, but rang Les in the

inner office, who was feverishly busy, in a flurry of paper. David, Les's son, looked up, but gave no sign of recognition, but he knew only too well who May was.

'Mr Smith will see you now,' simpered the dumb blonde, ushering May into the inner sanctum.

'How do you stick her,' she said when the door was closed behind her. 'She gets right up my nose.'

'Oh, she's all right. How are things? OK? Did you get the bag?'

'No. I went over the whole damned boat from end to end, even looked in the engine housing. Didn't find a thing. Tonight I'm going to tackle them head on.'

'Be careful. You don't want to spoil everything. Forget it. Leave it be now. Enough is enough.'

'I will not. It cost Sam his life. I'll get it if it kills me.'

'You've got quite enough without that. Don't forget, Manchester Airport, ten a.m., Saturday. I'll be waiting.'

'I'm all packed, and have most of my other belongings in a lock-up garage. I can ship it out later.'

'Good girl. But be careful. Forty-eight hours, and we're both free.' He placed some papers in front of her. 'Just sign these for me will you. Just formalities.'

'What are these for? I thought I had signed everything to free the monies.'

'Power of Attorney, nothing to worry about. Just so I can move everything for you as we planned.' May signed where indicated, without reading the papers.

'David doesn't know anything?'

'He hasn't a clue,' Les assured her. 'Don't worry. It's all right.'

May left and went on to see her mother. She took Maude a bottle of whisky, and a large pack of cigarettes.

Ash dripped from Maude's cigarette, as she changed channels on the TV.

'Oh, a guilty conscience, eh?' she said, seeing the whisky

and cigarettes. 'Having neglected your poor old mum ... I can see through you like me glasses.'

'I'm going on holiday. I'll see you as soon as I get back.' May tried to be casual.

Maude sniffed. 'Oh yes! Think I was born yesterday. Where's Sam? Inside again? Or are you doin' a bank with him?' Maude switched channels again.

'Neither,' she lied. 'Is there anything I can do? Get you?'

'These programmes are bloody useless,' she said, puffing smoke into the air. 'You could get me a subscription for that *Red Hot Dutch* programme. Sounds good. Much better than this lot.'

'They don't allow you to have it here.'

'Typical! And it's supposed to be a free country.' She lit another cigarette. 'Fetch me a glass, and a small jug of water. I might as well taste your whisky.'

'I'm having some money paid into your account.'

'Oh yes.' She flicked channels again.

'On a regular basis.'

Maude looked at her. 'You have got a guilty conscience and no mistake.' She turned as if disinterested, and tasted her whisky. 'Not bad. But I prefer double malt. Remember next time. If there is a next time, of course.' She looked May in the eye. 'Are you doing a bunk, for good?'

May dropped her eyes. 'No. Of course not!'

'I thought so,' sighed Maude, turning away, and pouring another whisky. 'You never were any good at telling me lies!'

Through the stop lock, and into a quiet wooded glade, an embankment rising to our left. No one was coming up, or going down. Gradually the trees thinned out and we were on a small embankment leading up to the Pool Lock aqueduct, which carried us over the Trent & Mersey Canal, with which we were soon to merge. There was a lock beneath us, down to our left, and 200 yards beyond, a further lock. The first down from our present level. These were the first two locks of the Red Bull flight, down which we would soon be travelling. Instead of turning right through 90 degrees into the Trent & Mersey Canal, we actually turned left through three 90 degree turns, a total of 270 degrees, turning right back on ourselves, and allowing us, for one brief moment, to enter Staffordshire.

As soon as we were over the aqueduct we took our first left turn into a large basin, with large, smart boats moored bow to stern along the whole length. The waters, we noticed, were taking on an orangey, ochre hue. A quarter of a mile, and we took another sharp left turn, under a quaint stone bridge, and then turned sharp left again. We entered Harding Wood Junction and were now squarely on the Trent & Mersey Canal. The waters were now bright orange, emanating from the deposits washed from the Harecastle Tunnel, behind us. It was unlike anything we had encountered previously.

The Harecastle Tunnel, 1½ miles long, is truly something to be experienced. We had travelled through it some years ago, when Richard was a young boy. It was christened 'The Hair-raising Tunnel', which has stuck.

Immediately facing us we saw not one, but two huge locks, the first of the six watery steps comprising the Red Bull Flight. So much was the volume of traffic here, that these locks were all duplicated, but now only one of each pair is in operation.

Down the first two steps, and we were beneath the aqueduct which, but a few minutes ago, we were travelling over on our final stage of the Macclesfield Canal. Below the aqueduct the descent was magnificent as new and gentler vistas opened up before us. A low stone wall separated the towpath from fields sloping towards Lawton Wood, and the main A50 Road, running from Stoke-on-Trent across the Cheshire

Ring to Warrington, close by the start of our excursion into the past. Beech trees soothed our other flank.

A half-mile respite between the Red Bull and Church locks gave a pleasing prospect of pastures and woodlands as the countryside unfolded, affording a pleasing view of Lawton Church as we bordered Church Lawton. The two church locks were also duplicated, as was Hall's lock beyond. Then almost immediately on to the three Lawton Locks, which are, in fact, treble locks. It seems that Thomas Telford designed this flight, replacing a staircase which Brindley had built, but which proved to be time-consuming and wasted far too much valuable water.

We had now dropped 111 feet and 5 inches since breakfast, and now luncheon beckoned. The canal bordered the pretty little village of Rode Heath, and here we found the Broughton Arms. As well as car parking spaces, this pub also has moorings all the way along its canal frontage. These, alas, were full, but thoughtfully, adjacent to the pub is a bridge over the waterway, so that mooring on the towpath side meant only a short walk over the bridge to our well-earned lunch, which we took in the open air at the rear overlooking the canal under a canopy of creepers.

We dallied a little afterwards for some shopping, for necessities and a few presents. On the canal one is never really far from anywhere. Its tempo of life is slow and measured. There is no rushing, for one simply can't rush, there is nothing to rush for. A feeling of freedom and tranquillity engulf the most cynical of us. We didn't rush back to complete our journey. There simply wasn't any need.

'I say, can we help?' Lucinda smiled kindly at Ern. 'We're just behind, and there are four of us, so we can give you a hand with the locks.'

Ern looked round, and saw *Turandot* behind him with

Rodney grinning benignly. 'Oh, yeah, you want to pinch my water and get in front again, do you?'

'Not at all. I wouldn't dream of letting them barge in front of you.'

'They did yesterday.'

'Did they? I'm sorry about that, but it won't happen again, I can assure you. We're going down the Red Bull, or are you going through the Harecastle Tunnel?'

'Down the locks. But it does take me a time on my own. So I wouldn't mind some help.' He realised that he was going to get it anyway, for Stan already had the lock open for him. He eased his way in. Stan closed the gate behind him, whilst Rodney opened the paddles in front.

'Oh dear, you've got a poorly finger as well.' Lucinda climbed onto the gunwale of *Hyacinth*, as it sank in the water.

'Yeah. Clumsy bloke shut it in a hatch. Don't think it's broken, but it is a bit painful.'

'Can I help?' she enquired.

'No. I'm all right,' he replied, overwhelmed by all the attention of this attractive young lady, and the surprising offer of assistance. For no one ever seemed to help him. He was usually left on his own.

'Follow on,' she shouted to Rodney as she stepped fully on board.

'I might as well stay with you. We're going down the locks, and as the lads are operating them for us they might just as well do it for you also.'

'Can't pay you!' Ern was defensive. This offer of help was too much.

Lucinda laughed. 'We don't want paying. I just thought we could help you, as we are going the same way. And you do have an injured hand.'

'It would certainly be a help,' Ern admitted.

'Another thing,' Lucinda laughed. 'We're just behind

you, and we'd have a long wait if we left you to operate the locks on your own.'

'You're not daft, are you?' Ern grinned.

'I hope not.' She knew now that she had got him.

All the time, she was careful to have *Colette* within her sights ahead. And Jo wouldn't suspect her being aboard this boat. Not, she was quite sure, that there was any real point in following them anyway, but Rodney insisted that he had his orders. He would carry them out to the letter, or die in the attempt. So much for his military upbringing, she thought.

Turandot was now bearing down on them, and they travelled in tandem. They reached Hardings Wood Junction in time to see Richard letting *Colette* out, whilst Jo was already on the lock ahead. Rodney and Stan went to the lock after Richard had gone. They were not going to mingle with him, but keep a safe distance.

Lucinda had been talking about boats, the weather, the scenery, and the orangey ochre colour of the water. In fact, everything but the questions she was intending to ask. When she considered she had sufficiently gained Ern's confidence, she started to include the odd question, getting gradually nearer the bone.

Ern, however, had been well schooled by May, and was going to follow her instructions to the letter. Otherwise she would kill him. Not that she wouldn't kill him anyway.

He had picked up the boat at Macclesfield for a friend, who had been holidaying with his wife, but was taken ill and rushed to hospital. His friend's wife was desperate, and as he had a week's holiday himself, he had offered to take it back to its moorings for them.

'How is your friend now?' Lucinda enquired sympathetically.

'Getting on all right now. Had a heart attack. Been poorly though.'

'You've heard from his wife?'

'Oh yes. She visits me regularly. Most nights in fact. Brings me groceries and things, as well as lets me know how he is.'

'You're going to see her tonight?'

'Yes, I'm going as far as Ettiley Heath tonight. She's going to stop off there to see that I'm getting on all right, and tell me how he is.'

'That's nice.'

'She came last night to Hall Green. Oakgrove Tuesday. She's very good, devoted to him. I've told her not to worry about me, but she's like that, insists, as I'm helping her, like.'

He had got it all off pat. Been practising it regularly, just in case. He didn't falter once, and was proud of the few extra pieces he had added himself.

'What do you do?' enquired Lucinda. 'I'm in PR.'

'What's that?' enquired Ern trying to avoid the question.

'Public relations. I publicise pop stars, baked beans, politicians. You name it, I do it.'

'I wouldn't know how to do that.'

'I say, would you mind awfully if I went to spend a penny?'

'Er, no I … er … mean yes, feel free.'

He didn't want her to go below, but felt that he had to oblige. It worried him, and he sincerely hoped she would not go anywhere near Sam. Although she would have to go through his cabin. But he couldn't leave her in that predicament, could he? No reason why she should find Sam.

Lucinda went below, found the toilet and noisily shut the door, but didn't go in. Instead she went quickly, and thoroughly, all over the boat. Not much food. Plenty of empty cans, a few clothes of both sexes, but little else. Nothing untoward in any way. All very innocent. It fitted in fully with his story.

She went back and opened the toilet door quietly, and

245

went inside. It contained a shower, wash basin, WC and toiletries and cleaning items. Nothing else. So she spent her penny, flushed the toilet and washed her hands. She shut the door noisily again and went up on the stern deck.

'OK?' he enquired.

'Yes, thanks. Nice boat.'

'Yeah. Wouldn't mind it myself if I could afford it.'

'What do you do?' she enquired again.

'Me? Engineering. Make springs,' he replied with confidence. He'd had time to think up a proper answer. He couldn't say that he was recently out of the nick, and the way things were going, was likely to be back there soon.

Rodney opened the gates of the bottom lock of the Red Bull Flight. *Hyacinth* moved off, turning right through Church Lawton for the church locks half a mile ahead. The descent with the lads working the locks had gone well, and *Turandot* was always behind. They had lost *Colette* momentarily round the bend, but there wasn't much between them.

As they emerged from the bridge under the A50 in Church Lawton, Ern noticed half a dozen policemen, some in plain clothes. They took no notice of him, and he didn't look in their direction. Lucinda surveyed them, though.

'Wonder what they are doing?' she enquired.

'Looking for drugs, I expect.' That at least was nothing to do with him. He spoke confidently, but was anything but confident.

Lucinda thought it was nothing to do with them, but did just wonder if they might have some news for Rodney. But they would not have come in those numbers just to pass on information, so she thought no more about them.

When they got to the first church lock, there was no *Turandot* behind them.

'Well, they've not got here yet.' Lucinda was now beginning to think that the police had been waiting to see

Rodney after all. 'I'll just open the lock. I'm sure they will be along in a minute.'

But no one came. She saw *Hyacinth* into the lock, opened the lower paddles for Ern, and as he sank in the lock she pushed the windlass on board.

'I'd better go and see if they've got lost.' With that she trotted off briskly, back along the towpath.

What have they got to do with the police? Ern pondered. He must work this out carefully, and get well out of their way. He still had *Colette* in his sights ahead, and he worked like a Trojan, rushing in and out of locks, often with the mooring ropes in his hands as he pulled the boat in, and towed it out. Twice he managed to do a change-over with a boat coming up, and twice he sailed out of locks, leaving the lower gates open and their paddles up. He didn't care. He just wanted to put as much distance between him and the police as he could.

'Oh sod it!' he said aloud, when he realised, after slipping under bridge 139, that *Colette* was moored just beyond it, and the occupants were in the pub.

For three days on the trot, he had managed to get ahead of the party he was supposed to be following. He didn't care if May did kill him. Let her! It would be a relief after all this. He would just keep on going now and stop in the basin at Wheelock.

'Sod 'em all!'

Rodney and Stan jumped aboard as they closed the bottom lock of the Red Bull Flight, and were enjoying the scenery when, ahead of them, they saw a group of men, including some policemen.

'Oh hell,' Rodney said with feeling, as he recognised Sergeant Tooth, who had a grin on his face and was politely signalling them in to the towpath, which they obediently did.

'Tie her up,' Sergeant Tooth ordered.

When this was done he, PC Jones and WPC Nonelly, with three plain-clothes men from the local force, went aboard.

'Let's go inside,' he said, indicating the saloon.

'Now then,' he said quietly, leaning back on the comfortable settee. 'We've found another body in a boat moored on the canal. Well, rather sitting on the bottom of the canal. Just near where you were moored three nights ago.' He looked round the group and saw sheer panic in their eyes. 'Now,' he said firmly, 'what exactly has it got to do with you?'

'Er … nothing,' stammered Rodney. 'We don't know anything about a body.'

'Don't give me all that nonsense again,' Sergeant Tooth snapped irritably. 'I've had enough of that.'

'No, really.'

'There has been trouble from you lot ever since Saturday night. We found you' – looking at Stan – 'loitering near a body at Thelwall.'

'There wasn't one,' stammered Stan.

'No. Because it was moved, wasn't it? We found it again, you will remember. Again near you, at High Lane.'

'Hello,' smiled Lucinda, appearing in the doorway of the saloon, somewhat out of breath, as she had run flat out all the way. She intended to miss as little as possible.

'This is Lucinda, Sergeant. She joined us yesterday.'

'Is she one of you lot?' One could hear the contempt in his voice. 'I haven't seen any woman aboard previously.'

'Oh no,' said Rodney. 'She's a friend. Just a friend.'

'You don't know what you've joined, miss.'

'Ms,' corrected Lucinda.

Sergeant Tooth glowered at her. He had thought she was, quite nice, but was rapidly changing his mind. Women were Miss or Mrs, none of this feminist Ms stuff for him. He took a deep breath.

'On Tuesday after you had gone, we found a second body in a boat, moored near where you were at High Lane. Or rather, sunk! Sitting on the canal floor. Both bodies have been identified, and both were involved in the bank raid in Wilmslow last Saturday.'

'Two bodies?' enquired Rodney with surprise.

'Yes, sir. Two bodies,' confirmed Sergeant Tooth.

'They are nothing to do with us, Sergeant. Nothing at all.' Rodney was so wound up he was expecting to be charged with murder at any moment.

'Look. You tell me a cock and bull story about following a boatload of drug traffickers, two hidden in the boat, never seeing the light of day. When I know full well that there are only four, not six, holidaymakers – parents with their son and daughter-in-law. And I've told you they are only holidaying.'

'Quite right,' agreed Lucinda. 'I told you, Rodney, it was all bollocks.'

Sergeant Tooth really was going off this young woman as well. 'Oh, and how, pray, do you know, young lady? And I must say I don't think much of your language,' reprimanded Sergeant Tooth.

'Sorry Sergeant,' Lucinda apologised. WPC Nonelly sniggered, and Sergeant Tooth noticed. 'I made friends with Jo and Richard last night. She took me all over their boat this morning.'

'I see.' Sergeant Tooth was interested. 'So you agree with me, that they are certainly not following drug smugglers. So what are they doing?'

'We were following them.' Rodney was emphatic. 'We've been ordered to.'

'Don't give me that load of crap,' Sergeant Tooth roared. 'If your bloody lot order you to stick your head in a gas oven you do it, do you?'

'Language, Sarge,' cut in WPC Nonelly cockily.

249

'Will you shut up when I am speaking?' After all it was of course all right for him, a man, to swear. But ladies didn't swear. He may be old-fashioned, but he was proud of being correct.

He took two deep breaths and cooled down. 'Your story about the people you are following is sheer rubbish.'

'Agreed,' emphasised Lucinda. Sergeant Tooth looked at her.

'But there are two deaths around you, of people involved in a bank raid. Coincidence? Now! And I don't want any more stupid answers. What have you got to do with the bank raid, what do you know of the deaths of the known people involved? And what is more to the point, where is the mysterious third person that took part in the raid? Was it one of you?'

He looked them each in the eye, and they turned to jelly. Pathetic, he thought. The crooks he usually interviewed had more backbone than this lot.

'Nothing at all,' pleaded Rodney. 'It's all news to me. We are simply doing as we were instructed. Following that boat, which we were led to believe contained drug smugglers.'

'I just can't believe what I am hearing. You are grown men, for Christ's sake!'

'I'm afraid they are right,' interrupted Lucinda. 'The whole thing is quite mad, but they really are following that boat load of holidaymakers.'

'How can you be so sure, madam?'

'I've known Rodney for years. He's a prat and he knows it, but he's dead straight. Couldn't lie to save his life. Poor thing.'

'Why should I believe you?' he asked, but for some reason, and it wasn't just because she was attractive, he did.

'It's the truth.'

'What about that boat you've been sussing out?' George enquired of Lucinda, regarding her recent mission.

250

'What's that?' enquired Sergeant Tooth. 'Another boat?'

'There's nothing there.' Lucinda shook her head. *Hyacinth* is the name of the boat.'

'Make a note of that, Nonelly.'

'Yes, Sarge.'

'It was moored between us and the holidaymakers last night and also, apparently, on Tuesday night at Oakgrove. Seemed a coincidence. So I sussed it out. Looked as if we were both following a boat load of tourists for no apparent reason.'

'Go on.'

'Well, I've been on board this morning. The man collected the boat from Macclesfield for a friend, who was taken ill suddenly, when on holiday with his wife. He is taking it back to their moorings for them. She meets him each evening when on her way back from hospital. Takes him food.'

'What's the matter with the husband?'

'Heart attack.'

'Sam had a heart attack,' interrupted WPC Nonelly.

'I know that.'

'Sam?' enquired Lucinda.

'Someone we know.' Sergeant Tooth was giving nothing away. 'Is he meeting her tonight? If so, where?'

'Ettiley Heath.'

'Check on the ownership of the boat. We'd better pay them a visit at Ettiley Heath tonight.'

'Why tonight, Sarge?' WPC Nonelly had a date.

'Because if there are two boats. I'd rather have them both, than just one.'

'He's not involved in anything.' Lucinda was definite.

'How, pray, do you know that?' Sergeant Tooth was getting a little irritated with everyone interrupting.

'I made an excuse to go to the loo, and went all over his boat as well. Nothing there except clothes.'

'You seem to have been very thorough,' said Sergeant Tooth.

'Thank you,' beamed Lucinda.

'But do you realise that in so doing you have committed a felony? The man on the boat could have you charged.'

'Charged? Why?' She jumped with surprise at the suggestion.

'Caught in the act, thieving.'

'I didn't steal anything.'

'Intent to steal. You opened doors, breaking and entering. Loitering with intent to steal. Gaining entrance by deception. False pretences. And a string of other charges I haven't thought of yet.'

'You wouldn't,' said Rodney.

'Wouldn't I?'

'You mean I'm a suspect now?' For the first time Lucinda was visibly shaken. 'I only told him I was in PR, when I actually deal in antiques.'

'Well, that's enough to charge you with for a start,' Sergeant Tooth had his tongue in his cheek.

'You're not actually going to?' pleaded Rodney. 'She only did it to help me, to prove that I was on the wrong tack.'

'Lad, you lot have been on the wrong tack from the start. OK.' He stood up. 'You can go now, but I want you to ring in with your map reference tonight, eight p.m. without fail, and eight a.m. tomorrow morning. Got that?'

'Yes, Sergeant.' Rodney was relieved.

'You, miss.' To Lucinda. 'Will you give your full name and address, and stay on this boat with the others?'

'Yes, Sergeant.'

'I shall also want to see some form of identification. Driving licence will do.'

'Oh, well, that's difficult.' She explained her story to Sergeant Tooth, who threw up his hands in complete surrender.

18

Suitably refreshed we continued with the two Thurlwood locks; both were duplicated. But owing to subsidence in the 1950s, one of the first locks was replaced by a guillotine lock. In theory boats entered a steel tank, which raised or lowered them appropriately. However the operation took longer, and boat users were dubious of it, so it became little used, and was demolished in 1987. I remember studying it carefully with Richard all those years ago.

A brief respite as we sailed quietly down a gentle valley bordered by open country and woodland. Reaching the twin Pierpoint locks, and on to the little hamlet of Hassell Green with two more. Then almost immediately into the Wheelock flight of another eight.

Richard and Jo worked valiantly at the locks, and by now were feeling the strain a little. I didn't help, by moving out of a lock too early instead of staying where I was, to allow an easy change-over with a boat going up. I should have waited for Richard's signal, but thought I knew better, and didn't. I recalled the wretched man among the bulrushes at the bottom of the Bosley flight.

It was hard work in the heat and we were getting to the bottom of what is known among boating people as Heart-break Hill. From Hardings Wood Junction we had dropped 242 feet 7 inches. Well named, Heartbreak Hill.

Wheelock, now a suburb of Sandbach, was well-known as the lorry building town. ERF and Foden are both here. Old warehouses line the canal, at the heart a wide open British Waterways wharf.

We pulled in, put out all the rubbish, and went in search of a newspaper. Just in case anything was happening in the world outside. The main Crewe–Sandbach–Congleton road runs right through this busy little town, which we negotiated safely, before making our way back to our floating home.

Richard and Jo now had a hard-earned rest in the cockpit, with another can of lager and their feet up. Richard was in good form, singing again, as we moved into very different country. For this is the domain of the salt works. The flat Cheshire plain.

We started to keep our eyes open for a pleasant, quiet site for our night's lodging. Through Ettiley Heath, past the motor works, and rounding a slight bend we found a pleasant, quiet, open stretch of water. Opposite were green fields, whilst from the towpath the ground dropped to rough scrubland with a small lake. Ideal. There was no other traffic about, and only one other moored craft, and that was a quarter of a mile ahead of us. It was nearly seven in the evening when we finally moored. Ten hours to travel 10 miles, with 27 locks, including the stop lock.

We got rid of the dust and sweat of the day. Duly replenished after a shower and change we sat down to a good meal, complemented by two tasteful bottles of a delicate Rhone wine. The only thing to spoil the peace of the setting was the darned Olympics yet again.

The telephone rang. 'May. That you? Ern here!'

There was a delay as May switched from the answering machine. 'Hang on, Ern. While it says its piece ... OK, go on.'

'There were police on the canal this morning. Bottom of the Red Bull. They didn't look at me, but pulled in the boat that was behind us last night.'

'Hell,' sighed May. 'That's all we need.'

'I haven't seen them, or the boat, since. But I did hear them talking about Ettiley Heath. So I've come well past that. The lot we want have got beyond Sandbach station. I know where they are. Nice quiet spot, with no one else about. Ideal for what you want. There is only one other boat in the vicinity, and that's at least a quarter of a mile away.'

'Where are you?'

'I thought it best to get well ahead, out of the way of both of them. I'm at Stud Green, just below the next lock, under bridge 162. I'll wait for you on the road to Marston Green. Bridge 161.'

'I've got that. You all right?'

'Sure.'

'Good. I'll see you there about nine o'clock.'

'See you.'

Ern sighed. A deep sigh of relief. She hadn't bawled him out. Even seemed to be concerned about him. Perhaps tonight, when they had got the cash, they would make it. He was certainly going to remember that!

After the long police interview, Rodney was very subdued. Another cock-up like this, and he would be up before his superiors. He prayed Sergeant Tooth would not be in touch with them again.

They had had no stop whatsoever since the police visit, and ate sandwiches on the hoof. At Ettiley Heath there was no sign of either boat. Rodney ordered Stan to run on ahead from that point, so that they did not come upon either *Colette* or *Hyacinth* without warning. Lucinda protested on Stan's behalf. Stan had done all the locking with Rodney. She suggested George for the job. He scowled, but went.

Just beyond Sandbach station he spotted *Colette*, signalled the boat on, and it moored just around the corner, out of sight. Rodney went out to make sure for himself.

'Look beyond. That will be *Hyacinth*. I'm sure it is. We'll be able to tell the police exactly where they are.'

Rodney returned with a revived smile of confidence. The police would be very pleased with his diligence and help.

Before settling down for the night, Margery joined me for a stroll ahead along the towpath. Swallows were flying low over the water. The air was still, and the cirrus clouds were high.

The boat ahead had a huge German Shepherd dog on a lead, tied to the boat. The lead was a long one, so long, in fact, that it trailed across the towpath. The dog lay on the grass on the far side from the boat. I looked carefully at it as we passed.

'I don't like that!' I said, looking at the lead across the towpath.

Margery didn't say anything. I expect she thought it was just me whingeing again.

At the end of the straight was a small canal bridge, and leading up to it, on the opposite bank, were a number of boats in various stages of fitting out, some complete, one little more than the hull with windows. We walked up to the bridge, and just behind it found a lock down into an attractive little pound, with another bridge at the end of it.

On the opposite bank, right up to the canal, was an elegant, mature house, with a well-maintained garden, complete with its own stone landing stage. Moored at it was a magnificent new narrowboat, with attractively shaped windows. This was a Rolls-Royce of the canal. Very upmarket, looking extremely fine in all-over navy blue livery, complete with its own crest upon the side of the cabin.

'Now I wouldn't mind that!' my eyes bulged.

'Nor would Richard,' Margery added.

We turned and walked back to our home for the night, as dusk started to fall. We were careful to avoid the lead trailing across the towpath.

May arrived ready for work, putting on her black woolly hat and gloves.

'Where are your gloves?' she enquired.

'Haven't got any.'

She went back into her car, giving Ern a black jumper, woolly hat and gloves. 'Sam's,' she said, as she picked up two 2 foot metal rods. 'One for you, and one for me.'

'We aren't going to use them?' They frightened Ern.

'Not unless we have to.'

'The other boat is well this side of them. It won't be any trouble.'

'Better not.'

She set off along the towpath.

Rodney met Sergeant Tooth at Ettiley Heath.

'They're some way up. Just beyond the station.'

'Then why on earth did we start from here?' Sergeant Tooth looked back from where they had come.

'It's not too far really.' Rodney lied. He could have changed the meeting place, but he hadn't thought of it. 'It is just around the corner from us.'

'*Hyacinth*?'

'No, *Colette. Hyacinth* is further on still.'

'Been quicker to have walked from Manchester.' Sergeant Tooth hadn't much confidence in Rodney, who was so eager to help.

'Who's in it?'

'*Hyacinth*?'

'Of course *Hyacinth*. I'm not interested in the other one.'

'I haven't had a chance to see.'

'Marvellous!' Sergeant Tooth sighed loudly. 'I'd like to

know who's on it. It's May's boat, but I can't see her being involved in anything like this.'

'You never know what people will get up to,' interjected WPC Nonelly.

'No, you don't.' He looked at her pointedly. 'But I know May. Her old man was a rogue, but she's a nice girl, straight as a die. Now come on. How much further?'

'Quite a bit to our boat. And *Hyacinth* is nearly half a mile ahead of us.'

'Struth!'

It was now getting quite dark. May and Ern walked silently along the towpath. They came upon the first boat, all lit up, and in the distance there were the lights of another boat.

'Not this one,' whispered Ern. 'The one ahead.'

'Good. That is far enough away. Let's try and get by without making a sound.'

They hadn't seen the German Shepherd, but there were two green eyes watching their every move. They walked on tiptoe, without a sound on the gravel. They were level with the rear of the cabin. Ern stumbled. His foot caught in the dog's lead, and he went headlong along the ground. The jerk of the lead pulled on the dog's collar, causing it to spring into action. It started to bark loudly.

A voice from inside the cabin yelled, 'Shut up!'

But the German Shepherd was aroused. It was being attacked on its own territory, and that was unforgivable. Ern got to his feet, but in so doing caught the lead again with his foot, causing another pull on the dog's collar. That was it. The German Shepherd snarled and pounced, burying his teeth into the crotch of Ern's trousers.

'He's got me! The bugger's got me!' he yelled in agony, at the top of his voice.

'Keep quiet,' whispered May. 'Where's he got you?'

'By the privates,' yelled Ern. 'Help! It's murdering me!'

A bearded man appeared on the stern of the deck of the boat. 'Hey! What the hell are you doing to my Colin?'

'I'm dying!' shrieked Ern.

'Come on. Good boy. Come to Daddy,' coaxed the bearded one, but the dog took no notice of him.

May could just see the dog in what little moonlight there was. Taking careful aim, she brought her metal rod crashing down on the dog's head. It yelped with pain, let go of Ern, whimpered and moved away.

'What have you done to my dog? Poor Colin. I'll get the police on to you,' roared the bearded one, who had now been joined by his wife.

Before the dog could recoup itself, May pulled Ern away, back in the direction from which they had come. He was doubled up in agony. She grabbed his right arm, and pulled it over her right shoulder, holding it tight with her right hand.

Ern screamed at being straightened up, but it was the only way May could move him. She took no notice of his pleas. Her left arm went around his waist and she dragged him back to the car. Ern held his crotch with his left hand. Behind them the dog barked furiously, whilst the man on the boat continued to shout abuse.

Eventually they reached the car, by which time the barking and abuse had ceased, and peace descended again. May lifted his left hand away, and saw it was bloody, as was the front of his trousers. She opened his zip, and took one brief look.

'I'm taking you to hospital. You'll have to be cleaned up, and given a tetanus jab at the least.'

She took off the black jumper she had given him, hat and gloves.

'I'm dying,' moaned Ern.

She took off her own work clothes. 'No you're not.'

She pushed the jumpers on the seat under him, to try

and prevent blood getting on the car seats, fastened his safety belt and sped off into the night.

When Rodney and Sergeant Tooth eventually reached *Turandot*, Lucinda decided to join them. Reaching *Colette*, they walked quietly, without speaking. No more than footfalls on the gravel. The occupants took no notice.

'This is it.' Rodney indicated the boat in front of *Colette*.

'You sure?' questioned Lucinda. 'Doesn't look quite the same to me.'

'Quite sure.' Rodney was emphatic.

'There were no lights on this boat before. Now it's lit up like a Christmas tree.' Lucinda was still doubtful.

Two green eyes watched them quietly from the grass verge.

Sergeant Tooth gave orders to surround the boat fore and aft, truncheons at the ready. He stepped aboard, tapped the cabin roof.

'Police,' he called.

Then one of the officers inadvertently caught his foot on the German Shepherd dog's lead, pulling his collar. He stumbled and righted himself, but by then all hell had broken loose again. WPC Nonelly was wearing trousers, and the brute also took a fancy to her pretty bottom, giving it a nip which caused her to yell, and hanging on to her trouser leg. PC Jones hit it with his truncheon.

The irate bearded boatman stepped out again on to the stern deck, followed by his wife.

'What the hell are you doing to my poor dog?'

'It's what your dog is doing to my officers. Get it under control immediately, or it will be put down, and you will be charged with assault.'

'Come on, Colin. There's a good boy.'

The bearded man collected his bruised dog, which was now whimpering again, and locked it in an inner cabin.

'That's not him, and this is not *Hyacinth*.' Lucinda said quietly.

'No. This is *Mallard*,' said the lady of the boat proudly.

'This true?' Sergeant Tooth shouted aggressively at Rodney.

'Yes, Sergeant. I'm afraid it is.'

Sergeant Tooth was livid. He got over his difficulties with the boat owner by pointing out that he might be charged with the assault of WPC Nonelly, who was actually only shaken. He would also be charged with failing to keep a dangerous dog under proper control.

Lucinda checked the WPC's pretty bottom, which had a pinch mark, but the dog had not drawn blood.

''Tis *Mallard*, Sarge. Its name is on the side.' PC Spriggs had it illuminated with his torch.

Sergeant Tooth gave Rodney the dressing-down of his life for wasting police time. He threatened to arrest him over the two bodies at High Lane.

'Are you sure *Hyacinth* is still ahead of you?'

'We haven't passed it, Sergeant. I can assure you of that.' Lucinda was emphatic.

'Right. Jones and Spriggs, I want you to follow on up the canal and check every boat you find, but don't disturb them in any way. I'll meet you, wherever possible, at each bridge, but we've got a hell of a walk back to the car. Thanks to him.' He indicated Rodney, as though he was a lump of dirt he had wiped off his boot. 'I'm sorry, lads. It's late I know, but I want that boat found, and soon. It can't be too far ahead now. It couldn't have got much farther in the time.'

'Yes, Sarge.'

'I want that boat tonight. Keep in touch by phone. We can't afford to let it get a chance to move again come daylight.'

'Can I help?' enquired Rodney, eager to make amends.

261

'Not bloody likely. I want it done properly.' With that he turned on his heel, and was gone.

'Rodney. You know you really are a prat,' sighed Lucinda. 'This isn't the job for you.' He looked drained. 'Come home with me, and I'll find you a proper job.'

Ern's injuries were messy, but thankfully not serious. However, he put up a creditable performance of sheer agony. He was playing hard for May's sympathy, but didn't get any. He was treated in Casualty, and discharged.

'I'm taking you home now, for a rest,' announced May.

He thought she meant her home, but she made it quite clear she didn't.

'They will have the boat marked by now I expect. So I'm just going to leave it be, and let them find it.'

After dropping Ern off at his small terraced house, without even one word of comfort, she went on to see Les.

'I've got one more chance tomorrow, and if I don't make that, I'll just have to leave it be. Much as I'm loath to let them keep it.'

'I should forget it. Saturday, remember!'

'Yes.'

Les seemed somehow on edge. There was something strange about him, almost as though he wanted to be rid of her. But she was tired too, after the evening excitement, and wasn't keen on dallying anyway. All the time in the world for that, soon enough.

She parked her car around the corner, but as always, in a different place. May wasn't going to let anything slip now. She entered her home from the rear. She could have no lights on, but she could have the TV on quietly upstairs, as long as there was not too much of a flicker visible from outside. It soon lulled her to sleep.

*

'Sergeant Tooth.' He pulled out his phone, before even reaching his car.

'PC Jones here, Sarge. We're at Stud Green. It's here all right. All locked up and no one about.'

'Well done, lads. I'll be there in a few minutes. I'll get the local boys to put up surveillance on it, and then we can go home.'

'I won't be able to sit on a car seat,' moaned WPC Nonelly, who was worried about her pretty bottom.

'You'll have to lie across the back seat and rest it.' He wondered what the Super would think of her pinched bottom. But there were more urgent things to think about than WPC Nonelly's pretty bottom.

'I wonder where on earth May is? She's not at home, nor on the boat. Her husband is dead, and she poor girl doesn't even know yet ... poor May.'

The telephone on the bedside table rang with a shrill urgency. A sleepy hand stretched towards it, and fumbled clumsily for the receiver. Eventually it was lifted.

'Yeah.' The voice was still very sleepy.

'Listen, don't say anything.' She couldn't anyway, and almost dropped off again.

'Emergency. Got that?'

'Yeah.' Something was now beginning to penetrate.

'Plans revised.' He was obviously worried. 'Must now go urgently! Urgently!' She was awake now.

'Meet me at the same place, but now five a.m. tomorrow morning! Got it?'

'Hell! Why?'

'Got it? Five a.m. tomorrow, Friday. Same place.'

The phone went dead.

19

There were boats about early, two travelling towards Wheelock, before I contemplated getting out of bed. The wash from their craft caused us to rise and fall on our moorings. When they had passed, stillness descended, and I dozed off again.

When I did eventually rise the sun was well up, and it proved to be another warm bright day. I stepped out into the cockpit, and took in the scene through all my senses. This was Friday, our last full day. Why go on? I thought. Why not stay here for a few days, sit down and let it all wash over us?

I sat down. The boat ahead was preparing to move off. I watched it go. I hope that they have taken that darned dog, I thought. It had barked twice late last night, but other than that, our night on this stretch of canal had been quiet, peaceful and uneventful. I wondered if anything ever happened here. Probably not.

We didn't rush over breakfast. I think we all felt the same: our last day, so why hurry? Yesterday had been a hard day, but six hours' boating would take us to our proposed overnight destination. There were four locks leading up to Middlewich, and another five around town. Nothing compared with what we were used to, and Richard and Jo were by now expert at locking. These were, in fact, the last locks we were to encounter.

At 10.45, a whole hour later than yesterday, we slipped our moorings, and continued our adventure into the unknown. I pointed out the boats which were being fitted out to Richard, who gave them more admiring glances. Under the bridge, and through the lock. Still moored outside the house on the far bank lay the beautiful narrow-boat Margery and I admired the previous evening.

'I wouldn't mind that,' said Richard enviously as he jumped back on board after the lock, and we slowly edged past it. He took it all in.

'If my numbers ever come up on the lottery, that's mine.'

As we cleared the bridge at Stud Green, we were aware of two young men in short-sleeved shirts, looking down upon us. Watching us. Moored just beyond was a boat that I thought I might have seen before, *Hyacinth.* But perhaps not. It seemed all shut up, anyway.

There was a turning point to our right, whilst we veered the other way to find a lock facing us. A huge chemical works flanked our right. Another lock came quickly, and then a relatively long stretch before the fourth. We were running along an almost straight corridor, with factories on our right, the towpath and road on the left, as we moved towards the centre of Middlewich.

The town was founded on salt, and there is still much evidence of its importance. We passed the Bisto Kids sculpture, a salt works, and stopped just after the fourth, rumps lock for Richard to nip across the road for a newspaper. Now a sanitary ware factory, huge salt lagoons. Pipes crossed the canal overhead.

We stopped just before the first lock around the town. Beyond the towpath was a large grass verge. We chatted together in the shade of some trees, before taking a look at a little shop full of canal memorabilia.

A sudden gust of wind took a grip of Jo's baseball cap and, whipping it off her head, sent it rolling across the grass, hither and thither. Richard ran for it, and virtually had his hand upon it, when another gust took it rolling off again, this time towards the canal. It stopped, but before anyone could reach it, yet another gust whipped it again into the air, and, unceremoniously, deposited it well into the canal.

It was certainly out of reach, but Richard was soon hanging over the side of *Colette* with the boat pole. He lifted it twice, but it fell back into the water. With a third last heave, he brought it, soaking wet, safely on board.

On board again after our brief shopping spree, we moved through the first lock, passing the Shropshire Union Canal junction to our left.

Then we were in the thick of it. There were boats everywhere. Queues for the locks going down, as we were, and seemingly, queues for those coming up. Never being ones to join the rat race, we moored and had our lunch, waiting until the mayhem had subsided.

Nosing around the boatyard, I learned the reason for the absolute pandemonium. There was to be, this coming weekend, a boaters' convention at the other end of town. The end we were going towards. Seemingly it is rather like a caravan rally, only with the caravans on water. The thought was terrifying!

After an hour and a half, as the caravaners went for their lunch, we found our chance and dived in, following one boat ahead of us. This meant that we, for the next three locks, had to wait whilst the locks filled again before we could enter, and these were truly deep locks.

At the first lock, I, and later Jo, was regaled by an old man who sat on the lower arm and helped a little, very little, to open the gate, with horrid stories of how he had met the Black Panther, who kept victims prisoner in the air vents above Harecastle Tunnel. He had every gruesome detail. To this day he is probably still terrifying everyone going through the lock with his gruesome story.

Leaving the lock, we had a T-junction before us, to the

left of our next lock down, while to the right was the dry dock, once home to Seddon's salt-carrying fleet. The importance of the canal to the town in the nineteenth century, for the export of its salt, was only too evident.

One more lock and we hit the Jamboree. There were boats of every size and description, everywhere. They were on both sides of the canal. A good job for us that it was a wide stretch. Pubs seemed to abound, and there was hardly a square inch on land which was not occupied by people. What was the attraction, I wondered, of having a boat of one's own, and herding together like this with other boat owners in a jam-packed mass? To me, the joy of the canal is getting away from everyone. But then it is possible that I am simply antisocial.

Passing one boat, I noticed a lady whom I recognised. She was taking down a pair of brief red knickers with black lace edging from her clothes line. She smiled and waved. Richard grinned, and pointed her out to Jo, who grinned widely. They waved back furiously, which greatly pleased Rose. Now I could see why she was here. Trade would, no doubt, be brisk. If that is the correct expression.

One more lock, the last of our week. Beside a pub, most aptly named the Big Lock, was a huge lock. It is known as the Big Lock as it is twice the width of a normal lock, although only a 5 foot drop.

It seems that, when the building of this canal started, it was intended that it should carry wide-beam craft from Preston Brook to Middlewich. They started building for the wide-beam craft, but found that the tunnels at Preston Brook were only built for narrowboats. So this wide lock stands as a lasting memorial to the canal builders of old who got it wrong, and made a monumental, but fascinating, blunder.

Once through the lock, boats and people quickly faded away and we once again, had the freedom of the cut. Wide open farmland greeted us on either side. Beautiful, gentle country, as we followed the course of the River Dane.

There are, on this stretch, three wide areas of water bordering the canal. Quiet lagoons, that it would be fun to sail into, and while away an afternoon. But warning signs instruct boat users to stay in the channel, and certainly not venture into these beautiful lakes, which came about through subsidence. Whilst there is no likelihood of further subsidence, in the 1950s these areas were used by British Waterways to sink, in watery graves, boats that they no longer required. What a waste. fifty years later people would have given their eye teeth for them.

We found here a heron, who became attached to us. It would perch on a tree stump or fence post ahead of us as we approached. Just before reaching it, it would fly off and settle on another stump, some distance ahead of us. It played with us for miles, but around the outskirts of Higher Shurlach we eventually lost it.

Poor Rodney was in a state of complete shock and in-decision. He was blindly following *Colette* at a safe distance, but realised now that there really was no point. Lucinda, whom he fancied, and he thought fancied him, seemed to have written him off completely. He really must be, he thought, a prat.

'Look.' Lucinda was trying to be a little more tactful. 'I know I've been hard on you, but only for your own good. To try to understand.'

He looked up at her. 'I know,' he sighed. 'But I don't know what to do.'

'Easy.' Lucinda felt at last that she was getting some-where. Letting him stew for a while seemed to have worked. 'Ring your superiors, and tell them that you have followed orders regarding *Colette*. But now that you have looked into the matter yourself, you find their information is incorrect.'

'I can't do that. It would be disobeying orders.'

'You won't be disobeying orders. Merely letting them know that somewhere there has been a mistake. A mistake, moreover, which is nothing to do with you.'

'Do you think so? They don't like admitting that they have made a mistake, you know.'

'The police will back you up, and you will probably end up getting a medal, or something.'

Rodney rang, with Lucinda at his elbow to make sure he didn't blow it. They were sure that there couldn't possibly be a mistake, but they would check it out. In the meantime, he was to continue surveillance.

'Told you,' said Lucinda with a smile. 'You really are a prat.' And she gave him a kiss.

David looked up from his desk in the outer office of Smith & Spindrift as the door opened and a familiar lady entered.

'He's not here,' said David dryly.

'When will he be back?'

'He won't.'

'What do you mean?'

'He's done a bunk. Cleared off. Left me to sort out the mess.'

'He can't possibly.'

'He has. Flown with his lady friend. In Timbuktu by now for all I know.' Or care, he thought. 'No trace in this country at any rate.'

May dropped into a chair. She felt faint. 'Gone with … his … lady friend?'

'Yes.' David looked across at the receptionist's empty chair.

'Trixie?'

'The same.'

'Trixie!'

'If it's cash you're worried about. I'm afraid it's gone.

He's cleared most of our clients' investments into a Swiss bank account of his own.'

'It can't be … He wouldn't.'

'He would, and he has. You and we' – he indicated his mother Sylvia, who had come out of the inner office – 'have nothing left. He's taken it all. Good job I'm not a partner in this firm, merely an employee.'

'I'm very sorry, my dear, but I'm afraid he's right.' Sylvia turned, almost tearful, back into the inner office.

'The bastard. What the hell am I going to do now?' May rose as if in a dream, and slowly, with faltering steps, left the office.

'Poor woman.' Sylvia watched her go from the doorway into the inner office.

'She's another one.'

'Another one what?' queried Sylvia.

'She's just another of his tarts. There will be more.'

'Will there?' Sylvia was surprised and shocked, Les was, she knew, no saint, but she didn't expect this. 'More?'

'Oh yes,' he went on while Sylvia sat down, visibly shaken.

'But,' said David, with a self-satisfied smile. 'I'm not going to tell them, but I've managed to intercept most of the monies he moved, clawed it back again. Into another Swiss bank account, in your name.'

'You have?'

'Yes. I guessed he was up to something more dodgy than usual. So I watched all his money juggling and got all the necessary paperwork ready. As soon as he did a runner, I moved it all on again. He'll never find a penny of it now.'

'But you didn't tell her. You said he'd got her money.'

'It wasn't her money. Like the rest, it's all the proceeds of thefts and robberies that he was holding for them. No, we're not handing a penny of their ill-gotten gains back to them. As far as they are concerned, he's got it.'

'And he told me you didn't know anything about the business. It seems he was wrong!'

After the exertions of the previous night, Sergeant Tooth was having a day off and, having spent the week running about the canal system, he decided to attend the convention in Middlewich. He might learn something of this fascination for water travel.

On the towpath he became aware of someone he knew. No, two people he knew. One was none other than Paul Boakes, the bank raid witness, who he was certain was dealing in stolen credit cards, but hadn't been able to prove. A cigarette was anchored to the right side of his lower lip. The other was Rose, that luscious, well-endowed – nay, very well-endowed – blonde, who was busy taking down her knickers from her clothes line.

Paul Boakes passed him on the towpath, after stepping off Rose's boat.

'Good day to you, Sergeant. It is a lovely day isn't it?' He smiled ingratiatingly and continued to the Big Lock pub.

If I know anything he'll need a few pints to build his strength up after that, the Sergeant thought.

'Oh, Sergeant. You've come.' Rose pounced on him. 'I knew you would.'

She jumped swiftly down on to the towpath to help him on board her floating Palace of Desire, making sure he didn't escape. She deftly put her knickers out again as she ushered him below, into her world of ecstasy. Before he could utter a word he was inside, with the doors bolted behind him. Psychedelic colours flowed slowly over the walls and across the ceiling, whilst *Tanhauser* emanated from the inner cabin.

She sat him down on the bed. 'I give a special discount to policemen,' she whispered, handing him a large glass of well-chilled Gewürztraminer. He noticed that she was now without her top and shorts. His blood pressure rose when he felt her ample firm breasts pressing against his arm, as she deftly undid his shirt buttons, unfastened his belt and slowly lowered his zip.

In his excitement he nearly spilled his wine. He drank it quickly, and with his trousers now around his ankles, he thought of Paul Boakes, who had recently been with her in the same situation. Though why he should think of him with Rose in this condition was a mystery.

'What was he doing here?' he enquired quietly.

'Oh, Sergeant. I can't discuss my clients' business activities. Now can I? You have my assurance of complete confidentiality. I am an adviser to the Department of Trade and Industry, you know.'

He grunted, still not realising that his trousers were around his ankles.

'I can show you my Servicing Charter, if you wish. I'm known for my reliability. And,' she giggled, 'lots of other things as well.'

'Yes, but doing it with a little creep like him, Paul Boakes ...' He spat the name out, as if it was an unpleasant taste.

'Oh, that's not his name,' replied Rose.

'It jolly well is.'

'No. Mr Evans. Vic Evans.'

'Vic Evans, my foot.'

'But it is, Sergeant,' she said anxiously.

Realising that the situation was a getting rather out of control, she crushed his face to her bosom. This usually worked.

'It isn't any such thing.' He pulled himself away from her, almost suffocating between those ample breasts. 'Vic Evans indeed. He's Irish, not Welsh, and his name is Paul Boakes, I should know.'

'So should I,' she replied with confidence. 'He used his credit card.'

273

'He did what?'

'He paid by credit card,' she said smugly. 'My bank manager, David, who is also a valued client, like you, Sergeant, set it up for me.'

'I've never been here in my life before,' he interrupted.

'But you will now. I know. Anyway, David has fixed me up. I have every facility here.'

'Have you got a slip signed by him?' Sergeant Tooth rose, and almost tripped over his trousers, which were around his ankles.

'Later, Sergeant, later.'

'Later? Now!' he shouted, pulling up his trousers and fastening his belt. 'Where is it?'

'Oh, all right, if it will satisfy you. Here.' She went into the inner cabin. The television was still running her pornographic movie.

He tucked his shirt into his trousers and buttoned it up.

'Here,' she said proudly. 'Now let's get started. Oh hell, you've got dressed again.'

'I've got the little sod.' Sergeant Tooth shrieked with obvious joy. 'I've got him by the short and curlies. The little bastard.'

'You can see him later.'

Rose's hand went to his belt again, but he pushed her off and unbolted the cabin door, with Rose hanging on to his legs. He stumbled up on the stern deck with Rose, wearing nothing but very scanty black lace briefs, still hanging onto him. On the stern deck he threw her off, and jumped down onto the towpath, firmly holding the credit card slip in his hand.

'I've got you. You smooth little sod,' he said aloud.

The crowd milling all around at the jamboree, on the boats, on shore, many with glasses in their hands, stopped what they were doing and gaped at Rose. The men in wonderment, the women in envy. Rose looked after

274

Sergeant Tooth in annoyance, her hands upon her hips, her breasts swinging.

'Sod it,' she said with feeling.

There was stony silence all round for a moment, followed by an eruption of spontaneous applause. Rose, suddenly realising that she was the focus of attention, turned it to her advantage by smiling and blowing kisses all round. The world at large was treated to a delightful display of her, ample – nay, very ample – bosom and her pretty bottom, when she eventually slipped down into the cabin.

In the bar of the Big Lock, Sergeant Tooth spotted Paul Boakes in a quiet corner, halfway down his second pint of mild. Paul looked away, as he did not want to be noticed, but it was of no use. He was a marked man.

'Come on, lad. You're nicked.' Sergeant Tooth was not bothering with the niceties. 'On your feet.'

'But I didn't think you were working today, Sergeant.' He smiled quietly. 'You're not in your working clothes.'

'It was my day off, but I'm never off duty, my lad.' Sergeant Tooth was being very firm with the little squirt. 'And if you don't get up soon, I'll march you out of here, with my hand on your collar.'

'OK.' Paul stood up immediately, but at the same time picked up his glass and drained the remaining half pint in one. He came out from behind the table.

'Right! Outside to my car.'

With that, Sergeant Tooth followed Paul to the car park, one step behind. He sat Paul in the front passenger seat. On pain of fearful reprisals, he sat quietly where he was as Sergeant Tooth drove him, without a further word being uttered by either of them, to the police station. Paul knew when he was nicked.

The mobile phone started to ring urgently. Its harsh, brittle cry caused George and Stan to look at each other. Them …

ringing us … That must be trouble!

George eventually plucked up courage to answer it. He took the phone to Rodney in the stern, who was sitting beside Lucinda, who was at the helm.

'S,' he whispered. 'In person.' Rodney's eyes and spirits dropped. He raised his eyes to Lucinda, and felt a little stronger.

Lucinda sensed trouble, after his previous conversation with the hierarchy of their clandestine operation. School kids, just playing, she thought. She switched off the engine, nodded to George to take over the helm, and sat down beside Rodney, her hand on his knee.

'Ponsonby-Smythe.'

'What the hell is going on?' a bucolic, staccato, bullying voice snapped.

'I beg your pardon?'

'Eh? What do you mean, pardon? What do you think you are doing? Eh? Eh?'

'I'm sorry, I am afraid I don't understand what you are talking about.'

'This bloody drug baron and his henchmen. That's what I am talking about! What have you got to say? Eh? Eh?'

'Nothing.' Rodney knew that S, a retired Colonel, suffered from gout, and was easily roused, particularly when deprived of an adequate ration of malt whisky. 'There isn't anything more I can say.'

'Nothing more you can say?' roared S. He didn't like people talking back to him. 'You are supposed to be following the most dangerous drug baron in Europe, and you lose him. Lose him! I find that he gets picked up by the police. The police!' He spat the word out as if it was indecent. 'They found him, skulking on a barge at Autherley Junction, on the Shropshire Union Canal. In a routine check of traffic. Where were you? Eh? Eh? Where were you? Putting your bloody feet up as usual. Having a joy ride round

276

Cheshire at the taxpayers' expense.' He was obviously livid. 'I shall require a full explanation, Smythe. This just isn't good enough you know. Don't know what the Regiment would think.'

Lucinda was listening. She looked Rodney in the eye, and nodded.

'You seem to forget, *sir* ...' he emphasised the 'sir', so that it sounded more like an insult. 'That you ordered me to come here, and follow a particular boat, even after the police told *you*' – he emphasised the 'you' – 'that it was harmless, and that there was definitely no drug dealer on board.'

'Nonsense,' protested S. 'Don't argue with me, Smythe, or I'll ... put you on a charge. Bungled the whole thing, you have.'

'Not only were you told by the police, before *you* sent me here, but after very careful investigation by myself, and my team I reported to *you* that I had been sent to follow the wrong people. I was nevertheless *ordered* to carry on surveillance of the boat in Cheshire. I have continued to follow those instructions, as *ordered*.'

'You can imagine this bloke leading the Charge of the Light Brigade,' whispered Lucinda in Rodney's spare ear, which she nibbled.

Rodney shook his head, she desisted and coyly put her head on one side.

'What's that? Be careful Smythe, or you will be in very serious trouble. As it is you will face disciplinary proceedings for neglect of duty. Got that?'

S was not going to have this young whippersnapper talking back to him.

Lucinda, stern-faced, nodded at Rodney. He was of two minds, but she was here, and he was there. He took a deep breath, and came out fighting.

'I shall not only, not be disciplined, but I shall not be

coming back. I have resigned. Got that? I have resigned.'

He switched off the phone, and left the choleric Colonel to splutter on alone. He smiled at Lucinda, and gave her a kiss.

'I'll put some backbone into you yet,' she smiled, and returned the compliment.

He called George and Stan to join him, although they had listened to every word.

'I am retiring, chaps. I think we'll have a little celebration. Open a bottle, George.'

'Great.'

'There is just one thing to be tidied up,' reminded Lucinda.

'Yes. I haven't forgotten.' Rodney was now feeling more sure of himself. 'One last job before I retire. We saw *Hyacinth* this morning, abandoned. The police have no idea of the whereabouts of the occupant, or why he has been following *Colette*.

'I propose we meet up with *Colette* tonight, to keep an eye on them, try and find out what our friend is up to. He's not been following them for nothing, and he might just stage something, as it is their last night on the boat. If so, we can nab him! OK?'

'Understood,' confirmed Stan.

'Your car is at Preston Brook, isn't it, George?'

'Yup.'

'Well, we can travel up there tomorrow, leave the boat in the boatyard, and arrange for its collection and hand the bill to S. My car is still at High Lane, so if you could drop Lucinda and me off there, on your way back to base, I'd be obliged.'

'Certainly,' agreed Stan, although it wasn't his car. 'No trouble at all.'

George and Stan started the engine and were away again. Lucinda and Rodney, hand in hand, went down into the cabin for a few quiet minutes together. The others realised that they just wanted to be alone. George, who was at the helm, called Stan to him in urgent conclave, without the chance of any eavesdroppers.

'You realise that it was us who bungled this job, don't you?' George was very earnest.

'Yes. But how? We definitely followed them to the boat-yard at Acton Bridge, and I saw them actually step onto *Colette*.'

'But suppose,' said George. 'They simply walked across *Colette* onto another boat moored the other side of it. We've often seen them double parked at boatyards.'

'Do you think so?'

'Well, if they were found at Autherley Junction they would have to have gone south from Acton Bridge, not north as we did. And remember, afterwards we never saw them again, because they weren't on *Colette*.'

'Oh hell!' Stan's face dropped. 'We have put our foot in it. What on earth can we say? Do?'

George was still very serious. He shook his head. 'We know nothing. Nothing at all. OK?' Stan still looked worried. 'We have simply followed, throughout, the people we were instructed to follow.'

'You think it will work?' Stan was still concerned.

'Most certainly. Just play it completely straight. And remember, neither of us will ever mention this again. They sent us on a duff mission.'

'Agreed.'

20

The salt industry may have declined, but industry flourishes, with ICI's vast lagoons at Broken Cross, and a little further on, its large Lostock works. Huge pipes carrying chemicals or effluent are suspended over the canal. Steam hissed. 'We could be on a *Dr Who* set,' said Richard.

An aqueduct carried us over the Wincham brook, where we were greeted by a number of derelict works. We went through Wincham and Marston, old salt mining villages on the outskirts of Northwich, where salt used to be mined like coal. The Lion Salt Works, closed some years ago, is now being restored as a museum.

Beyond Marston we entered the Marston New Cut. Such was the subsidence following the salt mining in the area that a whole stretch of the canal gave way, and had to be replaced. We wove our way all round Northwich, past the Cheshire Ring canal walk and the Marbury Country Park, to the little town of Anderton, which straddles the River Weaver, spanned by a huge swing bridge. The name 'Anderton', however, is famous all over the canal system. For here stands the Anderton Boat Lift.

The huge lift is capable of lifting craft 50 feet up or down between the Trent & Mersey above and the Weaver Navigation below, which is used to carry seagoing vessels. But sadly this marvel of engineering has stood idle now for a number of years. What a shame if it eventually goes the way of the guillotine lock, the site which we passed yesterday, but some years ago caused us considerable interest.

The canal eased itself around the outskirts of Barnton, and then buried itself under the town, into the Barton Tunnel. But we were used to tunnels by now and this, at 572 yards, wasn't half the length of the Preston Brook Tunnel which we met within our first few hours on the canal.

We emerged into a broad leafy pool, a small lane curling round the southern edge. A few yards ahead was the Saltersford Tunnel, this one only 424 yards long. Whilst we waited a few minutes, treading water for a boat coming south to emerge from the tunnel, we were conscious of a commercial working boat, towing a barge, emerging from the Barton behind us. Without so much as a by your leave, it chugged past us, as we waited, and straight into the Saltersford Tunnel as soon as the boat emerged from it.

We looked at each other, shrugged our shoulders, grinned, and followed him into the darkness. He was on business, and may have been in a hurry, whereas we were holidaying, not tied to anything. But an elementary courtesy would have been nice. We wouldn't have stopped him going ahead.

After the industrial landscape leading up to Barton, we now emerged into a quiet rural farming landscape. Below us to our left was the Weaver Navigation, with a large ship moving slowly along it. Strange to see large ships gliding peacefully through Cheshire meadows.

At 7.30 we moored for our last night, just through bridge 207. Half a mile away, and through two more bridges, well out of sight of us, was the boatyard, where tomorrow morning we were to hand back our home. An easy trip to base, whatever time we got up. Cattle grazed peacefully in the lush pastures opposite us, and beyond the towpath the fields sloped down to two pubs, The Horns and the Leigh Arms, half a mile away, just before the huge swing bridge carrying the A49 over the Weaver Navigation. Some distance ahead another boat was moored. We were certainly going out to dine, to celebrate our last night on the cut, at one of the hostelries we could see across the fields below us.

Sergeant Tooth had put the case of Paul Boakes safely to bed. It was now all up to the Crown Prosecution Service. He stretched himself at his desk, and felt pleased with himself.

His telephone rang. He winced. Don't they know it's my day off? I'm not really here. He lifted the phone.

'Geoff. That you? It's May.'

'Hello, May.'

'The police want to see me. There's a message on my phone. I've been away. I hope it is all right to talk to you. I don't know where Sam is. Haven't heard a word from him. I'm worried. He may be on my boat, it's not in the boatyard, and I've no idea where it is.'

'I'll be over directly. Make yourself a cup of tea, and sit down quietly.'

He was as good as his word. He had always liked and respected May. She was tearful and upset when she heard his news of poor Sam. He was very sympathetic – such a shock for the poor girl. He stayed for some time, holding her hand, and drinking tea which he insisted on making.

'Shall I get someone to stay with you?'

'No. I'll be all right. I'll go to Mum,' she lied.

'I'll be along tomorrow, and we'll go through all the formalities then. If you feel up to it. OK?'

'Thanks, Geoff.' She squeezed his hand, and gave him a kiss. 'You're very kind.'

He watched the tears rolling down her cheeks, and a lump welled in his throat. He wanted to crush her in his arms. That will have to wait, he thought.

May liked Geoff, but he was a policeman, and so she had given him a wide berth. However, in fullness of time she would cultivate a relationship. A policeman would give her an aura of respectability.

*

283

A good dinner, and a few drinks, rounded off the evening. Margery and I walked back to the boat full of the joys of spring. There was now a boat moored immediately behind us. Right up to the bridge in fact, but we took no notice as we climbed aboard.

We had all decided to give the cleaning a break until tomorrow morning, but as it was still light we set to, to give the boat a mop and a dust.

'Hello.' A girl's voice from behind startled me, as I stood on the cabin roof finishing the mopping down. I turned, and there was Lucinda with a young man.

'Hello.' I waved.

At that moment Margery popped her head out of the stern doors. 'I've swept inside, stem to stern. Have you done?'

'We've done the same thing,' Lucinda smiled. 'Just been for a quiet walk. Lovely on the canal, isn't it?'

'Hello Lucinda.' It was Richard, with Jo, who had come up behind Lucinda and the young man.

'This is Rodney.' Lucinda introduced the young man on her arm. 'This is Richard and Jo. I don't know your name,' she whispered to Margery.

'Come and have a drink,' suggested Richard, stepping into the cockpit. 'There's a bottle still in the fridge.'

Rodney ran back to his boat, which turned out to be the one moored just directly behind us, *Turandot*, I noticed. He returned with another bottle.

Margery emptied the dustpan, whilst I finished off mopping the stern deck. I looked at the boat behind, and noticed that there were two other occupants of the boat, both men, sitting in the growing dusk in the cockpit of their boat, just behind our rudder. They also were enjoying a bottle of wine, having clearly dined well.

Margery and I joined the youngsters in the lounge, and we had a fairly raucous evening. I managed to find two bottles of Cabernet Sauvignon I had kept quietly tucked away at the back of a cupboard, in case of emergencies. And this seemed a reasonable emergency to me. We went on till quite late.

A lone woman walked slowly along the towpath, first this way, then the other, taking everything in.

Turandot parked right behind them, thought May to herself. Ern had thought they were possibly police. Now they are partying together. Far too much of a risk tonight. But May was not disappointed. I can still put the fear of God into them. Screw the devils till they squeak. They'll get more than they bargained for! A slow smile crossed her face, and she walked on.

She had not noticed that the men in the boat behind had watched her with interest. A lone woman, walking backwards and forwards, along the towpath, paying particular attention to *Colette.*

Stan slipped ashore, and followed her at a safe distance. He noticed that once past *Colette,* her pace quickened. His assumption had been right, he thought. He followed her back through the boatyard, but lost her in the melee of the pub car park which, on Friday night, was thronging with people.

He saw her again. A plump, pretty blonde driving a car towards the car park exit. BMW thought Stan. Lucky Devil! He took the registration number. Well, almost, but two other cars, also anxious to leave, were vying with each other to get out first, and obscured her number plate. He ran through the parked cars to try and get a sight of the registration, but was almost knocked down by a third car, which reversed out of a parking space directly into his path. By the time he got to the entrance, May had vanished.

Eventually, in the early hours, the party on the boat broke up. They were happy, tired and anxious to crawl into bed.

Rodney, on his return to *Turandot*, had a run-down from Stan. He decided to speak with Sergeant Tooth in the morning.

They took it in turns to keep surveillance on *Colette*. George and Stan would not allow Lucinda to take a watch.

It was late, and she was tired. Her impromptu appearance had been a useful advertisement, as trade had indeed been brisk. Never a dull moment. The only difficulty had been a handful of wives hiding behind bushes, and on boats, on the look-out for errant husbands. One of which had in fact been caught red-handed trying to enter the cabin. She was just taking down her knickers for the last time, intending to go home and call it a day. She became aware that there was someone about, and on the towpath nearby she was conscious of a man looking at her.

'Hello.' Rose was never one to turn away custom, however tired she was.

'I'm sorry. I didn't intend to disturb you.'

'Come on board. I'm always pleased to see a new face.' Which wasn't what she really meant at all.

'Oh, I don't want to worry you. I just wanted to see you.'

'Well here I am,' she smiled. This must not be the big sell she realised. 'You are welcome to come aboard, and have a look.'

'But … I've had an accident,' Ern stammered. He was as shy with Rose as he had been with May.

'Never mind. There's nothing to worry about.'

He nervously took a step on board, but was very unsure of himself. He had often boasted, with men, about his prowess and experience. But in fact he was really very naive, and very conscious of the German Shepherd's attack on his privates.

Rose gently ushered him into the cabin, pegging out her knickers yet again. She sat him on the bed in the cabin. His

286

eyes caught sight of the large picture of Rose nude, and he stared in wonderment. Rose noticed.

'Would you like a glass of wine?' she enquired.

'I'd rather have a cup of tea, if you've got any.' he replied meekly.

'Oh good. So would I.' Rose seemed relieved. 'I'll just put the kettle on.'

She went into the small kitchen, switched on the kettle, and returned almost straight away. Ern's eyes were still on the picture.

'I'm better than that in real life.' Rose smiled, and slowly removed her top, allowing her breasts to swing free. 'There. How's that?' She stood before him proudly.

Ern couldn't believe his luck. May wouldn't have been anything like this.

'They're lovely. I haven't seen anything like them before.'

'Good. Now then, how about you?' she said. 'I'm standing here in next to nothing, and you've still got all your clothes on.'

Ern went into a sudden panic. 'I … Er … Only came to see you,' he replied feebly. 'You see, I was bitten by a dog yesterday, and I'm still a bit sore.'

'Where?' Rose enquired sympathetically.

'Down here.' He indicated.

'Let me see.' Deftly she took off his clothes, to inspect his problem. 'That's not very nice at all, is it? You'll have to look after that, but I'm sure it will be all right very soon. I do hope so.' She took to him. He wasn't the usual confident, pushy, sort she usually encountered.

The kettle whistled. Rose, in just her shorts, went into the kitchen, followed by Ern in just his shirt. Both enjoyed their tea and they talked of all sorts of things as they lay back on Rose's bed. Rose fancied retiring, and opening a boutique. With the right man of course, but the right man was difficult to find.

'Ridiculous, isn't it,' sighed Rose. 'I'm tired, and you can't. But you will come back again, won't you?'

'Oh, yes.'

She got dressed in her proper, as opposed to her working, clothes and helped Ern back into his trousers.

'My car's in the car park. Can I give you a lift, or have you a car here?'

'I came by bus. I've just come to see you. I didn't think, with this' – indicating the dog's bite – 'that I could drive.'

'You are a silly.' She gave him a quick kiss. 'The buses have stopped running by now, so you'll have to come with me.'

'Thanks.'

'You have got someone at home to look after that? To bathe it for you?' Rose enquired gently.

'No. I live by myself.' He was almost apologetic.

'Well, then. Why don't you come home with me? I'll bathe it for you. I'm just going to have my cocoa, and flop into bed. Even if you can't do it, we can still have a nice cuddle.' And cuddles were rare in Rose's experience. 'What do you say?'

'You sure?' Women weren't usually this kind to Ern. He had lived alone since his mum died, and been in trouble ever since.

'Yes. Be nice to have some company. I live alone as well.'

She switched off the lights, took her knickers down yet again, and padlocked the stern doors. She helped Ern down off the boat on to the towpath, and they walked arm in arm to her car. Not too swiftly, as his wounds still hurt. Rose was anxious not to rush him, or cause him any distress.

21

Saturday dawned bright and sunny, yet again. It was such a pity, handing back the boat after such a wonderful relaxing week. If it had been raining it would have been easier, but it wasn't. We didn't bother, or even feel like, rising early, and took our time over breakfast.

Lucinda and Rodney were in the bows of their boat when Richard started the engine.

'See you,' they shouted.

'We must keep in touch,' Lucinda said to Rodney, holding his hand as *Colette* sailed towards the bridge.

'Yes. We must,' he replied.

'I have spoken to Sergeant Tooth,' he said to Lucinda. 'He is very interested, but has no idea who the woman was. Unfortunately Stan couldn't give him a very clear description. Anyway he is having plain-clothes men at the yard to watch their arrival, just in case, and see them safely off the premises. *Hyacinth*, by the way, was used and abandoned by the bank robbers. Two, as we know, are dead. He wants you to give him a description of the third.'

'I wouldn't have believed it of that quiet little man.'

A nice couple. We had enjoyed their company. But I couldn't quite understand why there were also two other men, in the background, on the boat with this young couple. They were obviously holidaymakers, and certainly in

289

love. I mused on this, but didn't come up with a satisfactory answer.

Under bridge 208, we encountered other moored craft as we neared the boatyard. As we approached the final bridge, 209, which was on a slight left-hand bend. I noticed a man looking down from the bridge upon us.

Sergeant Tooth did have two plain-clothes men at the boatyard very early. They had instructions to watch *Colette*, and its occupants, from its overnight berth, into the boatyard. To keep a very careful eye open for any suspicious characters, taking note of anything out of the ordinary, ensuring that *Colette*'s occupants were seen safely out of the boatyard and on their way home. In no way were they to be in the least conspicuous. Only to move if they had the right man well and truly in their sights.

Colette slipped under the bridge. Ern crossed the road, and watched the boat run into the boatyard. Still in some pain, he then went down into the boatyard and stood, with others, watching the mooring and unloading.

''Ave a nice holiday, did you?' enquired the boatman, taking the bow rope and tying us up to the quay, whilst his assistant, a young lad, took the stern rope.

'Great time.'

'Good,' he said, leaving us to get on with our unloading.

Ern had felt well enough to drive this morning. Rose had dropped him off early, on her way to work, having made arrangements to meet again that night. He had parked his car by the pump out, whilst the cars of the boat hirers were parked neatly by the shop and office.

Once in the boatyard, the holidaymakers quickly transferred their goods to their respective cars, unaware that every package was being carefully scrutinised by Ern as it was transferred. There was no sign of the bag. So it was either still on the boat, or they had somehow removed it. But he couldn't see how. They seemed pleasant enough people, and he wondered if they ever knew that their boat had been used as a deposit. So who had taken the bag? It must surely have gone. May certainly wouldn't have missed it. Hell, no. May wouldn't have missed it.

The boatman gave the boat a cursory once-over, giving us a small package as a memento of the trip.

'That was great,' said Richard. 'I wouldn't mind doing that again. I'd even go through Manchester again. But I'd do it the other way round, and during a weekday, when the kids are in school.'

He summed up the feelings of us all.

When the occupants had gone, Ern went to have a closer look at *Colette*, as did a small group of onlookers. The young lady cleaned it out, to get it ready, and turn it round for the afternoon. The assistant looked in the nearside hatch under the cockpit seat, to check that everything was there. Lump hammer, mooring pegs, etcetera. They were all stowed, as they should be.

He saw also a tatty old leather bag, full of rubbish, it appeared, lying beside two empty beer cans and a plastic sliced bread bag, relics of a previous boat user.

Ern recognised the bag immediately, but he couldn't just snatch it. What should he do? Providence was in his favour.

'Looks as if they've left some rubbish in here,' the lad shouted, gathering up the bag, and putting the empty beer cans and plastic bread bag in it.

'Dump it,' shouted the boatman without looking.

The boy carried it to join the growing mountain of rubbish stacked beside the office building. He then went back to do some more tidying up.

Ern watched it all quietly out of the corner of his eye, without doing anything to show that it had in any way attracted his attention.

'Lovely boat,' Ern said to the lad, showing a keen interest in it.

'Super,' replied the lad.

When the coast was clear Ern got slowly into his car, and reversed through 90 degrees until it was beside the rubbish pile, between it and the boat. He got out, leaving the driver's door open, and walked round the front of the car checking all the tyres, but also making sure that no one was looking. He walked round the back of the car, checked the rear tyre beside the rubbish heap, and passing the bag, scooped it up quickly, empty beer cans and all. He threw it into the foot well of the front passenger seat and jumped in, slamming the door behind him.

Now, at last, he thought, I should be able to forget this life. The chip shop on the corner of his street was up for sale. He had always longed for a chip shop of his own, and now he could have one.

He would go and see Rose again tonight, although he was still rather sore. She had talked of retiring, and he felt he could persuade her. She wanted to start a boutique, but he was sure she would be just as happy with a chip shop.

The crowd of onlookers had now thinned considerably as the fleet had returned to base. Ern started his car, and noticed two young men talking together near the yard gate. As he approached it they straightened up, looked at his car, and moved purposefully into the gateway.

The telephone rang in the boatyard office on the following Monday morning.

'I say, I've made a terrible mess of things,' a young lady said with a laugh. 'I made friends with some lovely people on *Colette* last week. I'm supposed to be calling on them this week, and I've lost their address.'

'We don't give private addresses,' replied the boatman cautiously.

The girl, however, seemed so upset. It was urgent that she had it, and she did know the names of all the occupants, which was more than the boatman did.

'Well. I shouldn't,' he said. 'But as it's urgent … Hang on, I'll just look it up for you.'

'Thanks,' she sighed. 'You have saved my life. I'm ever so grateful.'

She put the phone down and smiled.

'Right, you devils, I've got you now!' said May.